A

TANGLED

WEB

By
K.J.RABANE

A Tangled Web

A Tangled Web

Dedication.
To Fran, Judy and Jin with love.

A Tangled Web

Acknowledgements

Many thanks to my family and friends for listening and to Nona for the final draft.
Cover image by Rebecca Sian Photography.

A Tangled Web

A Tangled Web

*Oh! What a tangled web we weave when first we
practice to deceive.*
Sir Walter Scott - Marmion

A Tangled Web

TABLE OF CONTENTS

A Tangled Web

Chapter 1

Walking along the red carpet on the arm of my son, I smile as the reporters aim their lenses in my direction and thrust their microphones towards me. The Olivia Maitland story was written and published after her death over forty years ago.

When I knew they were going to make a film of the book, which caused a furore when it was first published, I was anxious how it would affect my family. But I've been told the film adheres to the memoir in every respect. My fear that investigative journalists might try to research the past has been unnecessary.

"Ready?" my son asks, as we reach the foyer and hear the roar from the crowd as the actors playing Olivia and Ross reach the red carpet.

"I'm ready," I reply, knowing that now I'm the only one left, who knows the true story, the only one who can untangle the web of secrets and lies portrayed in the book.

It began long ago when John, Paul, George and Ringo were still strumming away in the Cavern Club. It was the early years of the nineteen-sixties and it started with a lie; it was a small one, just a little white lie. I *had* been to Oxford and *had* worked in the college occasionally, but it was to visit my niece Jane, not to study for my degree as I'd implied. I'd spent six weeks there, staying at her flat, typing her thesis and helping a couple of her friends with similar tasks. Anyway, the person I spoke to on the telephone seemed harassed, as if she was only half listening, which was why I found myself driving to Longacres under false pretences.

Living in London had become difficult. I needed a change. There were more than a few people demanding too much of me. The advertisement in the newspaper appeared to be the answer to a prayer. Olivia Maitland required a secretary/writer to help her complete her memoirs. In other words Olivia Maitland, jazz singer and wealthy fifties socialite, wanted someone to write her book and the word *help* was an ambiguity. I had no doubt that I could happily spend a couple of months on the Devonshire coast and then leave her to it. It would be fun. Olivia Maitland was a larger than life character in her sixties and I was sure there would never be a dull moment, in addition to which the pay was enticing.

I'd studied the route before I left London but, as I drove nearer to the Devonshire village of Little Minnock, I was surprised how desolate the countryside became. Perhaps it was the change in the weather; the sky had darkened and storm clouds hung threateningly on the horizon. The late-afternoon April sunshine had disappeared so I turned on my sidelights and drove onwards.

The ominous sound coming from under the bonnet of my old Morris Minor was worrying. I'd inherited it from my brother, who had recently moved to Australia and it had never let me down before.

As the first drops of rain fell against the windscreen, the engine spluttered and died. I shivered and wondered what was I going to do now? It was no use me looking under the bonnet, I hadn't a clue what was lurking there and had no intention of trying to find out.

A Tangled Web

Someone would pass along the road soon, I decided, so I sat back and waited for help to arrive.

Beginning to think I'd driven into *The Land that Time Forgot*, I wondered if I was the only person who had found this road on the map. The first faint stirrings of unease crept over me, as I looked down the road in the fading light. Trees to either side of my car appeared like spectres with outstretched arms and my imagination, which had always been fanciful at the best of times, took flight. What if no one came and I was stranded here all night? Should I start to walk down the road in the hope of finding a garage or a house with a phone?

I actually had my hand on the door catch when I saw the headlights of an approaching vehicle. A large, black, saloon slowed down, pulled over to my side of the road and parked in front of me. Then the driver's door opened and a tall, slim, man appeared and began walking towards me, with his head bent against the rain. So I slid the door catch into the locked position, just in case, and waited.

Chapter 2

Opening my window a fraction, as the stranger approached, I saw he was possibly in his late twenties with dark hair and piercingly blue eyes. To say he was attractive would be an understatement.

"Anything I can do to help?" he asked. He didn't sound, or look, like someone you wouldn't want to meet on a dark night. He was wearing a lightweight suit, which was now spattered with raindrops.

I replied, "My car won't start and I have no idea why."

"There's a garage a short distance away. I'll get someone to take a look at it for you. Are you OK waiting here? I won't be long."

I risked opening the window further. "That's very kind of you."

"No problem." He started to walk back to his car. "I'll come back with some help and wait until they fix it for you," he said.

The wind was howling through the trees as I called out. "There's no need to wait, but thanks." However, I don't think he heard me, as he walked towards his car and drove back along the road.

Minutes seemed to pass like hours and it was a relief to see the approaching headlights of a breakdown truck, followed by the black car with my Good Samaritan.

The man from the garage lifted the bonnet, tinkered with it, attached a few leads, grinned at me and told me I would soon need a new battery. I started to look in my purse to pay him but he said it had been paid for and there was no charge. It was then I realised that the black car was nowhere to be seen and my benefactor had disappeared. Feeling relieved, if slightly intrigued, I continued my journey along the road in the direction of Little Minnock.

I was driving down a narrow country lane leading to Longacres when the rain finally eased and I could see the road ahead more clearly.

Longacres had been featured in a glossy magazine story some time back but I seemed to remember it as being less grand than it appeared as I drove towards the house. Even though the rain had stopped, dusk had fallen and visibility was now poor. In the half-light I saw a Georgian style mansion, square and solid with a gravel driveway curving around a fountain opposite the front door. Majestic stone columns to either side of the doorway gave the house an elegant, distinguished aspect, the door stout, newly painted. I rang the bell and waited.

At first I wondered if anyone was at home for it seemed a while before I heard footsteps from within. Then a young woman, wearing a navy dress and high-heeled shoes, opened the door. Her hair was chestnut coloured and worn in a French pleat. She stared at me over the top of large tortoiseshell-framed spectacles. "Yes?"

"Anna Fairfax. Mrs Maitland is expecting me."

"Mrs Maitland is in the south of France." She hesitated. "Fairfax did you say? The ghost-writer? Come in." She stood aside to let me into the hallway. I'm Diana Huntley, her private secretary; I'm afraid you'll have to fend for yourself as I'm on my way to join Mrs Maitland now."

I looked at her askance.

5

"Don't worry. She's left you a note and Travers and his wife live in. They look after the place, so you won't starve." She smiled. "Your room is at the top of the staircase, second on the left."

And with another smile, aimed half-heartedly in my direction, she closed the door and I was left holding my suitcase wondering how I was going to carry it up the flight of stairs without giving myself a hernia. I'd never been known for travelling light and this was no exception.

I'd lifted my case over the first stair when a door at the back of the hallway opened and a man in his fifties appeared.

"Hang on, Miss. You don't want to cause yourself a mischief now. Let me carry that to your room."

"Mr Travers?"

"The same and you must be the young lady my missus and me are expecting."

Relived, that at least they were expecting me, I said, "Anna Fairfax, pleased to meet you, Mr Travers."

"Joe, miss. We don't hold with formality in these parts."

He was like something out of a Thomas Hardy novel, I thought, following him to my room.

"My Esther will bring you up something to eat once you've settled in," he said, putting my case at the bottom of a large double bed.

"Thanks, but tell Mrs Travers I'll come down, there's no need for her to bring food up to me."

"No trouble at all, Miss. You look all in; just you rest up now and there'll be breakfast in the morning room. Esther will give you a call. She usually wakes Miss Diana up at about eight. Will that suit you?"

6

A Tangled Web

Thanking him, I waited until he'd left the room before walking over to the window to close the curtains. The driveway was in darkness except for a light above the porch. My car was parked to the right of the fountain and another vehicle stood alongside it. It looked like a large saloon but I couldn't make out the colour. However I was certain it hadn't been there when I arrived.

I wondered vaguely why Travers had been so keen for me to stay in my room when it was barely nine-thirty but curbed my curiosity, closed the curtains and waited for Esther Travers to appear with my meal

Chapter 3

Sunlight, filtering in through my bedroom curtains, turned the pale yellow drapes into burnished gold and woke me from a disturbed dream. In an attempt to rid the nightmare from my mind, I ran a hot bath and, after dressing in a pair of denim jeans and a white shirt, left the house for an early morning walk through the grounds.

The dawn chorus was still in full swing as I inhaled the crisp morning air, thick with the smell of rain-washed grass and dew. There was a faint tang of the sea in the air and I relished the possibility of exploring the coastline during my stay at Longacres. No one was about as I walked down a path between two high hedges, which eventually led to a rose garden. Olivia Maitland's gardener had obviously made sure the gardens, were immaculately kept. Rosebuds, closed and waiting for the summer sun lined the path, beyond which I could see a lawn peppered with late-blooming daffodils.

The sunrise, which had woken me, promised fair weather and I felt optimistic about the task, which would keep me in such surroundings until I decided to move on.

Making my way back to the house, I saw two people approaching the car, which was parked alongside my own. I was too far away to see the man clearly but there was something vaguely familiar about the way he walked. The woman was tall with curly blonde hair and was carrying a small case, which she deposited in the boot of the car, then stood back and watched, as the vehicle accelerated down the drive.

My skin was tingling as I opened the door and went up to my room. It was nearly eight and as I ran a flannel over my face, I heard Esther Travers knock on my door.

"Breakfast is ready in the morning room, Miss."

"Thanks, Mrs Travers. I'll be down right away."

The layout of the house was relatively straightforward. To the left of the staircase on the ground floor stood the drawing room behind which was Mrs Maitland's study. On the opposite side, there was a music room, which faced the front lawn, a morning room facing the back of the house and a dining room leading off a short passageway. The kitchen and the staff quarters ran along the back of the house and the upper two floors contained family and guest bedrooms.

An appetising smell drifted towards me and I followed my nose towards the morning room. Surprisingly I wasn't alone. Seated and tucking into a plate of scrambled eggs and poached salmon was the young woman with curly blonde hair I'd seen earlier.

"Good morning," she said, putting down her knife and fork. "You must be the new secretary?"

"Anna, yes. I'm here to help Mrs Maitland write her memoirs."

"How do you do. I'm Diana Huntley," she said.

I was aware that my mouth had fallen open and that I was staring at her, but recovered enough to say, "I'm pleased to meet you," whilst wondering if I'd imagined the young woman in the navy dress who had opened the door to me upon my arrival at Longacres.

Chapter 4

Esther Travers seemed confused when I asked her about the woman in the navy dress, who had said she was Diana Huntley.

"Can't think who that could be, Miss."

The blonde was even less forthcoming.

"You must be mistaken," she said, which I thought was odd, considering the woman was presumably an imposter.

However, I had little time to concern myself with the problem, as after breakfast I asked to see the work that Olivia Maitland had left for me in her study.

"I've some business to attend to in Little Minnock but you'll soon find your way around," Diana Huntley said, backing out of the door.

Great, you've been such a help I thought, walking towards the study.

It was just as I'd anticipated; Olivia required a ghost-writer, not an assistant. So, it appeared, both of us had been a little creative with the truth.

I'd been reading through Olivia's diaries, which I'd found in the top drawer of her desk, for over two hours when the telephone rang.

"Er, who is that?" It was a man's voice.

"I'm Mrs Maitland's biographer, I expect you want to speak to Miss Huntley. She isn't here. May I take a message?" I answered.

"No. Tell her Ross rang. I'll try and speak later."

Before I could reply, he cut the connection. I made a note and placed it on the desk, which I presumed was hers and then carried on reading about how Olivia first met Frank Sinatra and Sammy Davis Junior.

Diana Huntley didn't return until dinnertime that evening. I heard her car draw up as I was washing. Being vaguely aware she'd entered the house, I dressed for dinner, and made my way down to the dining room

The table was laid for two people but there was no sign of Diana Huntley.

Esther Travers eased her ample frame through the doorway carrying a bottle of red wine and a serving dish. Placing both on the table, she sighed, "You'll be dining alone, dear, Miss Diana has been called away."

After pouring a measure of wine into a glass for me and removing the lid from the serving dish, she left me to eat my meal of braised steak and overcooked vegetables. But before she reached the door, I called after her.

"Is Miss Huntley likely to be away for long?"

"You can never tell, Miss. If I had a chance to go to the south of France, I wouldn't hurry back, I know that much." And with a shrug she left me alone.

The following day, after breakfast, which I ate alone, I entered the study to begin my work. The diaries were interesting in parts and tedious in others. Sifting through them gave me an insight into the early life of Olivia Maitland and I began to see aspects of her character, which weren't apparent from her public persona. For instance, the glamorous, self-assured performer, who had been married three times and had numerous affairs, had been born into an affluent family, according to her press release. But the generally accepted version of the story perpetuated by the newspapers was a fantasy. According to her diary, she'd been born into a poor Irish family, the eldest of a family of six, whose parents had died before she'd become famous. The younger children had been taken into care and Olivia had moved to London to seek fame and fortune. She'd played the clubs, slept her way into the limelight until she'd met and married Larry Farnsworth the racing driver. Upon his untimely death, in the Monte Carlo Grand Prix, she had inherited his considerable fortune and soon afterwards had reached the top of the charts in both the US and UK.

In addition to the diaries there was a scrapbook full of cuttings and programmes but these stopped when she married her second husband Grant Churchill. I remember my mother talking about him. He was a Harley Street surgeon, extremely good looking, charming and wealthy. According to my mother everyone was shocked when they heard Olivia had left him for a layabout with a cocaine habit by the name of Joshua Maitland. By this time Olivia was in her late forties and the newspapers were full of reports that she'd adopted a six-year-old child. Soon after, Maitland was found dead in bed from an overdose of a cocktail of drink and drugs, and Olivia was left to bring up her son alone.

I sighed, how much of this was actual fact or newspaper fiction? By anyone's standards it had been a colourful life. But how was I going to find something new and exciting to write about; most of this stuff was common knowledge, except for the early years, which were covered in her diaries and I wasn't sure how much of that, she was willing to reveal in the forthcoming book. Beginning to wish I hadn't been so creative with my application for the job, I stood up and looked out of the window.

As far as I was aware I was alone in the house except for Joe and Esther Travers. I saw a gardener attending to the border plants a short distance from the house. He looked youngish, mid twenties. He stopped weeding, looked around then lit a cigarette. I continued watching him until he became aware he was being observed. He stood looking at me for a moment then ground the cigarette under his heel and continued with his task.

It occurred to me that I should approach Olivia Maitland's memoir from a different viewpoint. Picking up my notebook, I went to interview Esther in the kitchen. Maybe she could enlighten me on aspects of her employer's life, which were not already public knowledge.

She was wiping down the surface of the large pine table.

"Miss Fairfax? What can I do for you?" Tucking a trailing grey curl behind her ear, she straightened up.

"It's Anna. I thought I'd take a break for a while and wondered if I could ask you a few questions about Mrs Maitland. It would help me to get started, if I could get more of a feel for her personality. Newspaper reports and diaries are all very well but you've worked for her for some time I understand."

I thought I detected a cautious expression as she walked to the sink to rinse out the cleaning cloth.

"Fire away then and I'll put the kettle on and make us both a cuppa."

I sat at the table and opened my notebook. "When did you start working for Mrs Maitland?"

She had her back to me. "Twenty-two years ago, just after she'd adopted Ross."

"I understand he was six at the time? So he must have known his 'other' mother?"

"He was a traumatised young boy; I understood his mother was on the streets and couldn't look after them."

"Them?"

"Him, I mean him."

"How long has Diana been her secretary?"

"Let me see now. It was just after my Joe had shingles, about six weeks ago it would be."

"And before that? Who did she replace?"

Esther bit her lip and put her cup down on the table with a slap. "Myrtle Strong."

The name rang a bell but I couldn't think why.

"It was all over the papers, because of Mrs M being famous like."

A memory stirred. "She died after a fall, didn't she?"

Esther sighed. "Lovely lady was Myrtle. She'd been born in Little Minnock. Everyone in the village was devastated when it happened. She fell down the main staircase. An accident they said."

I looked up. "You don't think it *was* an accident?"

She picked up her cup and took it to the sink then began vigorously washing it. "Yes, I expect it was, Miss. Now if you don't mind, I'd better be getting on. There's dinner to prepare and I've shopping to do."

The brush off, I'd no doubt, so being bored with the diaries I decided to a spot of digging where Myrtle Strong was concerned. I suppose you could say that was the catalyst from which the rest of it stemmed, although I didn't realise it at the time. I wonder what

A Tangled Web

would have happened if I'd just stuck to transcribing
the diaries and let the past lie undisturbed.

Chapter 5

Pulling on a warm jacket, as a cool wind was sweeping across the lawn and threading through the trees, which were now in bud, I walked towards the gardener. Esther Travers said his name was Tom Trevellyn and he'd been working at Longacres for a couple of months. He had his back to me and was planting a rose bush.

"It's Tom, isn't it?" I said, as I approached.

"That's right and you're the new secretary."

I didn't put him right; after all it was as near to the truth as to make no difference. "Do you mind if I could interrupt you for a moment? I'm working on a book about Mrs Maitland and I wondered if I could ask you a few questions."

He straightened up and faced me. He was better looking than he'd appeared from a distance. His eyes were hazel coloured and his face tanned, the sun had bleached his hair and his body was muscular. But there was something about him that made me feel uncomfortable. I couldn't quite put my finger on it, call it a sixth sense, if you will, but I felt the hairs on the back of my neck stand up for no accountable reason.

"Don't know what I can tell you. I hardly know her. Only bin working here since last summer. Don't see much of her anyway. She told me what she wanted and left me to it."

"No problem, I really only need some background information. What you thought she was like as an employer but if you can't help me it doesn't really matter." I started to turn back to the house. "Oh by the

16

way. You were here when Myrtle Strong fell down the stairs, weren't you?"

"I'd be careful if I were you," he muttered. "Asking too many question might land you in trouble."

"What on earth do you mean?" I asked, stopping in my tracks.

He didn't answer, just shrugged and carried on digging.

Later, reading through Olivia's diaries during the year she adopted her son, I began to feel as though I was getting somewhere. I glanced at my notes and realised I had enough information to complete the opening chapter. I decided to concentrate on aspects of her personality rather than the peripheral characters populating the pages of her diaries and had typed three pages when the desk telephone rang.

"Hello, not now Ross dear. Sorry, sorry, hello, Anna isn't it. It's Olivia Maitland here. How are you getting on? I wonder if…"

It was a bad line and I missed the rest of her words, being left with just a crackling sound. Should I try and ring her back, I wondered, but I'd seen Joe and Esther leaving for Little Minnock earlier and had no idea how to contact my employer. I thought perhaps she would ring again, if there were a problem. So putting, the phone call to the back of my mind, I carried on typing.

It was getting dark when I heard the spluttering sound of a car's engine and knew Esther and Joe had returned. There was no mistaking their old Austin as it ground to a halt in the drive.

I'd switched on the light in the study earlier but it was still dark in the rest of the house. By the time I'd reached the hallway I could hear Joe talking to his wife in the kitchen. As I drew nearer, their conversation drifted towards me.

"It's no good, girl. She'll find out, bound to. Tom said she was down in the rose garden asking questions earlier. I knew it was a mistake to agree to it. You mark my words, there'll be trouble."

"Ross said there'd be nothing to worry about. So I'm going to put the kettle on, make us some tea and forget about it all. Tomorrow's another day, as they say."

The feeling I'd had earlier persisted. There *was* something funny going on in Longacres and somehow I'd landed right in the middle of it.

In bed that night, I tossed and turned until the clock on my bedside table read two-thirty. I slid out of bed and walked towards the window. It was a clear moonlit night. The rose garden was limed in moonlight as was the terrace and beyond it the lawn. I opened my window a fraction and inhaled the cool night air. I had been standing there for at least five minutes when I saw the headlights of an approaching car. It swept up the long drive and purred to a halt beneath my window so I could no longer see it. The faint sound of a door closing reached my ears as I wondered who had arrived at Longacres in the middle of the night.

Interrupted sleep meant it was late when I awoke. Esther Travers, knocking on my door at a quarter past nine, woke me.

"Are you awake, Miss?"

I groaned and managed to croak, "Sorry, Esther, I overslept. Thanks for waking me."

"I've brought you up some breakfast," she said opening the door whilst balancing a tray on her arm.

"That's so kind of you. Thank you."

"My pleasure, dear."

"Did we have a visitor in the middle of the night? I thought I heard a car."

"Car, dear? No. You must have dreamt it. There's just Joe and me, no one else."

I picked up my mug of coffee and said, " Right. I'll be down in a bit. Thanks again for breakfast."

"Don't hurry. It's a nasty day; rain's set in. It'll be set for the day, I shouldn't wonder."

As the door closed behind her, I sighed. What on earth was going on? What was so important that Esther had lied to me about the car? Determined to find the answer to these questions, I finished breakfast, took a bath, dressed, and went downstairs.

A policeman was standing in the hall taking to Joe and Esther was sobbing into her handkerchief.

Chapter 6

I thought it best to make for the study, as unobtrusively as possible, but Joe stopped me.

"Awful news, Miss. Jim has just called in to tell us. It's Miss Diana…"

At this Esther sniffed loudly.

"What's happened?" I asked.

The police constable stepped forward, cleared his throat and answered me. "Miss Diana Huntley was drowned after falling from the cliffs in the south of France. The news was relayed to the station this morning by Mr Ross, as the telephone line to the house is down."

Turning to Esther, I took her arm. "I'm so sorry. This is terrible news. You look shattered. Let me make a pot of tea." Leading her towards the kitchen, I said, "Would you like a cup, constable?"

"No thanks, Miss, have to get back to the station."

Joe walked him to the door then followed us both to the kitchen where they sat at the table in stunned silence as I put the kettle on.

"This must have been such a shock for you," I said, stating the obvious but feeling I should say something.

Esther looked at her husband as if I wasn't there. "What are we going to do now?" she asked.

"Hush, hush, we'll manage. You'll see, just don't worry."

I frowned. "Do you want me to go into Little Minnock and ring for someone to fix the line?"

"Jim will see to that, Miss. Then we can ring Ross and see what's to be done."

20

"Good." I handed them their teacups and said, "I'll be in the study. If you want anything, if I can do anything, just let me know."

Joe murmured, "We will, thanks." But Esther just bit her lip until drops of blood fell on to the table-top.

I couldn't concentrate on work. The words wouldn't come, none that made any sense, because I couldn't concentrate on a past life lived through jottings on a page when the present was far more absorbing. As I sat at my desk I heard the sounds of activity from the hallway, followed by an expletive from Joe. Opening the study door, I saw Tom carrying a large case towards the front door. Joe walked behind him. They were concentrating on their task and so I partially closed the door and watched them.

"Ross said to put it in the outhouse. There'll be someone by to pick it up later."

"Have you packed everything?"

"As instructed. It's all gone."

Their voices became indistinct as they approached the door and Tom lowered the case to the step before turning around. Our eyes met as he drew the door towards him and I saw him hesitate, but it was only for a fraction of a second then he closed it with a loud slam.

It was nearly half past eleven and I hadn't seen Esther since breakfast; usually she looked in about eleven with a mug of coffee and some of her homemade biscuits. Making for the kitchen, I looked up the main staircase and thought I caught sight of her.

"Hello? I'm going to make some coffee. Would you like a cup, Esther?"

The kitchen door opened and Esther said, "Sorry, Miss. I'll bring your elevenses in, the kettle's just boiled." She looked flustered and I wondered whom I'd seen on the staircase.

"No need. I'll sit in the kitchen with you, I'm in no hurry."

"Er, yes, well, all right, dear, if that's what you want. Only I'm a bit busy, what with the news about Diana and all."

She waited whilst I sat down then set a plate of biscuits in front of me and, after handing me a mug of coffee, made a pot of tea.

"Will Mrs Maitland be retuning to Longacres soon, do you think?"

"I can't say. Ross wasn't sure when I spoke to him. He did say he might pop home for a while but he didn't say his mother would be joining him."

"I just thought it might be easier if I could work with her, rather than extracting my information from her diaries."

But Esther Travers wasn't listening. She was looking out of the window, a deep furrow creasing her brow. What secrets she and her husband were keeping were a mystery.

It was the following day that I received the news from Joe about my imminent future. It appeared Mrs Maitland had instructed him to inform me that she wished me to travel via the Blue Train to the south of France where her son would meet me.

"She apologised for not speaking to you directly, Miss but she has a cold and is losing her voice. I'm to ring Mr Ross to let him know if you are agreeable," Joe added.

The thought of an all expenses paid trip on the Blue Train was incentive enough, without the prospect of staying at the Maitland's villa, a short way along the coast from Monte Carlo.

"I'll pack, right away," I told Joe and skipped up the stairs to my bedroom.

Premonitions are all very well in hindsight and I would be lying if I said I knew this trip was going to end in disaster. Humming the chorus of '*love me do*', I packed my mini skirts, cotton tops and pedal pushers, making a promise to buy something chic, with the first pay cheque I received in France.

An hour later I saw Esther as I walked towards my car.

"Won't be long, just popping into Little Minnock to buy a few things for the journey tomorrow," I said.

"Right you are." She walked away from me in the direction of the rose garden where Tom was standing watching us.

Driving towards the village I felt elated at the thought of spending a few weeks or maybe more in the sun. The atmosphere at Longacres was making me paranoid. I'd begun to feel that there was some sort of conspiracy going on between Joe, Esther and Tom but the further I drove away from the house the more ridiculous it seemed.

The village of Little Minnock comprised a main street lined with small shops, a church, village green, a cafe and a pub. Parking in an area close to the shops, I saw a young woman loading carrier bags into the boot of her car. Her curly blonde hair was tied back but she was wearing a dress I'd seen her wear before. She looked up as I pulled into a space opposite her then closed the boot, hurried into her car and drove away.

I watched Diana Huntley until I could no longer see her car and wondered why on earth a corpse would be driving past me with a boot full of shopping. Mark Twain's insistence that the reports of his death had been greatly exaggerated sprang to mind as I walked towards the shops, confusion my uncomfortable companion.

Chapter 7

Unable to concentrate on my shopping I walked to the Walnut café and ordered a strong black coffee. Sitting at a table overlooking the street I began to wonder if I'd been seeing things. Perhaps the woman was someone who looked like Diana, wearing a similar dress; perhaps I was more in need of a change of scene than I'd thought. Although I tried desperately to find an alternative to the obvious, I knew I was wasting my time. I was absolutely certain I'd seen Olivia's private secretary, there *was* no mistake and she knew I'd seen her.

Later, driving back to Longacres, I considered whether I should tell Joe or Esther about Diana but decided that either way they would say I'd been mistaken.

Tom was wheeling a barrow of cuttings towards the potting shed as I drew to a halt in the drive. He stopped, and as I got out of the car, said, "Off to the sun tomorrow then? OK for some."

"Yeah," I replied, walking towards him. "Do you know, I've just seen Diana Huntley alive and well in Little Minnock."

I waited for the smart reply but to my surprise he frowned and bent his head towards me. "It's like I told you, the other day, I'd be careful if I were you." And as Joe opened the front door, Tom continued pushing his barrow in the direction of the potting shed.

"Get all you wanted in the village?" Joe asked.

"And more," I muttered, out of earshot.

I nodded.

"Need a hand to carry it in?"

"No, thanks."

"Missus has put the kettle on if you fancy a cup."

Unable to face the thought of making small talk over yet another cup of tea, I replied, "I think I'll have a lie down. My head's thumping. Tell Esther, I'll not be bothering with dinner, I'll heat up a tin of soup later."

"OK are you? You look a bit pale." He took a step towards me.

"I'll be fine once the tablets kick in," I replied, walking past him and into the house.

After a good night's sleep fortunately undisturbed by dreams, I awoke to a misty morning, damp, and still but with the promise of sun on the horizon. Such mornings were commonplace as we were so near to the coast. Once breakfast was over and Joe had driven me to the station, I began to relax and forget the intrigue at Longacres, whether real or imagined.

The ferry crossing was smooth and uneventful and before long I was sitting in comfort on the Blue Train watching the French countryside rolling by.

Olivia's villa was on a hill overlooking Beaulieu sur Mer, a coastal village situated between Nice and Monte Carlo. I'd seen it pictured in magazine articles and there was a framed photograph in her study showing her sitting in the garden on a lounger, whilst smoking a cigarette in a black and gold holder. I couldn't wait to see it.

I was reading a paperback novel by Agatha Christie, a glass of white wine in my hand, when I heard someone say, "The Butler did it." I looked up from my book, faintly irritated by the interruption and saw a

26

flash of red hair and a wide grin. "It's a joke, don't look so annoyed." He held out his hand. "My name's Paul Harrison otherwise known as Red for obvious reasons. And yes I do know about the Beatles but they weren't around when my mother was having me back in the dark ages. Mind if I join you? Can't find anyone under fifty to talk to on this train and it's a long journey."

He sat down opposite me before I could answer so I replied, "I can see it might turn out to be."

"Great, someone with a sense of humour, at last."

I smiled in spite of myself and put my book down, knowing there was no chance of me finding out 'who done it' in the immediate future.

"Fancy another?" Red asked walking to the bar.

"Chablis, please."

When he returned he handed me my glass of wine and placed a large glass of orange juice on the table in front of him.

"Don't drink, in case you're wondering," he explained. "Uncle, an alcoholic, caused enough havoc in the family to make Dylan Thomas turn TT."

"Rotten for you."

"Yeah. Where are you going?" he asked, stretching out his long legs in front of him.

"Beaulieu sur Mer. You?"

"We're to be neighbours, I think. Villefranche is just a short train journey away."

I sighed, "So I'm unlikely not to see you again then?"

"Not a chance." He grinned and whether it was after two glasses of chilled wine or not, I began to think I rather liked this seemingly uncomplicated man. At least the long journey wouldn't be dull.

The night passed in gentle slumber in my couchette, rocked by the motion of the train and I awoke to bright sunlight creeping through a gap in the curtains. After washing and dressing in a cotton dress, I picked up my book and went to the buffet car where I hoped to read another chapter during breakfast.

"What kept you?" Red was tucking into a plate of bacon and eggs. He looked up and smiled.

I put my book down on the table-top, sat down and ordered a plate of scrambled eggs and a black coffee.

"I see you're determined to find out if I'm right." He nodded towards my book.

"I can see that's not going to happen any time soon."

"That's the ticket. After we've finished here why not join me in the salon and tell me all about yourself. It will help to pass the time."

He was incorrigible and I must admit the thought of spending the whole journey on my own was not an agreeable one. Far better to be accompanied by an entertaining companion and Red was certainly that.

Later, sitting in comfort and watching the flat French countryside, medieval towns and winding rivers slide by as we journeyed southwards, I asked Red why he was travelling to the coast.

"It's a bit of a long story so I tell you the bones of it," he replied, "My parents died a couple of years back in a boating accident.

"I'm sorry," I sympathised but he shrugged and muttered something about, 'life happens, nothing to get beat up about' then continued, "Having inherited some money, I studied for my degree in French and decided to travel. Friends of mine have a villa in Villefranche,

28

so I thought, why not start in the south and work my way northwards, spending a month or so in Paris on the way."

"Sounds idyllic."

"Right. Now how about you?"

"Me? Oh nothing so interesting. I've been working for Olivia Maitland, on her memoirs and as she's intending to spend the summer in Beaulieu, she wants me to join her."

"Not interesting? An understatement, my dear girl; working for Olivia Maitland must be fascinating."

"I've yet to find out. I haven't actually met her yet. We've only spoken on the telephone."

"Well then, I insist we make a date to meet in Beaulieu so you can tell me all about it."

So, as the miles sped past, Red and I arranged where and when to meet and sat back to enjoy each other's company for the rest of the journey.

Chapter 8

I lost my travelling companion in the exodus from the train at the station in Nice. The platform was crowded and somehow we got parted without saying goodbye. Soon after, I saw a tall man, wearing cream cotton slacks and a mint green shirt, walking towards me. I recognised him instantly. He was the man in the black saloon car, who had called at the garage when my car had broken down on the way to Longacres.

"Miss Fairfax? I'm Ross Maitland." He held out his hand. "I trust you had a pleasant journey?"

"I did, thank you," I replied. His greeting was formal so I didn't tell him about Red, or my journey southwards. He instructed the porter to carry my case to his car and we threaded our way through the crowd out of the station and into the heat of a French afternoon.

Ross Maitland talked little on the drive, other than to point out a few landmarks. I supposed it was because he was concentrating on the road, which wound upwards towards the villa. A warm breeze threaded through my hair and I was grateful that he was driving an elegant Mercedes sports car, which purred along the winding road, rather than his black saloon.

At first sight the villa was impressive by anyone's standards and mine were naïve, to say the least, where luxury was concerned. Through the large gates, which slid open when Ross pressed a button on the wall, I could see the house at the end of a long driveway, its cream stucco walls gleaming in the sunshine. Manicured lawns and bright borders, box hedges and a shrubbery led to the main entrance above which was a long balcony presumably leading off a master bedroom. As we drove up I turned my head and saw the magnificent view of the coast, which lay behind us. It was breathtaking. Both sea and sky were sapphire blue and met on the horizon. In the distance a motorboat cut through the water leaving a trail of white spume behind it and I saw a cruiser sailing near to the coast.

"I can see you're impressed," Ross said, opening the passenger door for me.

"Who wouldn't be?"

"Pierre, put Miss Anna's case in the blue room, please," Ross instructed, as a thin-faced man, in his fifties with slicked back hair, approached. "I've to drive into Monte Carlo but mother will be somewhere about. I'll probably see you at dinner," he said as I watched him get back into the car.

"Thanks for the lift."

"No problem," he replied turning the key in the ignition and disappearing down the drive before I could catch my breath.

Pierre was waiting for me on the step and showed me into the house. "Mrs Maitland is on the terrace. She said she would see you after you've settled in and unpacked your things."

My room overlooked the back garden and pool area. I saw a figure stretched out on a sun lounger under a striped umbrella but, although the woman was lying face downwards, I recognised the Wallis-Simpson-thin body as belonging to that of my employer.

Although not excessively large, my room was spacious with a double bed the covers of which matched the curtains at the window. They were a pale shade of cornflower blue. The floor was made of yellowed marble, in the centre of which was a blue patterned rug. French windows led to a small balcony. I opened them and stood outside, inhaling the scents of the garden before tackling the task of unpacking my case.

A while later, dressed in a pink and white sundress, I went downstairs in search of Olivia Maitland. She was sitting up reading a book. I thought she looked amazing for a woman in her sixties. Her dark hair was obviously cut and coloured by Sassoon, in a style favoured by the fashion designer Mary Quant. It made her look years younger than her contemporaries. However, as I drew closer and sat in the chair opposite her, I could see her tanned skin was creased by fine lines and when she removed her large sunglasses, around her eyes there were similar deeply-etched patterns.

"I hope you had a good journey," she said, her husky voice, instantly recognisable.

"I did, thank you, Mrs Maitland."

She smiled. "It's Olivia, my dear. Now, Ross tells me that you've completed the first chapter, which is why I've asked you to come out here and spend the summer with me. I'm dying to read it and as Esther said you were asking questions about my past, I thought you might prefer to ask me in person."

I wasn't sure at first whether this was a reprimand but could see no evidence of it. "I'm very grateful. Not only am I to live here for a while, which to me looks very close to paradise, I also have the pleasure of getting to know someone who I admire greatly."

Aware I was sounding sycophantic, I added. "Thanks again, Olivia, for giving me the opportunity."

"My pleasure. Now if you don't mind." She picked up her book. "Oh, and please feel free to use the pool and whatever else takes your fancy."

I thanked her again and left her to read, thinking this was going to be great. Olivia obviously wanted peace and quiet to relax and not be bothered about trivialities. It would be easier to discover traits in her personality by living with her for the coming months besides which Ross Maitland was someone I was looking forward to seeing on a regular basis and hopefully getting to know.

My first dinner at the villa was held outside on the terrace. Nick and Jacky Ferris, who lived nearly and were pleasant enough company, joined Olivia on one side of the table. They were a retired couple and he had been an oil executive working for Shell. Jacky told me she had been his secretary before they married and had their daughter Avril. I sat facing them alongside an older woman, who had been involved in the music business and was staying at the villa whilst trying to encourage Olivia to make a new record. Her name was Velma Houston and she was from New York. I found out later that she and Velma were extremely close friends.

The meal was informal, beautifully prepared and suitable for the warm night. Each course was light and full of flavour but I noticed that my employer toyed with her food absentmindedly. I could see how she retained her slim figure and felt aware of my own indulgence as I cleared my plate.

Conversation flowed easily. Velma and I talked constantly throughout the evening. She was entertaining and amusing. It was only when Nick and Jacky stood up to leave that I realised Ross hadn't joined us for dinner. As if reading my thoughts, Velma handed me another drink and said, "I wonder what happened to our handsome host, tonight?"

"Who?"

"The delectable Ross Maitland, honey. I can see you've yet to fall under his spell. But mark my words, you will."

Olivia appeared then, having walked her guests to the door. "I'm bushed. I'll leave you two night birds to it and see you in the morning."

I slept well that night, lulled into slumber by the sound of crickets rubbing their legs together and moonlight stroking my skin through the open French windows. When I awoke, I smelled bacon cooking and looked at the time. It was eight thirty six. I sighed, a quick shower, throw something on and look ready for work before Olivia showed her face.

She was sitting at the breakfast table in the dinning room reading a newspaper.

"Did you sleep well?" Her voice sounded even huskier this morning.

"I did, rather too well, I think."

"Oh don't worry about me, Anna. I'm an early bird, always have been. No one is going to clock-watch you here. I'll get around to reading your work sometime later today but there's no hurry. Enjoy the sun, take your notebook on to the terrace or go for a walk into town whenever you feel like it. In short – be my guest."
She picked up her cup then said, "Oh and by the way,

have a word with Pierre, he'll show you a car you can use during your stay. It's a bit of a walk into Beaulieu."

"That's fantastic and I promise I'll still crack on with chapter two, I'll not let you down."

"That's agreed then. If you want to talk to me about my life, first thing in the morning is always the best, remember that and we'll get along just fine."

I spent the rest of the morning working in the study, a book-lined room on the first floor with views of the coast and of the small terrace at the end of the garden on which I could see Velma and Olivia sitting on deckchairs.

Making a mental note to speak to Olivia in the morning to gain some first hand information, I finished work at lunchtime and, after a light lunch, took a siesta before driving into Beaulieu Sur Mer. There was no reason for me to consider the possibility that I would be unable fulfil my intention of speaking to Olivia, in the morning, no reason at all.

Chapter 9

The sun was hot on my back as I watched the bathers running up the sand and flopping down on deckchairs. They lay beneath striped umbrellas clustered together along the stretch of beach like fish on a slab. The water looked so inviting I wished I'd brought my bathing costume with me, as my forehead felt damp in the searing heat. In order to find some shade I walked towards a café.

"I thought if I sat here long enough you'd be sure to show up. Red's grin lit up his face as he stood up. "I've kept a seat for you just in case. You look as if you could do with a cool drink. Garçon!"

"The answer to my prayer," I replied, sitting down at his side at a table in the shade. "I'll have a lemonade, please, with plenty of ice."

"And how are things up at Villa Maitland then? Nose to the grindstone and all that?"

I shrugged. "Nothing of the kind as you can see. Olivia is so laid back, there's no pressure and she's encouraged me to take time off to enjoy the scenery."

"So you're having a good time then, excellent." He picked up his glass of orange juice and smiled at me over the rim. "No excuses not to join me in some sightseeing then?"

"None. I was hoping I'd see you actually."

"Good, How about meeting me here tomorrow afternoon. I'll hire a car and take you into Monte Carlo or Saint Tropez, whichever you prefer."

"No need to hire a car. I have one at my disposal and I'll be glad to meet you here at, let's say two o'clock tomorrow afternoon?"

36

"Two it is. Now, tell me what she's really like."

I spent the rest of the afternoon chatting with Red and strolling along the beach, until the sun began to sink on the horizon and I saw that it was time to get back to the villa or I'd be late for dinner.

The villa glowed pink in the setting sun as I parked the car in the garage and hung the keys in the cabinet as Pierre had instructed. No one seemed to be about so I went up to my bedroom, showered and dressed for dinner. I was descending the main staircase when Ross Maitland appeared in the hallway.

"Hello, I wondered where you were. I'm afraid Ma is unwell and won't be joining us this evening." He was plucking at the cuff of his cotton shirt.

"Oh, I'm sorry to hear that. Is there anything I can do?"

"Er, no, thank you. I'm not sure if she's had too much sun or eaten something that's upset her. Anyway, I expect she'll be up and about in a day or two." He pointed to the dining room. "After you."

We were alone at dinner. Velma had a headache and had requested to have some food sent to her room. The staff were French and my limited knowledge of the language made conversation with them difficult. Pierre however spoke excellent English and liaised with the them kitchen whenever necessary.

"Have you been to this part of France before?" Ross asked.

"Never." For some reason, I felt tongue-tied in his company and I'd not mentioned the help he'd given me on the road to Longacres as I was sure he hadn't recognised me.

"And first impressions are good?"

"They are. Beaulieu is fantastic, I'm in heaven."

He smiled at me and I felt the butterflies in my stomach flapping their wings.

"As Ma isn't going to be much help to you for a day or two, why don't you let me show you some of the countryside tomorrow? We could drive up the coast to Monaco and have lunch in a little place I know on the hilltop."

"I'd love to, if you can spare the time," I said a bit too eagerly.

The rest of the meal passed in a flash, all I could think about was spending the day alone with him; my proposed meeting with Red in Beaulieu the following day totally forgotten.

After dinner, Ross excused himself saying he had work to do. I had no idea what he did for a living having assumed he had no need to work. I watched him walking up the staircase as a sudden surge of loss swept over me. Ridiculous, I scolded myself, I didn't know anything about the man and had only spoken to him briefly; I was being foolish. However, the thought of the following day was like a warm secret I was keeping and as I stepped into the garden I was smiling.

Strolling along the avenue of box hedges that let to a stone seat. I sat down and watched the stars shining in the clear night sky. What must it feel like to live like this, to have no money worries, to travel when and wherever you desired? Did Olivia and her son know how lucky they were?

After a while, I felt a cool breeze sweeping in from the coast and shivered. Inhaling the scents of the night, I retraced my steps and reached the terrace, when I heard voices.

"You could at least have made up something," Ross Maitland said.

"It was awkward. She saw me. "What was I supposed to do? I had to think quickly. You know I'm no good at this sort of thing."

"It complicates matters but we'll sort it out
- promise."

I shivered again but it had nothing to do with the breeze. I wondered who was the woman Ross Maitland was meeting so secretively and why.

Chapter 10

Unable to sleep, I tossed and turned until eventually I drifted into dreams filled with Ross Maitland, disturbing, fascinating scenarios that shocked me awake at six thirty, bathed in sweat.

Not wishing to wake the rest of the house by turning on the shower, I walked to the French windows, threw them open and stepped on to the balcony. Sunrise on the horizon bathed the garden in shades of pale primrose through to custard yellow. There was a light breeze rippling through the trees like a whisper and I thought back to the conversation I'd overheard last night. In the cold light of day, it seemed innocuous enough. Overheard conversations were often only partly illuminating; best to forget the whole thing and look forward to spending the day with Ross.

He was sitting on the terrace eating breakfast and when he saw me he raised his hand. "Join me?" He was smiling and once more, it had the desired effect. I took my seat and, soon after, Pierre arrived with breakfast.

"Nice to see you've a healthy appetite," he said, as I finished eating. "Ma eats like a bird."

"How is Olivia today?"

"Bit better, I think. She approves of me showing you around and said to tell you to enjoy yourself; plenty of time for work later."

"I can't believe she's so kind."

"That's Ma for you. Too kind for her own good sometimes."

I looked up but his remark held no malice. He put down is knife and fork, wiped his mouth with his

40

napkin and said, "I'll leave you for a short while as I've some planning to do. I mean for us to have a 'special' day out today."

"Sounds intriguing but please don't go to any trouble."

"It's no trouble. My pleasure. Be ready at ten?"

"I'll be waiting."

I think I changed my clothes three or maybe four times before I was satisfied. He was waiting near the front door as I hurried downstairs to meet him.

"You look lovely," he said.

"I wasn't sure how the fashionable women of Monte Carlo dress," I said following him to the car.

"You'd put them in the shade whatever you wore." He turned the key in the ignition and accelerated down the drive and into the open road.

My pleasure at hearing his compliments was tempered by the conversation I'd overheard the night before. Was this his way of 'sorting it out', whatever 'it' might be? All I knew was I didn't have a clue and was determined not to let it spoil the day.

Ross drove through Beaulieu and out towards Monte Carlo. The majestic Riviera coastline sped past us until he suddenly turned the car into a layby. "This is a view that is too good to miss, when seen for the first time," he said, turning to face me.

The coastline lay below us, the curve of the bay, cradling Monte Carlo in its arms, cruisers and yachts of every description nudging up against each other, the Casino and garden visible from our vantage point.

"Well?"

"I'm speechless, for once."

"So I've created the desired effect."

A Tangled Web

At first I wasn't sure if he was being sarcastic but he smiled and said, " Ready for more of the same?"

"Lead on."

After he'd parked the car in the marina, I picked up my sunhat from the back seat and put it on. The temperature was rising as it was approaching midday. Ross took my arm and steered me towards the cruisers lined up in the dock.

"Where are we going?" I asked

"Trust me. You'll soon see."

Fortunately, I was wearing cotton pedal pusher slacks and pumps because I was being guided along a wooden jetty towards a cabin cruiser, which was moored there.

Ross jumped aboard and reached out his hand to me. "Careful, here, let me help you climb aboard."

The cruiser was not the largest in the marina but it was beautifully designed. A sundeck with cream leather loungers and chairs led to a lower deck where there were two cabins and a lounge with a well stocked bar area. Ross showed me around with obvious pleasure at my reaction to the furnishings.

"Are you ready for a trip around the coast?" he asked.

"Fantastic."

"Good. Then I suggest we go back on deck, you can relax and I'll get to work."

I suppose, I'd thought such luxury would come with a crew as a matter of course. I'd not considered the possibility that Ross would handle the boat alone. My concern as to his competence was unnecessary however as he guided the cruiser out of the marina and into the open sea with obvious dexterity.

A Tangled Web

Relaxing on deck, I closed my eyes and felt the sun on my face, whilst inhaling the salty air. "I'm making for Saint Tropez, if you're wondering." Ross called to me from the wheelhouse.

Brigitte Bardot was known to frequent Saint Tropez along with others in the film industry and those wishing to catch sight of them. I glanced down at the cotton pedal pushers I'd bought two years ago and at my scuffed pumps and sighed. What did it matter what I was wearing, no one would be looking at me anyway. But I was wrong, someone was most definitely looking at me but who it was, I had yet to discover.

Chapter 11

Ross moored in the marina at Saint Tropez and suggested that we find a restaurant, where he knew the seafood was exceptionally good.

"I'm ready for anything. This day is getter better by the minute."

To my surprise, he laughed out loud, took my hand and steered me through the throng of holidaymakers who were desperate to see a face they recognised from the silver screen. Reaching the thoroughfare he led me to a restaurant where, to my relief, my cheap clothes wouldn't be an embarrassment. The atmosphere was fashionably relaxed. A couple of hippies sat at a table outside sipping their drinks and attacking a shared fish platter.

We were inside the restaurant when I realised Ross was still holding my hand. "It's cooler in here," he said, as a waiter approached.

The waiter recognised him immediately and showed us to a table overlooking a secluded courtyard where a fountain played in the centre of a terrace spilling bougainvillea flowers like a waterfall over a high, stone wall.

"This is just lovely," I said, sitting opposite him.

"As are you." He was holding the menu in front of him so I couldn't see his eyes and began to wonder if I'd heard him correctly. Perhaps he was talking about the food on the menu, I thought stifling a chuckle at the prospect.

"The lobster is excellent," he said, when the waiter arrived to take our orders.

A Tangled Web

I wanted to appear as if I ate lobster on a regular basis so taking Ross's suggestion, I ordered the same. When it arrived together with an array of implements redolent of those used in an operating theatre, my look of dismay must have been obvious.

When the waiter left us to eat our meal, Ross said, "Don't worry, it looks more difficult than it is. Why don't I show you and you can have a stab at it yourself?"

"Perfect, otherwise I'm likely to remain hungry." So much for my attempt at sophistication."

He stretched across the table and patted my hand. "Don't try to be anything, other than your delightfully uncomplicated self, Anna. Believe me you are a rarity in today's world."

Was this a pass? I'm not sure, even today, after all that's happened, and was even less so then. So I smiled and ignored his remark, saying something fatuous about the lobster to stem the heat rising up from my chest and threatening to turn my face as red as the seafood on my plate.

Ross was right, the lobster was excellent and after we left the restaurant, he suggested we go back on board the cruiser, open a bottle of champagne, sit on deck and join the people watchers from an advantageous position.

The afternoon shadows began to lengthen as we chatted, drank champagne and enjoyed the vibrant atmosphere. Long legged beauties in shorts paraded the length of the beach and limousines drew up near the harbour depositing their cargo of starlets eager to be seen with the 'in' crowd.

"You're quiet."

"At the risk of repeating myself, I'm totally speechless."

The afternoon had turned into dusk. Lights twinkled on the shore and my head was spinning, not only from the champagne but also from an overload of new experiences.

"Shall we take a walk? The air is cooler now." He reached over to help me up.

"Great, it will clear my head."

"You are OK?" He sounded concerned.

"Of course. I'm enjoying every minute."

Looking back I suppose it could have been my own fault. But I know that's an excuse. I wasn't drunk. Nowhere near it. I knew exactly what I was doing. Ross steered me towards the wooden planks making up the short jetty attached to our berth. I was standing on them when they gave way and I was plunged into the water. I felt a sharp pain in my leg as my head went under and my feet tangled in what felt like rope. I tried to struggle to lift my head above the water but my ankle was trapped and I couldn't free it. I started to panic as my breath left my body.

The next thing I knew, an arm was around my waist lifting me up to the jetty and a familiar face was peering down at me, his red hair turning a distinct shade of orange in the dying rays of the sun.

"Thanks for your help," Ross said, taking me from Red's grasp.

"Are you hurt?" he asked, ignoring Ross.

"I don't think there's too much damage. It was just a shock."

"I'll get you back on board and see to that graze on your leg," Ross said.

"Shouldn't she see a doctor?" Red was angry.

"Thanks for your concern but I'll see to things from here on," Ross replied, helped me back to the deck, avoiding the planking through which I'd fallen.

I looked back towards the promenade, once I was seated and saw Red dejectedly walking back to the harbour. Then I remembered I'd planned to meet him earlier and had forgotten all about it once Ross had suggested this trip. Planning to make it up to him and to thank him for coming to my rescue, I allowed Ross to clean up my cuts and bruises, one eye on the harbour.

"I'll get you back to the villa and you can rest," he said. The atmosphere had cooled between us, the fun having gone out of the day.

He was silent throughout the journey. In the darkness, which swirled around us as we drove upwards from the coast, I kept seeing the broken plank. The wood around it wasn't rotten; I wasn't that heavy, so why had it given way?

Chapter 12

Ross helped me up to my room. "Ring down if you need anything. Try and have a good sleep and I'll see you in the morning."

I started to thank him for the day but he walked away as if all he could think about was putting distance between us. My head ached and my damp clothes still felt uncomfortable even though they had partially dried in the warm air. Stripping off, I stood in front of the mirror thinking I looked a sorry sight. My hair curled unfashionably, my cheeks were stained and massive bruises had formed around my grazed thigh and lower leg. Feeling the need of a shower and a good night's sleep, I let the water soothe my aching body and was standing near the French windows in my dressing gown when I heard the sound of a raised voice coming from the terrace. It was too indistinct for me to make out what was being said but it sounded like someone talking on the telephone, someone who was angry, and I was sure it was Ross. I shivered and decided to seek the comfort of bed and sleep induced oblivion.

Thankfully I awoke from a dreamless sleep the next day but it was only to find rain lashing against the windows and a howling wind rattling the sun blinds above the terrace. The air was still warm and I remembered reading somewhere that storms were not unusual at this time of the year.

There was no sign of Ross at breakfast but Velma and Olivia were already up and about. I thought Olivia was still looking unwell but she seemed to be restored to good spirits and was keen to show me some

photographs and magazines articles about the time she
was popular with US audiences.

"When you've finished, I'll be in the study; come
on up. I'm sure what I have to show you will be of
help. By the way, I liked what you did with chapter
one. I read it whilst I was recovering in bed." She
wiped her mouth with her napkin and left the breakfast
room.

"Great. I won't be long," I promised.

"There's no hurry. Take your time."

Velma put down the newspaper she'd been reading.

"She's not well you know. She's putting on a face,
that's all."

"I'm sorry to hear it. I'll take care not to tire her."

"Ross not about?" She looked at me, as if I should
know his whereabouts."

"No idea."

"Did you enjoy yesterday? I gather he was showing
you the sights."

Normally I would have told her all about my
accident on the jetty but something stopped me. So I
simply replied, " Yes thank you, lovely," and picked up
another piece of toast.

Olivia was on the telephone when I entered the study.
She hesitated then replaced the receiver and said,
"Anna, do come in, my dear. I was just talking to Ross.
He told me you had an accident yesterday. Are you
quite recovered?"

"I am, thanks. It was nothing, really."

"Ross says he's worried about you and to keep an
eye on you. He's at the airport."

My stomach did a flip and I tried to act
unconcerned.

"He has some business in the UK." Olivia picked up a photograph album. "Now let's get down to work. I'm sure you'll be interested in these."

The rest of the morning passed remarkably quickly. I soon fell under her spell and became fascinated as her early life unfolded in front of me via the photographs, many of famous and not so famous faces. Olivia had a story to tell attached to each of them and before I knew it I had a notebook full of facts and a renewed enthusiasm for the task ahead.

After lunch Olivia retired for her siesta and I began transcribing some of my notes on to an electronic typewriter. The phone rang at just after two and I picked up the desk extension.

"Mrs Maitland's residence."

"Anna? It's Red." He sounded breathless, as if he'd been running. "Are you OK?"

"I'm fine. What's the matter?"

"I need to see you right away. Can you drive down to the café in Beaulieu?"

"Now?"

"Yes. I'll see you in half an hour?"

I agreed, put the phone down and frowned. I felt bad where Red was concerned. He'd accepted the fact that I'd stood him up in favour of a day out with Ross, freed me from the depths (a slight exaggeration) and was anxious about my welfare. I switched off the typewriter, the very least I could do was to meet him. Work would have to wait.

The storm had passed, leaving behind a warm day with the sun trying it's best to break through the clouds. As I parked the car, I could smell planters full of recently washed spring flowers spilling their perfume into the afternoon air.

The café where Red sat impatiently waiting for me was draped in waterfalls of Wisteria, which shed petals like confetti in the strengthening breeze.

"At last!" He breathed a sigh of relief.

"What is it?" I sat down opposite him and ordered a black coffee as a waiter hovered at my elbow.

"I'm afraid yesterday wasn't an accident." He seemed nervous, looked over his shoulder and reached for my hand.

"What on earth do you mean?"

"After you left the jetty with Ross Maitland, I took a look at the wooden planks. I couldn't understand why you would have fallen in such a manner; the wood looked new."

I remembered thinking along similar lines at the time. "And?"

He waited until the waiter handed me my drink then continued, "The boards had been sawn through. They were put in place to look as if they were secure when in actual fact they were anything but."

"I don't understand, anyone could have fallen through them."

"Not exactly. You see the struts you stood on were removable. Most cabin cruisers have them on board. They aren't fixed. The owner of the boat simply attaches them to the jetty in order to make it easier for people to pass from the cruiser to the jetty."

I shook my head, confused. "It was all so sudden. I suppose I just thought I'd stepped onto some rotten wood." I knew this wasn't the exact truth but didn't want to admit it to myself."

"Where is he now?" Red asked anxiously.

"Who? Ross? He's in the UK."

He sighed. "Right, that's good."

"You can't seriously think that Ross cut through the decking in order to cause me harm? What on earth for – he hardly knows me."

"Let's just say, I'm happy he's not staying at the villa at the moment. Do you know how long he'll be away?"

"Er, no."

"In that case, let me know as soon as he returns. I suggest you take care never to be alone with him."

I gave a nervous laugh. "I can't believe what you're saying. Ross Maitland didn't do it. Why would he?"

He took my hand in his and said, "I suspect that Diana Huntley asked the same question."

Chapter 13

Leaving Red to drive back to Villefranche, I sat in my car and tried to make sense of his suspicions, none of which made any sense. He'd told me that he'd met Diana Huntley in London in November the previous year and kept in touch with her ever since. When she told him she was going to the south of France with her employer, he'd asked her not to forget about him and to let him know all about how the other half lived. His curiosity as to her welfare was aroused when he received a frantic phone call from her stating that she was afraid someone was trying to kill her. Her voice was slurred as if she was drunk at the time and there was the sound of a party in full swing in the background.

At first he'd thought she was imagining things, as he'd heard nothing more from her. Then came the news that she'd died in an accident. He contacted the police, told them about the phone call but discovered some time later that there were no suspicious circumstances surrounding Diana's death.

He said when he'd met me on the train he was planning to do some investigating himself. He'd made up the story about him studying French. He had some time off work and intended to take a look into the circumstances surrounding her death. The coincidence, of finding that I was working at the same Maitland's villa, had been too fortunate to ignore.

He hinted that he suspected Ross of being involved in some way, not only with Diana's death but also with my accident.

A Tangled Web

Driving back to the villa, I thought how preposterous his suggestion seemed. Why would Ross Maitland have killed Diana and engineered my fall? It didn't make any sense.

There was a pale blue E-Type jaguar parked in the drive alongside the Mercedes. I wondered if Olivia had invited some of her famous friends to visit and began to feel excited at the prospect.

When I entered the hallway, I could hear voices coming from the music room overlooking the front terrace, which faced the sea. I'd started to climb the stairs to my room when Pierre opened a door to my left.

"Excuse me, Miss. Mrs Maitland asked if you would join her on the terrace when you are free."

"Thank you, Pierre, I will, just as soon as I've freshened up."

I rushed up the stairs, changed out of my shorts into a cotton sundress, dragged a comb through my hair and hurried to meet Olivia's guests.

The late afternoon sun was sinking on the horizon filling the room with shades of gold and touching the heads of the couple standing with Olivia at the window. They were drinking champagne and laughing with their hostess.

"Anna! Do come and meet Brigitte and Hank."

The woman had her back to me. She was young, her blonde hair pinned up in a French pleat from which strands had been artfully left to curl to her shoulders. I held my breath, was this Brigitte Bardot, the French film star, everyone was talking about? When she turned to face me, I could see there was a distinct resemblance, the features, the make-up but this woman was no ingénue, she was nearly forty, if she was a day.

"Hello, nice to meet you. Olivia has been singing your praises, all afternoon." Her eyes swept over my cheap sundress as if assessing my monetary worth then, deciding I failed miserably in that department, she dismissed me by turning to face her companion. "Hank, be a dear and fetch a refill." She handed him her empty champagne glass.

Hank, a short, thickset man, in his early fifties hurried to do her bidding and I wondered at their relationship.

"What have you been up to this afternoon, my dear?" Olivia asked as Pierre arrived with a tray and handed me a glass of champagne.

"Oh, nothing much. I met a friend in Beaulieu, who is staying just around the coast in Villefranche."

Someone appearing from the direction of the lower terrace, which overlooked the rocky coastline, suddenly distracted her attention. I held my breath. It was Ross with a young woman who was holding on to his arm like a leech. I recognised Ruby Dent immediately. She was a young jazz singer who'd been making her name on the London club scene.

Under other circumstances, I would have been thrilled to meet a minor celebrity such as Ruby Dent but the way she fluttered her coal black lashes at Ross destroyed any hint of pleasure I might have felt at the prospect of meeting her.

The champagne was making me light-headed. I hadn't eaten much all day, Red's uncomfortable revelation having robbed me of an appetite.

Ross reached the terrace as Brigitte enveloped him in an embrace. "Now the party's really started," she cooed. Hank coughed and moved closer.

"Hank, good to see you again." Ross extricated himself for Brigitte's clutches and stepped forward to shake the older man's hand. Then he saw me.

"Er, Anna. I don't think you've met Ruby." He turned to his companion. "Ruby this is mother's biographer." He made it sound more important than it was and for that I felt unaccountably grateful. Perhaps it was from a lack of self-confidence in such elevated company, although I would never have considered myself to be so shallow.

Ruby stepped forward and to my amazement kissed my cheek. "Hi, Anna, Good to meet you."

I wanted to dislike her, if only because of the proprietorial way she'd clung to Ross whilst walking up the garden but my instinct was just the opposite. I took to Ruby Dent straight away.

As evening shadows lengthened, Velma arrived with Nick and Jacky Ferris. Food was served on the terrace and afterwards someone suggested that Ruby and Olivia should sing for us.

"Not me darlings, a lifetime of Players full-strength have taken their toll on my vocal chords but Ruby, please do, if only to save everyone from listening to me." Olivia blew Ruby a kiss, as Ross, to my surprise, walked over to the grand piano, sat down and started to play Blue Moon, a particular favourite of mine.

I'd heard Ruby Dent sing on the radio but was unprepared for a live performance. She was fantastic. I was no expert but even to my ears her vocal range was incredible, her pitch was perfect. She captivated her audience with a toss of her head, a look from beneath those thick black eyelashes, and with her haunting melodic voice. When she'd finished I joined the others in encouraging her to continue and was thrilled that she accepted our praise and entertained us until the moon coated the lawn in silver and the guests drifted away one by one.

Ruby was staying in the room next to Velma's but she was a night owl and sat talking to Ross long after Velma and Olivia had gone to bed. I chatted to them for a while then left them when my continual yawning became an embarrassment.

"See you in the morning then," Ruby said. "Bright and early?"

"You'll be up, bright and early?" I asked incredulously.

"That's me. I don't sleep much, afraid of missing something."

I grinned. "Night then."

Ross stood up and walked with me into the hallway.

"You are OK aren't you?" he asked looking down at me with an expression I found difficult to assess. "I've been worried about you since your fall."

"Fine. I'm fine."

"Right, well goodnight then." He bent down and kissed my cheek then walked back to join Ruby.

Chapter 14

Ruby was sitting on the terrace eating breakfast when I joined her the following morning. "True to your word, you really can't sleep," I said.

"Always been the same, even when I was a child."

The early morning sun showed me a Ruby I'd not been aware of last night. She was young, probably no more than twenty. Her skin was translucent and her chestnut hair which swung to her shoulders, shone with health.

"How do you know Ross?" I asked, but failed to sound as offhand as I'd anticipated.

"Yeah, everyone falls for Ross."

I blushed and was furious for doing so.

"It's OK. He's not available though; most of us have tried at one time or another. He's impervious to our charms."

I shuddered at the thought.

Ruby grinned. "No, no, not that, don't get me wrong, he likes women well enough."

"He's in love with someone?"

"Been in love, unrequited, I heard."

"Diana Huntley?"

"What? No. she was one of the ones that tried and failed. I'm not sure but I think it was some years ago now."

Footfalls across the floor, followed by Velma's appearance, curtailed the rest of our conversation. But I did notice that Ruby had failed to answer my question as to how she'd met Ross. Deciding it was unimportant and probably had something to do with his mother being in the same business, I bit into a croissant and felt the butter sliding down my chin as Ross walked up the lawn from the direction of the sun terrace, a newspaper tucked under his arm.

"It's going to be a another hot one," he said, sitting at my side and opening the paper.

"When are you going to take me to Saint Tropez, Ross? You promised," Ruby asked.

"Did I?"

"You most definitely did. And if it's going to be a hot one why don't you take Anna and me out on the water today?"

He looked uncomfortable at the suggestion.

"Look, if you don't mind, I've got rather a lot on, Ruby. I'm way behind with work as it is," I said.

She smiled and draped one leg sensuously over the side of her chair. "Looks like it'll be just you and me, babe?" She smiled at Ross.

"Sorry to disappoint you. Like Anna, I've too much on today. Some other time, I promise."

Undeterred, Ruby jumped to her feet. "You and your promises, Ross Maitland." She poked his arm as she passed his chair. "I'm off to persuade Nick and Jacky that they are desperate to visit the coast."

We watched as she squeezed through the hedge at the bottom of the garden, a short cut to the Ferris's property, until she disappeared out of sight.

"They don't know what they're in for," Ross exclaimed, picking up his newspaper once more.

"Right then, I'll see you later I expect." I stood up and as I passed his chair he caught hold of my hand. "You must be careful," he said.

"Careful?"

A Tangled Web

He coughed, seemed embarrassed and let my hand drop. "Erm just watch where you're walking. I mean, just take care, that's all."

Walking upstairs to the study, I thought it decidedly odd that this was the second time I'd been told to be careful. Tom Trevellyn, the gardener at Longacres, had said the same thing and for the life of me I couldn't understand why.

Olivia didn't make an appearance until mid-day by which time I had almost finished writing chapter two. However, she was decidedly disinterested in my progress. She stood by the window smoking and complaining about the heat. My attempts at trying to get her to talk about how we should continue with chapter three hit a brick wall.

"I'll leave it up to you, dear. You obviously have things in hand. I've a headache; I think I'll take a walk to clear my head." She walked to the door. "No need to continue with this today. It's far too hot. Why don't you take the afternoon off to enjoy yourself? Tomorrow's another day."

As the door closed behind her, I thought, at this rate, I was unlikely to finish her memoirs this side of next year and wondered how long I would be content to continue, however accommodating my employer became. But the sound of Ross, calling out a good morning to Hank, put all thoughts of terminating my employment out of my head for the foreseeable future.

Olivia was right about one thing, the temperature was rising; most of the sunbeds on the terrace were occupied. Ruby, Hank and Brigitte were alternatively sunbathing and cooling off by diving into the pool.

A Tangled Web

Nick and Jacky were talking to Velma and drinking cocktails but there was no sign of Ross or Olivia.

Packing a canvas duffle bag with my bathing costume and a towel, I decided to drive to the breach at Beaulieu. However, when I reached the main stretch, I could see I wasn't the only one with the same idea.

The prospect of finding an unoccupied patch of sand and a deckchair was daunting. I leaned against the wall overlooking the beach and saw a familiar face peering up at me.

"Are you stalking me, Miss Fairfax?" Red grinned.

"Absolutely."

"Why don't you come down and join me then?"

"I don't think so. Too crowded for me. I think I'll drive further along the coast and look for a quiet cove."

He clambered to his feet, scattering sand in all directions much to the annoyance of his neighbours. "Fancy some company?"

"I do actually. Shake some more sand off and you've got a deal."

Once Red was sitting alongside me, I asked him if he knew of a suitable place nearby, away from the crowds.

"There's a cove a mile or two along the coast. Of course, it might be busy today, you never know, what with this heat, but you have to climb down a rocky stretch to get to the beach, which I think discourages most people."

"Sounds just the place," I said, "point me in the right direction."

Chapter 15

It was, as Red had suggested, not the easiest of walks down to the cove, which was why there were only a few people brave or foolish enough to have attempted the descent. It was worth taking the trouble though. The sand was soft under our feet and the sea as blue as amethysts.

"What d'you think?" asked Red.

"Perfect."

We spread out our towels on the sand near a rocky overhang, which provided a certain amount of shade. I think I was the first to nod off. Red was talking about someone he'd met in London and his voice drifted away on the breeze. The dream was pleasant, the details indistinct, and I awoke to hear a shriek of laughter from the beach. A young couple were fooling about in the shallows.

"Enjoy your nap?" Red was bending over me dripping seawater on to my legs.

"I did. Enjoy your swim?"

"Great. Fancy joining me, now you're awake?" He grinned and pulled me to my feet.

The water was cool and slid over my body like a sheet of satin. I lay on my back and floated for a while then followed Red and swam around the rocks and into a small beach where a cruiser was moored. The beach was nothing more than a strip of sand only accessible by boat. I heard laughter coming from the shore and to my dismay saw Ross and Ruby Dent lying side by side on the sand. So much for Ross being too busy, I thought. Feeling a sudden dip in my spirits, I turned around and swam back to the cove.

"Had enough?" Red asked.

"Yeah, something like that."

"Huh! No stamina, if you ask me." He followed me up the sandy beach and slumped down beside me. "Hey, what d'you say we drive around the coast to Nice tomorrow?"

"Not sure. It depends on Olivia. She's not likely to let me have tomorrow off as well."

"OK then. What if I give you a ring at ten? Let me know how the land lies and we can make arrangements then."

I agreed but, rather than being thankful for the invitation, the sight of the couple on the beach had put a dampener on my enthusiasm for his offer.

As things turned out Red and I didn't meet the next day. Olivia was in a mood to work and I made up for the time I'd wasted on the beach in a frantic burst of industry. Eventually, I had a rough draft of the third chapter in sight and Olivia seemed pleased enough. Whether she'd tired herself out during the day or not, she appeared as usual for dinner and drinks afterwards on the terrace.

Ruby was drinking heavily but there was no sign of Ross, neither at dinner nor afterwards. At a quarter to eleven, I decided I'd had enough, left them to it and went to bed. I was at the bottom of the stairs when the front door opened and Ross entered.

"Anna, I'm glad I've caught you. There's something I need to talk to you about. It's important...I"

He didn't finish his sentence as Ruby, swaying slightly, closed the door to the dining room behind her and threw herself at Ross. "Come on Rossy wossy, we're drinking out on the terrace. I wondered where you'd got to." She draped her arms around his neck and started to steer him towards the garden. "Anna's no fun, she's off to bed. You'll keep me company won't you, darling?"

Ross raised his eyes at me and mouthed, "In the morning?"

I nodded and went upstairs to bed.

There was a slight breeze blowing through the window but it was pleasantly cool after the heat of the afternoon. I stood on the balcony for a while until the sound of Ruby crooning a melody to Ross became monotonously repetitive. Closing the French windows a fraction to block out her voice, I climbed into bed unaware that I was listening to Ruby's swan song and that the events of the coming day were set to cast a long shadow.

Chapter 16

I wasn't sure what time it was when Ross crept into my room. There was a faint glow showing through the curtains but the sun always rose early so it could have been any time from half-past four onwards.

Still only half awake, I felt his hand over my mouth and began to struggle.

"Keep still, it's only me. I don't want you to make a sound. Do you understand?" he whispered in my ear.

I nodded as he removed his hand from my mouth. "I need you to get up now, as quietly as possible, pack your things, or as many as you can take in a small bag. Make sure to take your passport. There's a flight leaving in two hours from Nice. I'll drive you there as soon as you're dressed. Don't worry about money, I've seen to all that."

Feeling as if I was still dreaming, I managed to whisper, "What on earth's happened? Where and why am I supposed to be going?"

"Please, Anna, don't ask any more questions. Tom Trevellyn will meet your flight and drive you to Longacres. Once you are home, I'll ring you."

"But...."

He ignored me and began packing my things in my small case. I slid out of bed and took over from him.

"Can't I even have a shower?"

"No. Just hurry, please."

The drive to the airport was undertaken in silence. I did try to get Ross to explain why I was leaving in such a rush but he told me he couldn't say more at the moment. He would be happier once I arrived at

Longacres, he said. It seems odd to me now that I should have let myself be swept along without asking to speak to Olivia. His insistence that I should leave immediately seemed so urgent and he *was* my employer's son so I supposed he was indirectly informing me of her wishes.

At the airport, he left me walking to the checking in desk, waited until I reached the entrance to the departure lounge, and raised his hand to me as I looked back at him.

Later, feeling the aircraft leaving the runway and heading for the clouds, the sensation of living in a dream still persisted. Why didn't I insist on talking to Olivia before leaving? Why didn't he want anyone to hear us? Red's warning about Ross filtered into my brain and however hard I tried, I couldn't still the voice telling me I was making a big mistake by trusting Ross Maitland.

Tom was waiting at the airport. He looked different. He was wearing a collarless lightweight jacket, cotton shirt and denim jeans. He took my small case and loaded it into the boot of the saloon car I'd seen Ross driving the first time I'd met him on the road to Longacres.

"I don't know why I had to leave in such a hurry but it's good of you to meet me," I said, as he opened the car door for me.

"No problem," he said.

"Did Ross say anything to you about it?"

"Look, if I were you, I'd sit back and relax. Ross will ring you, once I've spoken to him."

I sighed. So he was as tight lipped as his employer. There was nothing more I could do so I took his advice and waited until we reached Longacres.

A Tangled Web

There was drizzle in the air as we arrived at the house and, although it was warm, the temperature was nothing like I'd experienced in France. I shivered and carried my bag inside leaving Tom to park the car.

"Good to see you again, Miss." Joe said. "Esther is in Little Minnock shopping but I put the kettle on as soon as I heard the car. I'll bring you up a cup of coffee, just as you like it and leave you to unpack."

After thanking him and reaching my room, I found I couldn't stop shaking. It was a relief to lie down on the bed and close my eyes. Was there something going on at the villa that Ross Maitland wanted to hide from me? Did it have something to do with Olivia? Was he afraid she'd reveal something about her past, which was damaging in some way? One question followed another until I thought I'd drown in a whirlpool of doubt.

The coffee was strong and black and helped restore my equilibrium. I was getting out of the shower when I heard the phone ring. Dressed in a bathrobe, I answered the extension on the landing. I thought I heard the faint click of the phone being picked up downstairs but as no one spoke I couldn't be sure.

"Anna?" It was Ross. "Was you flight smooth? Are you settled in at Longacres?" His voice sounded strange, his conversation stilted."

"You said you'd explain. What is it Ross?" There was silence from the other end, followed shortly afterwards by the sound of weeping in the background. "Ross, what's happened? What is it?"

"I'm sorry, Anna. The police are here at the moment and well, there's no easy way to tell you. It's Ruby. She's dead, I'm afraid."

I gasped and was left holding the phone, hearing the disconnected line buzzing in my ear. Someone had cut the connection.

There was a small piece about Ruby on the six o'clock television news. I sat alone in the drawing room and watched the announcer saying.

The young jazz singer Ruby Dent, who has been making her name on the London club scene, has been found dead in her room at Olivia Maitland's villa in the south of France. The French police are looking into the circumstances surrounding her death and their findings will be made clear later.

Was this why Ross wanted me out of the way? Was he involved?

I heard nothing from him or Olivia during that day or the next. I couldn't concentrate on work and sat at my desk staring into space. On the third day after I'd arrived back at Longacres, the newspapers were full of it. There were no suspicious circumstances surrounding Ruby's death. She'd been in the habit of using purple hearts, otherwise known as speed and had taken an overdose, apparently.

The following day, Esther and Joe appeared to be preparing for the arrival of Olivia, who it seemed couldn't bear to stay at the villa a moment longer.

It was in the evening, half eight or so when I heard Olivia arrive with Velma. I kept out of their way until I was needed. Why? I suppose I was afraid to bump into Ross. However, I needn't have worried; when Joe told me he was still in France, I couldn't be sure whether I felt disappointed or relieved.

A Tangled Web

At breakfast the following day, I was surprised to see both Olivia and Velma seated in the breakfast room. Olivia's eyes were red-rimmed. She greeted me with, "Anna, how are you, my dear, such terrible news." She dabbed at her eyes with a handkerchief and continued, "I still can't quite believe it. Ruby was so young, such fun. What a waste."

"It was a shock to me too. She seemed so vibrant, so unlikely to take her own life."

Both Olivia and Velma exchanged a glance then Velma said, "Appearances can be deceptive. She was head over heels in love with Ross. Unrequited love can be so traumatic in the young, I always find."

Suddenly I lost my appetite. This wasn't right surely? Ruby wasn't heartbroken over Ross. I'd chatted to her about him and knew she thought it was all a game. She'd tried to net him in London, she'd told me, and liked the idea of seeing him squirm like a fish on a hook now that they were thrown together again in France. This wasn't about unrequited love, I was certain about that. But not so certain that it was an accident; one accident could be a mistake but two was getting to be a habit.

Chapter 17

For the next few weeks I immersed myself in the work I'd been hired to complete, tried to forget my misgivings where Diana and Ruby's deaths were concerned and watched summer unfolding in the Devonshire countryside. The trees surrounding the estate and in the woods were dressed in so many shades of green it would have been impossible to count them. Tom's expertise had ensured that the rose garden was a delight and the borders and planters were well stocked with flowering plants right through the summer months.

It was nearly a month later, when the sun was high in the sky and we hadn't had rain for a week or two, that I saw Ross.

I'd decided to take a late afternoon stroll down to the creek. The air was thick with the scent of roses as I cut across the garden to reach the stile leading into the woods. Midges gathered around my head and I flicked them away with an impatient hand as I took the overgrown pathway, which would eventually lead to the creek. I'd discovered this route two weeks ago and jealously guarded its secret.

Parting a few branches, which had grown across the path, I came to the spot where the ground fell away towards a stretch of sparkling blue water threading its way though the countryside.

Removing a picnic rug from my duffle bag, I spread it on the dried grass, searched to the bottom of the bag, found my book and a thermos of iced lemonade and lay back to enjoy the rest of the afternoon.

The words ran into each other and, as the shadows lengthened, I fell asleep. I was dreaming about Ruby when I was roused into wakefulness by the sound of voices.

"She's asleep. I've been watching her ever since she left the house."

"And there's nothing unusual, no one poking their nose in where it's not wanted? What about Joe and Esther?" It was Ross speaking. By this time I was fully awake and knew I wasn't mistaken.

"The same." I couldn't be sure who the owner of the second voice was but I thought it might be Tom Trevellyn.

Looking around in the faded light I wondered where they were. A cabin cruiser was moored at a jetty, which I recognised as belonging to the Maitlands. It was too far away for me to hear if anyone was aboard but the woods to my rear offered ample concealment in the form of thick summer foliage, which was where the men probably were.

I was about to pack up my things when I heard a rustling sound behind me followed by footsteps crunching over the dried grass.

"Ah, here you are. I wondered where you'd got to." It was Ross. He was wearing shorts and a pale cotton shirt with the sleeves rolled up to his elbow; lowering himself to the ground he sat down beside me.

"How long have you been home?" I asked.

"I arrived early this morning. I wanted to speak to you about Ruby." He turned to face me. "I stayed on at the villa because there were some inconsistencies surrounding her death, which needed to be investigated."

"I don't understand. We were told it was a drugs related incident."

"So it was. Look I can't explain now." To my surprise, he took my hand in his. "I'm going to be away from Longacres for the next two weeks and if you are concerned about anything unusual happening I want you to tell Tom Trevellyn about it."

"The gardener?"

He laughed, a harsh, bitter sound, incongruously competing with the gentle lapping of water against its banks and the humming of insects in the trees.

"Will you do as I ask?"

"Of course but surely, if you are worried, shouldn't you be telling the police of your concerns? Especially if you suspect that Ruby's death was no accident."

He sighed, stood up and stretched out his hand to help me to my feet. "Time to get back to the house, I think. It will be dark in the woods soon."

I followed, as he parted the branches and we walked back along the path I'd trodden earlier. Light still filtered through the leaves but Ross was right, I wouldn't have fancied being in the woods alone as darkness descended, especially in view of recent events. I was even more certain now that Ruby's death was suspicious and the thought sent a shiver down my spine.

"I'll walk back with you to the house but then I have to drive into Little Minnock. Perhaps I'll see you later at dinner," Ross said helping me over the stile.

I was surprised how quickly dusk had fallen. I must have been asleep longer than I'd thought; I'd left my watch on the dressing table in my room and had lost track of time.

"Thanks, for walking me back," I said, as he turned towards his car.

"No problem. My pleasure." He raised his hand without turning around.

As I entered the house I felt uncomfortably aware that I was no nearer to making up my mind about Ross Maitland. Red's warning was still something I found difficult to ignore and returned to haunt me just when I thought I'd put it to rest.

I hadn't heard a word from Red since my hasty return to Longacres. It wasn't in the least bit surprising. He had no idea that I'd left the south of France, as I didn't have any way of contacting him. He'd told me he was staying at a friend's place and I had no idea where it was except in the region of Villefranche.

"There you are, my dear. Did you enjoy your siesta?" Olivia was standing at the foot of the stairs wearing a flimsy pale blue and white kaftan and holding a large straw hat. "Too hot for me. I'm to linger in a nice cool bath before dinner. Have you seen Ross anywhere about?"

"He's gone into Little Minnock."

"Really? How tiresome." She turned away and climbed the stairs ahead of me. "It's a mystery what that boy gets up to." At the top of the stairs, she strolled along the landing towards her room leaving me to walk in the opposite direction to mine.

It was dark by the time I opened my bedroom door but I was surprised to see the French doors were closed and the atmosphere inside was hot and stuffy. I was sure I'd opened them before I'd left the house and supposed that Esther must have closed them.

Switching on a sidelight, I walked towards the window in order to stand on the balcony for a while to

73

cool myself down in the breeze sweeping in from the sea. As I reached the French doors I saw a scrap of material wedged between the lock and the frame. It was pale blue cotton, the type used in men's shirts, the sort of shirt I'd see Ross wearing earlier.

Chapter 18

Dinner was a dismal affair that evening. Olivia picked at her food, complaining about the heat and a pounding headache. She left us sitting on the terrace at nine o'clock and went to bed to sleep it off. Ross spoke little, sipped at his wine, and watched the moonlight creeping up the garden as if his life depended on it.

Only Velma seemed unconcerned by her companions lack of conversation and chatted on about the time she first met Olivia in New York and how they had been friends ever since. Fortunately there was no necessity for me to join in her recollections, other than to nod and murmur the occasional yes or no at the appropriate time and to sit back and let my mind try to make some sense of recent events.

An hour or so later, Velma began to yawn and left Ross and me alone. He was the first to break the silence.

"Make sure you lock your bedroom door at night," he said.

His remark was so unexpected and unconnected to anything that I almost laughed. "What is it? Why? I've been hired to write your mother's memoirs, nothing more. Is there an axe murderer lurking in the woods?" The whole cloak and danger thing was getting to me. I'd drunk too much wine and was beginning to find the whole thing ludicrous. First Tom Trevellyn tried to warn me of impending danger then Red continued by suggesting that Ross might mean to harm me, and now Ross was at it. It was all too ridiculous, especially as no one had explained why anyone would wish to harm me.

He leaned towards me, his face pale in the moonlight. "Just a precaution," he replied, with a tight smile. "We're very isolated here and apparently there have been a few burglaries in Little Minnock lately."

It was a pretty lame explanation and I could see by his expression that he knew it to be so. I stood up, swayed slightly then straightened up so as to appear more sober than I felt.

"If you'll excuse me, I think I'll turn in."

He stood up and walked with me to the bottom of the main staircase then put a hand on my arm. "Remember what I said, Anna."

"Oh yeah. The burglaries!" I shrugged and climbed the stairs, whilst being aware he was watching me until I reached the landing.

Thankfully I slept until morning without focusing on Ross Maitland. I rose early, showered then went for a run around the grounds. An elderly man was planting the borders with summer flowering pansies and marigolds. There was no sign of Tom.

The sun was warm on my back promising another blisteringly hot day. The thought of being stuck in an airless study for most of the day wasn't an enticing one so when I reached the woods I decided to run along the banks of the creek where it would be cool.

There was a mist rising up from the water, which was thicker in places than others. I thought I heard the slop, slop of oars but couldn't be sure and I wasn't able to see the banks on the opposite side because the mist had thickened since I first broke through the cover of the trees. In the distance I could hear the rushing sound of the weir but had no intention of extending my run in that direction as my stomach was warning me not to miss breakfast.

Then I saw it. A small punt was being rowed in the centre of the creek. A figure was hunched over the oars but the mist was still swirling over the water and the image became indistinct. The craft was heading in the direction of the weir. I called out a warning but my voice was lost on the breeze and muffled by the mist.

Turning back to retrace my steps I ran straight into Tom Trevellyn.

"Hey, steady on, what's the hurry?" He grinned and held on to my shoulders.

"There's a punt, in the creek, it's heading for the weir," I gasped, the words spilling out of my mouth in a rush.

"Right. You go back to the house, I'll see to it." He ran ahead of me and I could hear him calling out a warning as I hurried back through the woods, satisfied that the unwary boatman would have to be deaf not to have heard him.

After taking a quick shower, I headed for the terrace, where breakfast was being served. Olivia and Velma were walking back from the lower terrace having breakfasted overlooking the coast.

"It's going to be another hot one," Velma commented. "I'm off to Smugglers' Cove. If anyone's brave enough to join me, you're welcome." She smiled encouragingly at me.

"Have fun," I replied, and as Olivia approached. I looked up from my plate and said, "I won't be long."

"No hurry. In fact I've left some notes on the desk, which should keep you busy for an hour or two. I've a headache, too much sun yesterday, I expect. I'm going to take it easy today. When you've finished, take the afternoon off; it's far too hot to work anyway."

77

Later, as I climbed the stairs to the study, it occurred to me that Olivia's headaches seemed to be increasing. I'd not heard her say she'd consulted a doctor and wondered whether this was a normal pattern for her. Although she was in her sixties she was fit and looked far younger than her years; perhaps I should mention my concerns to Ross when I next saw him.

However, I didn't get the chance as I heard Ross was in London on business and wouldn't be expected to return for a while. Over the next few days the temperature rose and I saw little of Olivia. She left work for me every morning and most afternoons I spent either in the garden, lying on the beach at Smugglers' Cove, or shopping in Little Minnock.

It was during one such shopping expedition that I saw Red again. He was sitting on a bench near the village green, reading a paperback. At first I thought I was seeing things.

"Red?"

"Anna!" He rose to his feet looking nonplussed. "What are you doing here?"

"I could ask you the same question."

"Staying here, actually. I bumped into an old friend in France and he suggested I finish the summer at his house in Little Minnock as he was planning to go trekking in the Himalayas and the place would be empty." He shrugged. "You know me, something always seems to turn up. I was way out of funds anyway and had planned to return from the Riviera and well this seemed a good place to stay for a while. And may I say, it's getting better by the minute." He tucked his arm in mine and led me towards the teashop on the High Street. "But what are you doing here?"

A Tangled Web

"Working. Olivia has a house nearby."

"How convenient. Couldn't be better, in my opinion."

We spent the rest of the day together, and afterwards I realised I was looking forward to having Red living so near. He made me feel secure and was fun to be with, neither of which I could attribute to Ross Maitland, who always made me feel slightly uneasy. It didn't occur to me to question the fact that Red staying in the village was extremely coincidental. I accepted it without question.

A week after my first meeting with Red, Ross returned from London and my previous feelings of contentment were to disappear like breath on a mirror.

Chapter 19

The routine, which had been established a Longacres, changed dramatically the following day. The house was alive with activity. Olivia, her headache obviously no longer plaguing her, was up and about at the crack of dawn insisting that we begin early as we had so much work to cover before her guests arrived. She didn't elaborate but I found out later it was her birthday the following day and she'd invited some friends to stay for the weekend.

It was nearly four o'clock by the time I'd finished work and was able to drive into the village in order to buy a gift for Olivia.

What could you buy a woman who had everything? I wandered aimlessly from shop to shop eventually finishing up in *The Old Curiosity Shop* a sort of junk/antiques place presided over by a Pickwickian character of indeterminate age.

"Caught in the act." I felt a hand on my shoulder and turned to see Ross smiling down at me.

"OK. I admit it. But I'm struggling to find anything suitable. Any ideas?"

"I'm sure anything you buy will be acceptable. Mother's not the diva some folk think as no doubt you've discovered by now."

Walking towards a pile of old sheet music, I left Ross picking up a book, in which he suddenly appeared to have taken an interest. The doorbell pinged and I heard a customer enter but didn't look up, as I'd just found exactly what I wanted. Under a stack of yellowing sheet music I found *Hey Baby Blues* and *Moonshine Monday* a couple of Olivia's early successes. I removed both copies from the stack and walked deeper into the store where I was fortunate enough to find a cream leather folder, which although yellowed with age, still looked good and complemented my purchases exactly. I was so pleased, I was only dimly aware that the doorbell had pinged again and Ross had left the shop.

After paying for my gifts, I went into the street and, with a self-satisfied expression, began walking towards my car. Placing my purchases on the seat at my side, I drove past the village green and to my astonishment saw Ross obviously having a heated exchange with someone. I couldn't hear what they were saying and it wasn't until Ross turned away that I saw a flash of red hair and an instantly recognisable face.

What was going on? Driving towards *The Green Man* pub, I decided to find out. The small car park was quiet and I managed to find a spot, out of sight of the village green, where I waited until I saw Ross's car drive past the pub and out of the village in the direction of Longacres.

Red was walking towards me as I made my way back to the green.

"I thought it was you," I said. "What's going on?"

He grinned and slid his arm through mine. "Off to the pub for a cool beer, coming?"

I had little choice, if I wanted to know the answer to my question so let myself be guided back to *The Green Man.*

By now it was nearly six-thirty and the evening clientele had decided to make an appearance. Eventually Red joined me at a table overlooking the beer-garden.

"Well?" I looked up at him.

"OK. I could stick to my story about staying with a friend, who just happened to be living in the vicinity and, hey, what d'you know, it just happened to be in the village where you did your shopping. Or I could tell the truth."

"Always a good option, I find."

He grinned and lifted his pint glass to his lips. "Part of it's true. I am staying at a friend's place as I told you when we met the other day. But, I did know it was close to Longacres and I was concerned about you when you disappeared from France, without contacting me, after Ruby died."

"You knew Ruby?"

He looked uncomfortable. "Yeah, sort of."

"Why were you concerned about me?"

"I'd prefer not to answer that one at the moment. Let's say I wanted to make sure you didn't have any more 'little' accidents."

I spluttered. "You aren't serious?"

"Deadly," he replied, without the trace of a smile.

A shiver ran down my spine and although the evening was warm, I felt as if I would never feel its warmth again. The reason for his altercation with Ross was staring me in the face and it left me feeling as if the bottom had fallen out of my world.

He must have realised my changing mood because he reached across the table and took my hand. "Don't take any notice of me. I'm just looking out for a friend, that's all. It was fortunate for me that Tim lived in Little Minnock and was planning a couple of weeks, maybe months on a climbing expedition. His place was empty and he was pleased to have someone looking after it for him, whilst he's away – simple as!"

I tried to smile but it was a weak attempt. "Come on, cheer up. Your old friend Red is here and looking forward to you showing him around tomorrow. What d'you say?"

What could I say? His mood was infectious and before long he was making me laugh and cheering me up no end.

"What's the matter?" he asked as I looked at my watch and frowned.

"I've missed dinner and I should have at least rung the house."

"Bit late now?"

"Just a bit."

"Right then, let's see what *The Green Man* can offer and hope it doesn't turn us the colour indicated on its sign."

It was late when I arrived back at Longacres. Ross was pacing back and forth in the drive. He waited until I closed the car door then, with a face like thunder, said, "Where have you been? You missed dinner?"

I started to apologise then changed my mind. "I didn't know I had to check in with you Mr Maitland. I'll apologise to Esther about not informing her I wouldn't be dining tonight, so you've no need to be concerned."

He was trying hard to recover some equilibrium but failing miserably. "Er, right, as long as you're OK then." He walked away in the direction of the rose garden leaving me to enter the house alone.

Was Red right to be concerned about my safety at Longacres, I wondered? And, unable to come to a satisfying conclusion, I climbed the stairs to bed.

Chapter 20

Breakfast was eaten in almost complete silence. Olivia was eating hers in her room, with instructions that I should join her in the study at nine on the dot. I sensed my unexplained absence from dinner the previous evening hadn't gone unnoticed by my employer. Ross stood up as I entered the breakfast room, nodded in my direction, and, sometime later, I heard the sound of his car being driven at speed down the driveway. Velma had a summer cold, sniffed her way though a plate of scrambled eggs then left with just the briefest attempt at excusing herself, so I was left with a plate of uneaten croissants for which I'd lost my appetite.

The morning passed without the usual laid-back attitude I had come to expect from Olivia. She dictated without her normal good humour then as lunchtime approached, she said, "You have plenty to keep you occupied this afternoon, Anna. Will you be joining us for dinner this evening?"

I felt the hackles on the back of my neck rise in annoyance, what was it with this family, did they think they owned me?

"I don't think I will, I'm meeting a friend," I lied.

"I see. Well don't forget to inform Esther."

"Certainly, "I replied, feeling I'd been rebuked by the Headmistress for some trivial misdemeanour.

As soon as I was able to leave the house I went in search of Red and found him, as before, sitting on a bench on the village green reading the local newspaper.

"Escaped again, I see."

For a fraction of a second I felt how apt his words were. "Fancy another meal in *The Green Man*?" I asked but to my surprise he shook his head.

"Sorry, sorry, if I'd known we were going to meet." He hung his head. "Made other arrangements for tonight. But tomorrow, definitely tomorrow, same place, same time?"

I sat down on the recently vacated bench and sighed. It was all very well making a point but the thought of sinking my teeth into an overdone steak in the pub in preference to Esther's dressed crab and salmon was almost too much to bear. However, I had no choice and after the briefest of meals, I left *The Green Man* and headed back to Longacres where I intended to have an early night with Agatha Christie.

Intentions are not always fulfilled because as soon as I drove up to the house, Joe Travers met me and handed me a note.

"It's for you, Miss," he explained, before leaving me and walking towards Tom Trevellyn who was wheeling a barrow towards the potting shed.

In the fading light I read.

"Will you meet me as soon as you read this. I'll be waiting on the bank of the creek by the boat. R"

I looked up at the sky. The sun was sinking but it was still light enough to see my way through the woods. Although I didn't fancy walking the same route once darkness descended, I was aware that I wouldn't be alone so crossed the stile and entered the woodland path without any fear.

It was much darker than I'd anticipated, a thick canopy of foliage obscuring what little light there was. Increasing my pace, I walked in the direction of the creek. I was used to this path now, having often walked it in the afternoons when my presence wasn't required in the study. But it was a different proposition in the rapidly gathering gloom.

Above my head, an owl hooted and the rapid flapping of bat's wings made me shudder at the prospect of taking a wrong turning in the wood. So it was with a degree of relief I heard the lapping of water against the banks of the creek and parting the branches stepped onto the grassy knoll where I'd previously seen Ross.

The boat was moored as usual at the jetty; it was the Maitlands' cabin cruiser lit from within and showing the outline of someone standing on deck.

Although the sun was still hovering on the horizon, rain clouds had gathered making it difficult to see clearly. I think I was aware of someone talking and of music drifting towards me from the cruiser. The attack was so sudden, I neither heard nor felt the initial blow, all I knew was darkness had descended and I was in no position to know why.

Chapter 21

It was still dark when I awoke. I stretched out my hand and touched a wall, the surface of which was damp. My head ached and I felt a lump like an egg rising from beneath my hair. There was a crust forming over the lump, which was presumably from dried blood. How long had I been unconscious, I wondered? Long enough for blood to have clotted, so longer than ten minutes presumably.

Then I smelled a distinct odour rising from the neck of my blouse. Chloroform? So I'd been sedated; in that case I could have been here for quite some time. But why? How was I any threat to anyone? I'd trusted Ross, in spite of Red's warning. Now it was beginning to look as if I'd been mistaken to do so.

Diana Huntley and Ruby's faces swam before me. Their deaths took on an altogether more sinister aspect in view of the position in which I now found myself. What was going on? None of it made any sense.

Trying to stand was not an easy task. My legs felt like jelly and the pounding in my head made me giddy. There was a musty atmosphere in my prison, the sort of smell that rose from a damp face flannel left to go mildew. I wrinkled my nose. Where was I? It must still be night-time but I couldn't tell due to the absence of a window. I started to feel around the walls, which were cold and clammy and dripping with damp. After completing my search, which was fruitless, the answer hit me – I was imprisoned in a cellar; was there such a place in Longacres? Possibly, it was a large old house. In that case there was always the chance someone would hear me if I shouted loudly enough. And there must be a staircase leading upwards. In the darkness, I began searching again but found nothing, no stairs and no door. What sort of prison had no door? To my shame, I sank to my knees and wept like a child.

After a while realisation began to dawn; my prison was rocking gently to and fro and there was something else. I listened and heard it again, the sound of water, the rhythmic slapping of ripples under my feet. I was in the bottom of a boat.

Remembering that the last thing I'd seen before passing out was the Maitlands' cruiser moored at the jetty; I came to the inevitable conclusion. Why had Ross imprisoned me, and what did he intend to do? The more I thought about it the more confused I became. My throbbing head made rational thought difficult; the pain obscured everything else, even the sound of voices nearby didn't immediately come to my attention until I heard the pounding of feet on the deck above.

I shrank back in a corner fearing discovery and to what it might lead. There was a scraping sound followed by the hatch opening and a flashlight illuminating the darkness. Blinking in the harsh beam, I saw the outline of someone lowering the ladder and climbing down.

"Thank God!" The voice was muffled but I thought I recognised it. Tom Trevellyn lowered the flashlight and came towards me. "Are you OK, Anna?"

"I think so," I croaked.

He put his arms around me and lifted me towards him. I staggered against him as he steered me towards the ladder and the hatch through which I could see moonlight.

Only dimly aware of Tom helping me back to the house and the commotion once Esther and Joe were roused from sleep, I was made to sit in the kitchen and given a tot of brandy before anyone began to question me.

"I'll ring Sergeant Boynton at the station," Tom said, after I'd explained what had happened.

"We should wake the missus." Joe looked anxiously at his wife.

"Where's Ross?" Tom asked, as he went to pick up the telephone in the hall.

"He was here earlier, at dinner," Esther frowned. "But we haven't seen him since and I think his car's gone. You know what he's like, comes and goes as he pleases."

Tom hesitated. "Perhaps you should wake Mrs Maitland. In any case she's bound to hear the police car arriving, it's on its last legs, much like its owner."

I tried to smile but the effort involved made my head swim.

Olivia descended the stairs as Sergeant Boynton arrived. She was wearing a pale blue silk negligée and her hair was tied up in turban. I thought she looked exotic.

"Joe, show the sergeant into the drawing room, please, then bring in Anna and Tom, there's a good chap."

She was seated in an upright chair, the sergeant standing, his notebook open and pencil raised in anticipation.

"Anna, sit here, my dear, next to me. What a dreadful ordeal." Her hands shot to her face when she saw me. "Perhaps you could make this quick, sergeant, I think Anna has suffered enough for one night."

"Aye, Mrs Maitland. Now, Miss, if you can tell me exactly what happened this evening."

I explained as much as I knew, which wasn't very much. In reality, I had no idea who my captor was or why. When I'd finished Olivia instructed Esther to help me up to my room and see I was comfortable. As I left the drawing room, I could hear Tom telling his version of the night's events. He said he was walking along the riverbank, as it was a warm night and he couldn't sleep, when he noticed the tarpaulin on the cruiser had been disturbed and went to investigate.

Once I was settled in bed, it occurred to me to wonder why Tom Trevellyn had lied to the sergeant. There was no tarpaulin on the deck and to my knowledge there never had been.

Chapter 22

I didn't mention Ross's note to the police. Perhaps it was a mistake not to do so but something made me hold back the information. Where was he, I wondered, surely he couldn't have done this to me? At length the painkillers kicked in and I fell asleep. It was nearly three o'clock.

I awoke from a dream where I was being strangled, I'd tried to call out but the words wouldn't come, however hard I tried. Looking out of the window at the dawn breaking over the sea, I thought I must have slept for an hour or two but when I glanced at my watch I realised it had been merely half an hour since I'd closed my eyes.

After such a traumatic experience I should have been glad to rest but my brain was active and I couldn't sleep. Opening the French windows I sat on the balcony and watched the sun coming up. The sea was as blue as the sky and both were streaked as if with tinsel, twinkling in the dawn light. I closed my eyes and took a deep breath trying to rid myself of the remnants of the dream but my meditation was interrupted by the sound of a car being driven at speed towards the house. My eyes shot open in time to see Ross Maitland closing his car door and running up the front steps to the house.

In less than five minutes I heard a soft knocking at my door and went to open it. He was looking down at me with an odd expression.

"You're OK?"

"Do you know what time it is?" I asked, suddenly annoyed.

"Yes, of course, I apologise. I've only just heard. I came straight away," he began, backing away from the door.

"Come in," I urged. " I need to talk to you."

He stood awkwardly moving from one foot to the other.

"Did you send me a note asking to meet me at the creek yesterday evening? " I demanded.

He hesitated. "Er, I…"

"Well! Yes or no?"

"It's both actually. Look, come and sit down and I'll explain." He led me to the balcony and pulled out a chair. "Please."

I sighed, drew the folds of my dressing closer around me and waited.

Ross looked over the balcony and around to either side then sat opposite me. "I did write a note asking you to meet me but I never sent it. As far as I was concerned it was still on the dashboard of my car. It was a shock to realise that it had disappeared."

"Why didn't you send it?"

"My intention was to get you to come to the creek without anyone knowing of the meeting. But before I could hand it to Joe to give to you, I had a phone call which made it impossible for me to meet you yesterday evening. So I left the envelope on the dashboard, went back inside to pick up my wallet and drove into the village."

He'd been driving a green open-topped sports car throughout the summer months and I could see how it would be possible for someone to remove the note, whilst he'd been looking for his wallet.

"I see, and you didn't notice the note had gone when you got back to the car?"

"No, I didn't, I was preoccupied. Believe me it's even more important for you to take care, after what had just happened." He leaned forward and took my hand in his. It felt warm and a comforting. "In fact I want you to stop working for mother at Longacres immediately."

I gasped and shook his hand away. "Whatever for? The police will deal with this. They'll find out who attacked me and that will be an end to it."

Ross stood up and looked out towards the coast. "I wish I could believe it," he said softly. "Please do as I say, Anna. I've typed a note to mother from you, explaining that you've been called away on family business and regret you can no longer continue your employment, all you have to do is sign it."

"I see so you've thought it all out."

"I haven't slept. I will of course continue to pay your wages until you find another situation."

"There's no need. I'll soon find something and I'm not destitute." I was indignant.

"I wasn't suggesting....." He turned to face me. "I'd be happier, please, at least let me give you this." He handed me an envelope. "Call it severance pay."

In the clear morning light I could see he was struggling to remain calm. "If you wish," I replied coolly as I stood up.

To my surprise he came towards me, put his hands on my shoulders and kissed the top of my head. "Where will you go? Back to London?"

He was still holding me. I could feel the warmth of his hands through the thin cotton of my dressing gown. "I expect." I replied, but the words came out like a croak.

"Please let me know your address and telephone number. I will explain why I need you to do as I ask, I promise, but it can't be now, there's too much at stake."

The fight went out of me then. I took the envelope with the money and the letter he'd prepared, promised to write to him letting him know where I was and watched him leave my room as quietly as he'd entered.

That morning I left Longacres before anyone in the house was up. I didn't see Ross Maitland as I drove away from the house but saw Tom Trevellyn standing in the doorway of the potting shed. He was smoking a cigarette and watching me through narrowed eyes.

The summer would end, autumn would pass and it would be during the first snows of winter that Longacres and the Maitland family would make headline news.

Chapter 23

I can't deny feeling sorry to be leaving and one of the reasons was Ross. In spite of the warnings I'd received from Red, who seemed to have disappeared off the face of the earth and was no longer staying at his friend's place in Little Minnock, I'd become fond of Ross Maitland. His insistence at my leaving left me confused and annoyed. However, there was nothing I could do about it and could only wait until he contacted me to explain the situation. He'd given me over two hundred pounds and wouldn't hear of taking any of it back. It was a fortune in the early sixties, when the cost of a fashionable suit of clothes was five pounds and shoes retailed at twenty-nine and eleven pence and I felt very uncomfortable at accepting such a sum.

However, once I'd driven to Lyn's house and told her I was in need of a bed until I found a suitable flat, I decided I would give every penny of the money back to him at the earliest opportunity.

Lyn was working for a small fashion magazine, which was giving Vogue a run for its money. She was a good friend and although we hadn't seen each other for months, it was as if we'd never been apart.

"I could ask Rosie if she has any work going," Lyn offered. "Someone's always leaving to get married."

So, after a successful interview with Rosie Kline, I began working as a reporter on *Hatchers* magazine. I was a hired as a junior but it was work and far enough away from Longacres and Ross.

After a week or two, I did as he'd asked. I wrote to him giving him the address of my recently acquired flat and my telephone number. But I heard nothing back from him or Olivia and decided to put the events of the summer far behind me.

When autumn leaves began to fall and the Beatles were hot news, I thought I saw Red again. He was walking in front of me down Oxford Street. I was about to call out to him when he rushed into Selfridges and I lost him in the crowd.

He'd told me little of his background, and what he had seemed to shift focus every time he told me, but as far as I was concerned he was good fun and entertaining company. It would be good to catch up with him again.

Two days later, I saw him again and this time I was sure of it. I was leaving work and heading for the tube station. He was talking to a guy who was leaning out of a car window. He looked up at me and I raised my hand but was left holding it in the air as he turned away and hurried towards the zebra crossing and all I could see was a flash of red hair amongst the shoppers.

Thinking it very odd that he hadn't acknowledged me, I entered the tube station and, after descending into the bowels of the earth, waited for my train to arrive. In the claustrophobic interior of the tube, I sat alongside a man with body odour and a girl whose hair was so thick with lacquer it sparkled. When my stop arrived, I hurried down the tunnels, and up the escalator to reach fresh air only to find it clogged with traffic fumes. Such was life in the city and I ached for the house in Devon where the air smelled of the countryside.

Red was standing outside my flat when I arrived home.

"Hi," he said, "got a minute?"

For some reason, I was reluctant to ask him inside. "What a surprise. OK, there's a café nearby, if you like. How did you find me?"

He grinned. "I was thinking more like the pub at the end of the road." He didn't answer my second question.

I followed him towards *The Bell* determined to discover why he'd ignored me earlier.

The pub was busy. It was crowded with after-work drinkers and early Christmas shoppers. Red found us a seat in a corner and brought over two glasses and a bottle of red wine from the bar and placed them on a small table nearby.

"You want some answers, am I right?"

"You could say so."

"Mmm, well, let's have a drink first." He handed me a glass filled to the brim with wine. I didn't comment on the fact that he'd told me he didn't drink alcohol, wondering if this was yet another white lie.

"Do I need this?" I asked, with a frown.

"I think somehow you might."

The wine was warming and, as the wind scattered the last remaining leaves from the trees, I waited to hear his explanation.

He'd finished the first glass and was starting on a second before he began. Then placing his glass firmly on the table, he said, "First, I'm afraid I've been lying to you, Miss Fairfax."

I was slightly taken aback by his use of my surname but said nothing.

"My name is not Paul Harrison. When I first saw you, you were reading a magazine with a picture of the Beatles on the back page – it was the first thing that came into my head."

"Couldn't you have used your real name?"

"Not really. I think it's time I came clean for once and told you the absolute truth. There's something about you that makes me useless at lying."

"Huh, I don't think so!"

"OK, I asked for that."

I sighed then asked, "Well, what is the absolute truth then?"

"My name is Paul. Paul Weston and I'm a Private Investigator."

"And I'm supposed to believe this?"

He slipped his hand into the inside pocket of his jacket and removed a business card. It read;-*Weston investigations. –Paul Weston 129, Clackett Lane, Brighton. Tel No Brighton 35476.*

"And?"

"I was hired by Mr Nicholas Ferris, who lives…."

"At the neighbouring villa to the Maitlands' property." I finished.

"Exactly. Some time ago he became concerned about the death of a woman called Diana Huntley, who was a friend of Avril, his daughter. Everything pointed to her death being accidental but Mr Ferris was not so sure and, prompted by his daughter's friendship with Diana, decided to hire me to see what I could find out."

"And did you discover whether it was accidental or not?"

"My investigation is still on-going. There's nothing I can prove at the moment, which is why I've been warning you to be careful of Ross Maitland."

"Ross? You don't think he's involved, surely?"

"Let's say, I'm glad you are no longer involved with the family and leave it at that for the moment."

A shiver ran down my arm. "So why are you in London?" I asked.

He bit his lip and looked away. "Ross Maitland is staying at his mother's house in Belgravia and Avril Ferris is staying with him."

Chapter 24

A cold wind blew down the street as I said goodbye to Red. He had my telephone number and promised to keep in touch should he have more information concerning Ross Maitland. I was inclined to tell him not to bother but curiosity held me back. He suggested we should meet, have a drink, go for a meal, perhaps the cinema but I said maybe it wouldn't be wise, under the circumstances, and we left it at that.

The news about Avril and Ross staying together in Belgravia had unsettled me. Inside my flat, I switched on the electric fire, put on the kettle and made a hot drink. I was about to sit down and switch on the television when I noticed an envelope on the mat in the hallway. There was no address just my name. I slit it open and read.

Dear Anna,

Forgive me for not contacting you sooner. I owe you an explanation and due to unforeseen circumstances have been unable to contact you before this. I will be waiting for you in the foyer of the Savoy Hotel at eleven o'clock on the fifteenth.

Ross.

My indignation reached new heights. I sighed, there was no room for manoeuver in his mind – was it, meet me or else – or, meet me if you want but if you don't it doesn't matter – either way it felt insulting. He'd asked me to leave Longacres and I'd agreed without making a fuss, now he assumed I was again at his beck and call and would come running to the Savoy on the fifteenth, regardless of any appointments I might have on that day. The fifteenth was in two days time and it was a

Saturday. At least I wouldn't be working. What was I thinking? Was part of me already making plans to meet this man?

The following day, work at *Hatchers* magazine went into overdrive. Apparently Laura Bentley had been due to do an exclusive interview with Mary Quant at half eleven and had called in sick. I couldn't believe it when Rosie poked her head around my door.

"Anna, you're needed PDQ. It's your big break. What d'you know about Mary Quant?"

My heart began to race, "You mean?"

"I mean, baby, you've just got an hour to get your butt over there."

From then on it was manic. I picked up the standard questions from Laura's desk, together with details of the venue. Arriving with five minutes to spare accompanied by a young photographer who seemed to know what he was doing, I was shown into Mary's workroom. I'd seen photographs of the emerging fashion designer but wasn't prepared for how pretty she was in the flesh. Her trademark dark hair shone and was cut to perfection complementing her regular features and luminescent skin. She was wearing a skirt, shorter than I'd seen on any catwalk, and I noticed sketches on the wall under which were written the words, *Mini Skirt - Hot Pants*. I'd heard of neither and so decided to ignore Laura's standard questions and focus on the designs Mary was working on for the following year.

The rest of the day was taken up with producing copy for the magazine and liaising with the photographer whose name was Jeff. At the end of the day I was exhausted and fell into bed at ten thirty, after taking some painkillers to ease a pounding headache, the legacy of working too hard and eating too little.

When I awoke, I soon realised there was no way I was going to miss being at the Savoy at the appointed time; wild horses wouldn't have stopped me. I bathed, and then, dressed in a warm woollen trouser suit and silk blouse, I headed for the tube station. There was snow in the air but I anticipated it to be too early for it to come to much.

It was a short walk from the tube station to the hotel. The doorman smiled and stood back for me to enter. Once inside the foyer I looked around for Ross, then not seeing him, glanced at my watch; I was five minutes early. Heading for the cloakroom, I left my thick scarf and gloves with the attendant, used the ladies room to freshen up my make-up and walked back into the foyer. There was still no sign of him.

Sitting on a sofa in front of which was a low table, I ordered a pot of tea and waited for him to arrive, feeling more and more aggrieved by the minute. By the time I'd drunk two cups and was starting on a third, I realised he wasn't going to show.

Mentally kicking myself for not ignoring his note, I made my way to the shops on Oxford Street for an afternoon of retail therapy but only ended up buying a pair of fur mittens and a cream fur hat.

It wasn't until the next day, when the Sunday paper was delivered, that I read the news of the death of Olivia Maitland at her country house Longacres, situated in the heart of the picturesque Devonshire countryside.

It was a shock to say the least. Apparently, Olivia, who had been suffering from a weak heart, died peacefully in her in sleep in the early hours of Saturday morning.

I tried to remember having heard of Olivia's heart condition at any point during the time I was working for her and failed miserably. Something was very odd, it didn't add up; surely I would have been told about her heart condition before?

Chapter 25

The Monday morning newspapers were full of Olivia's demise. My phone started to ring whilst I was grabbing a bite to eat before work. It was Lyn.

"Are you OK?"

"Fine."

"Did you see the news? Olivia Maitland..."

"Yeah, I know."

"Well?"

"They say she had a heart condition."

"You never mentioned it."

"I didn't know."

"Has he been in touch?"

"Ross? No. And I don't expect him too. I'm closing that little chapter of my life. Hey, don't forget to look out for my piece on Many Quant."

"Go on, tell me – what was she like?"

Having successfully changed the subject, I gave Lyn a brief run down on the fashion designer, finished breakfast and pulling on my coat, fur hat and gloves, headed for the office.

Red was standing on the pavement outside my flat.

"At last," he said, falling into step alongside me. "You've seen the papers?"

I nodded.

"It's like I said, nothing is what it seems chez Maitland."

"If you don't mind, I think I'd like to talk about something else. I've had enough of the lot of them."

"By that you presumably mean Ross Maitland?" He grinned and slid his arm through mine.

"Yes, him too."

"Well, I haven't the luxury of forgetting him. I'm still being employed by Nick Ferris and I've some spade work to do."

He left me at the entrance to the tube station. "Have a good day and don't work too hard," he said, before becoming lost in the morning rush hour traffic.

The weeks passed, Olivia was buried in the churchyard at Little Minnock; I sent my condolences via a sympathy card. My piece on Mary Quant was well received, after which I was given more assignments effectively keeping me busy.

Christmas arrived and with it a small parcel wrapped in brown paper and stamped with an unreadable postmark. I turned it over wondering who could have sent it. Red sprang to mind as I hadn't seen or heard from him for a couple of weeks. It was just like him to send me something to arrive with the last post on Christmas Eve.

I looked out of the window and saw flakes of snow drifting down like a Christmas cliché out of a darkening sky. In spite of the heat from my coal fire, I shivered and removed the brown paper layer from the parcel. Inside was a box wrapped in gold paper. I contemplated leaving it under the tree until the morning but my curiosity got the better of me. The box bore the name of a Hatton Garden jeweller and inside, nestling on a bed of black velvet, was a gold chain necklace with a diamond dropper attached to it.

Holding the necklace up to the light from the window, I saw that the diamond dropper sparkled and shone, dispersing all thoughts of it being a piece of costume jewellery. This wasn't the sort of gift Red would have sent, I was sure of that. Picking up the box

A Tangled Web

I saw a small card resting amongst the folds of wrapping paper.

To Anna,
With all my love,
Rx

I was still no nearer to discovering the sender and refused to admit to it being Ross Maitland. Perhaps Red had been paid for his investigation and was feeling generous. He'd ring later, I decided, and placed the box containing the necklace under the tree for the morning.

Lyn and I spent Christmas day at her brother's house. He lived in Chelsea in a house he shared with his wife and three children. Roy had the same curly hair as his sister and the same lop-sided grin. I loved visiting him; he always made me feel like an honorary sister and his house was usually crammed full of colour, bohemian friends and laughter.

The day began with champagne and conversation then the most enormous Christmas lunch imaginable, games, and more champagne, soon followed by an afternoon tea consisting of Christmas cake and mince pies. After the children were in bed, Roy and his wife Bea played the piano and sang. It was the excuse needed for some of their friends to accompany them with a guitar and percussion instruments in the shape of spoons, an empty chocolate box and a pepper grinder.

Finally, Lyn and I curled up on the bed in the spare room and fell asleep as the promise of dawn lit the sky.

The men were going to watch a rugby match on Boxing Day. Lyn and I helped Bea clear up some of the mess from the previous day then took the children out for a walk after lunch.

A Tangled Web

I arrived back at my flat at a quarter past six, snow was falling and the temperature inside had reached freezing.

Ignoring the coal fire, which required some measure of industry to create an ambient temperature, I switched on the electric fire and the boiler, poured a measure of brandy into a glass to warm me up and sat down. The box containing the necklace was still under the tree. I picked it up and looked again at the diamond glittering in the light from the lamp. This had to have come from Ross. But why?

Chapter 26

After work on New Year's Eve, I headed back to my flat through the slush and avoided the early evening drinkers spilling out from the doorway of *The Bell* in my eagerness to get inside out of the wind. I've always disliked New Year and this one was no exception. It wasn't simply the amount of work I'd done during the day, or that Lyn was spending the festivities with her new boyfriend in Scotland. There had been plenty of invitations from colleagues at work but I'd turned them down, by inventing a previous engagement.

I was inserting my key in the lock when I heard footsteps behind me. Turning around I was shocked to see Ross, his head bent against the wind, smiling down at me.

"Happy New Year," he said, "any chance of letting me in out of this cold wind?"

Unable to answer for the shock of seeing him, I nodded, held the door open for him to come in, and followed him inside.

"What on earth are you doing here?" I asked.

"Sorry. I know, I should have phoned."

Taking off my coat, I held out a hand for his but he caught my fingers and drew me to him, then to my complete astonishment, he kissed me. "A very Happy New Year, my dear Anna," he said, still holding me tightly against him.

"Did you send me the necklace?" I asked, stepping away from him.

"Of course."

"Why? I don't understand."

He removed his coat and hung it on the hallstand. "There's no reason why you should. It's my fault. I never did explain, did I?"

The fight went out of me then, indignation gave way to concern. "Sit down, I'll put the kettle on, unless you want something stronger?"

"Tea, will be fine, for the moment. You might want something stronger later though, after you've heard my story."

He helped me to light the coal fire and we sat drinking tea, as the flames licked the coals and warmth seeped into the room.

"Right, I better begin." Ross sat up in his chair and stared into the depths of the fire. "You met Diana Huntley when you first arrived at Longacres."

I was about to interrupt him but he shrugged.

"At least you met two of them. The young woman who spoke to you first, as you might have guessed was the real Diana. The other, she was a different story, one which it's not mine to tell."

"I'm sorry?"

"I know it sounds mad but it's so difficult to explain. For some time I'd been under the impression that any woman who grew close to me was in danger. I know it sounds as if I'm paranoid and without stating actual events, it certainly sounds as if I'm making this up. But please believe me, Diana Huntley's death was the culmination of odd little accidents which befell earlier girlfriends of mine."

I fell silent, Ruby's face dancing back at me in the firelight.

"Ruby and I were friends but nothing more, nevertheless someone thought otherwise."

"Oh no, surely not Ruby?"

"I see you are getting the picture. It's why I was so insistent that you should leave Longacres. I wanted to keep you safe."

"But we're not...."

"No, we're not. But I think it's more than obvious how I feel about you."

He turned away from the fire and looked at me and for the first time I saw the longing in his eyes.

"Not to me."

"But now I think you see what others have seen?"

He leaned forward and took my hand in his.

"But why would someone wish to hurt me? I haven't made any enemies at Longacres or at the villa, at least not as far as I'm aware."

"It's not been about you, my love. It's about me. But now I feel the danger has passed."

My mind was racing, trying to make sense of it all. Realisation dawned as his eyes met mine. "Olivia?" I croaked.

"She's always been overly protective of me but I don't seriously think she would do any of it. However, I believe she was indirectly involved and with her death the danger is passed. I know it doesn't make much sense and I'm not in a position to explain further. Diana and Ruby's deaths may be coincidental but I couldn't take the chance, especially after you'd been attacked. The police think it was robbery, as the bar on the boat had been ransacked but I wasn't so sure that's why I insisted you leave immediately."

I turned away and watched the flames dancing over the coals. " I didn't know Olivia had heart trouble."

"No. Neither did I. But the post-mortem results showed prolonged damage suggestive of heart disease."

"I'm sorry. I liked her and can't believe she had anything other than your best interests in mind. I'm sure you'll find out your suspicions are groundless and that there'll be a simpler explanation for it all."

He sighed. "I hope you're right."

"Would you like something stronger?" I asked, picking up the teacups and taking them into the kitchen. "I know I could do with a stiff drink."

"Please."

Whilst I was pouring brandy into the glasses, I felt him standing behind me. He placed his hands gently on my shoulders and turned me towards him. Then he bent his head and kissed me.

I still remember what that first real kiss was like. It sounds fanciful but I knew with certainty that he was 'the one'. It felt as though, if I let him go now, I'd regret it for the rest of my life.

Afterwards, we sat on the sofa together and I felt the heat of his body against mine as we continued making love. He was a gentle and considerate lover and I fell completely under his spell.

Ross spent the night in my bed and in the morning he asked me to marry him. I had no doubt about my reply and gave little thought to what the consequences of my decision to become his wife would be.

Chapter 27

We were married in a registry office in Richmond. Lyn and Julian, an old friend of Ross's from school, were our witnesses. We dined in Claridges and spent the night at my flat before driving to Longacres the following morning.

"I promise we'll have a honeymoon, my darling girl, but it will have to wait until the summer months. I have too much work on at the moment. Olivia's business interests must be looked after and although I'm up to speed on most things, there are loose ends to tie up, since her death. You know how it is."

"You don't have to explain, Ross. I'm just happy being with you," I replied, placing a reassuring hand on his arm as he drove towards Devon.

The sky was littered with ominously black clouds making it seem later than it was but it was still only early afternoon when we drove along the road where I'd first seen my husband.

"Joe and Esther will be shocked," Ross mused as we drove in through the gates and continued towards the house. "I expect it will take them time to get used to the idea of having you as their new mistress."

"They're not going to be the only ones," I commented. "I don't feel like the mistress of Longacres. I still feel like the hired hand."

Ross laughed and put his hand over mine as he stopped the car. "Whichever way you look at it you are definitely no longer the hired hand." He kissed my fingers. "You'll manage."

Ross was right of course. It was obvious as soon as Joe Travers opened the door. He could see Ross and I

A Tangled Web

were a couple by the way my husband's arm was around my waist and, in order to make sure there was no room for speculation, he said, "Joe, will you see to it that my wife's case is taken up to the master bedroom, please. You know Anna, of course."

I could see the smile sliding from Joe's face to be replaced by a look of confusion. "Aye, Master Ross, will do," he said.

He was halfway up the stairs when Esher opened the kitchen door. "There you are. Oh…" The rest of the sentence was left hanging in the air as she took in the scene. Ross was kissing me as we stood at the entrance to the drawing room and there was no mistaking the passion in our embrace.

"Esther, just in time to be the first to congratulate us."

"Congratulate?"

"Anna and I were married in London two days ago."

She held on to the doorframe, her face deathly pale but managed to contain her surprise at Ross's announcement by saying, "Er, I hope you'll both be very happy, that I do."

It was strange to be suddenly thrust into being the mistress of Longacres. I was a child of the sixties and loved the emergence of the British bands on the pop scene, the changing fashions and the relaxation of fifties attitudes of behaviour. Ross, although only a couple of years older, was still 'old school', however, he embraced the differences between us with good humour and was keen to understand how ideas were changing.

113

A Tangled Web

We'd been living together as man and wife for just two weeks when Ned Mason, the old gardener, who shared looking after the estate with Tom Trevellyn, decided his arthritic knee wouldn't allow him to continue and he handed in his notice. I suspected it was an excuse; he didn't like the idea of me replacing Olivia in the scheme of things. If I'd thought Ross was 'old school' Ned was prehistoric.

In the middle of February it snowed and continued doing so. Each day began with leaden skies and the thin coating of fine snowflakes covering the garden gradually built up into snowdrifts near the hedges and foot deep layers over the paths and driveway.

We were effectively snowed-in and spent long mornings in bed, whilst snowflakes tapped at our windows, and afternoons cocooned in warm clothes and wellington boots, taking our exercise by walking through the woods and along the frozen bank of the creek.

Even since, whenever it snows, I remember how happy we were, isolated from the outside world, during the honeymoon period of our marriage and how time has a way of changing things.

At the end of March the frozen ground began to recover from the onslaught of winter. Tom Trevellyn started to tidy up the debris left by the retreating snow and Ross decided it was necessary to employ another gardener.

"It's too much for Tom to manage on his own. I know Ned wasn't much help in latter years but he was another pair of hands. I'll put an advertisement in the local paper," he said, whilst we were out walking one afternoon.

But before he could employ a new gardener he announced, "I'm afraid I have to leave you for a week or two, my love. There's some business I have to attend to in the States."

"Should I come with you?"

"Much as I'd love it. I'd be travelling around quite a bit and you'd only be a distraction. The quicker I can get to my meetings and sort out our business interests the quicker I'll be back home."

"I'll miss you."

"Me too," he'd replied, packing his case. "Oh by the way, I've told Joe to see to interviewing someone to help Tom, I thought you'd rather not be bothered with it."

"Oh, right, yes, of course." I wondered if it was because he didn't trust me to make the right choice. Perhaps he thought I'd be more inclined to find someone who looked as though he belonged to *The Rolling Stones.*

I missed him as soon as his car disappeared from sight. Weeks stretched before me devoid of the one person with whom I wanted to spend my time. The day after Ross arrived in New York and telephoned to tell me how much he missed and loved me, I decided to do something positive to make the time pass more quickly. Mooning around Longacres like a lost soul was going to make the hours, without my husband, stretch interminably.

The study smelled musty, although Esther had dusted and polished as usual. I opened the windows and felt the chilly bite of spring air in my nostrils. Olivia's recording machine was on the desk together with her journal and first chapters of her memoirs were in the top drawer.

I picked up the memoir only to discover no one had worked on it since I'd left at the end of last summer. Slightly surprised, I switched on the recording machine and found a similar story. The tape began where I'd stopped it all those months ago. Olivia's voice filtered into my ear and I felt a sudden wave of sadness sweep over me.

It seemed she'd been in the middle of recording the next chapter when, on the tape, I heard the sound of the study door opening and Olivia saying, "Oh it's you, come in. What a shock, Miles didn't say you were coming today."

The machine whirred and clicked; she was obviously unaware that it was still recording. A male voice, which was slightly indistinct, began to speak. It sounded as if he was too far away from the microphone of the recording machine to make his voice clear but I heard enough to make me curious.

"He's up to no good. I told you exactly what was going on. You have to do something, go to the police, consult a psychiatrist, whatever – but you have to do it now, before it's too late." Unfortunately that was all I heard, as the continuous spooling of the tape was followed by a click as it ran out.

I leaned forward. The tape machine also recorded dates and times in tiny figures on an electronic display panel. The details were so small I had to screw up my eyes in order to read them.

Catching my breath in disbelief, I looked again but there was no mistake. Olivia's last recording had been on the day before she died. The urgency of the warning issued on the tape, combined with the date, was difficult to ignore. I slid the cartridge out of the machine and put it into my pocket, determined to place it somewhere safe. My next task was to discover who had been speaking to Olivia for, although he sounded vaguely familiar, the recording wasn't clear enough for me to be sure and I had no idea where to begin looking.

Then I found a journal in the bottom drawer of her desk, which put all thoughts of the cartridge firmly from my mind.

Extract from Olivia Maitland's Journal

Chapter 28

"Livia Ryan, you get down here at once and start cleaning this place. There's the baby to change too. I've to get to work, I haven't got all day to wait for you to get up, my girl."

I wake up with a start. It is all so real; I'm back again in Ireland, with a drunken father and a mother who supplemented the family's income by joining the oldest profession.

"You OK?" The voice is thick with the after effects of a cocktail of booze and drugs. Josh is propped up on an elbow and looking down at me. "You were dreaming, shouting all sorts of shit."

"Yeah, I'm fine. Like you said, I was dreaming." I reply with the remains of the dream still clinging to me like a helpless child.

"Have I ever told you, you've got a great bod, Liv?" His voice is thick with longing but I'm in no mood to indulge him.

"Yeah. I've got a studio session in less than an hour, so hard luck, buddy."

I slide my legs out of bed and head for the shower room.

The dream has unnerved me, memories of my childhood always do. I thought I'd managed to erase my early life as effectively as I'd re-created a new persona for the magazines and newspapers, My parents were dead, my siblings God only knew where and marrying first Larry and then Grant had made sure I'd never have to worry about being poor again, even if my blossoming career went down the pan.

Joshua Maitland was a mistake. I've always known it but he has something I can't resist. It is difficult to pinpoint exactly what that something is but I suspect it's all to do with sex appeal; the first man who had made me lose all sense and reason.

I've tried cocaine; most of my contemporaries in the industry have if nothing else experimented with drugs. But it's not for me. I hate the loss of control, the frightening loss of stability. It is the same with alcohol; I've seen how it destroys relationships and have no intention of going down that road. OK, I like champagne, who doesn't, but I've never drunk enough of it to make me insensible.

However, Josh never knows when to stop and it's heroin with him. I hate seeing the needle marks and the glassy-eyed stare reminding me of a fish on a slab. I've paid for him to go to re-hab but a lot of good it has been. The clinic is in the States, the first of its kind, exclusive, expensive and a waste of time.

It is during my time in America, waiting for Josh to dry out, that I first meet Velma Houston. I like her from the start; we are roughly the same age and have the same sense of humour.

We are at a party.

"Olivia darling! I'd like you to meet someone. The party is being held by a friend of Velma's. "Jake Bernstein – Olivia Maitland."

I can't believe I'm speaking to the man who has been responsible for making and breaking countless careers in the music industry. He's tall, thickset, and in his late thirties, with a shock of prematurely white hair and twinkling blue eyes.

"Hi, Kid. Velma's told me all about you. How'd you like to come to Burleybank, tomorrow afternoon around two?"

Burleybank is the Mecca of recording studios, from which the new music radio station, USA Radio, broadcasts throughout North America.

Lost for words, I finally manage to stammer, "I do, I mean I will, thank-you Mr Bernstein."

"Good, good, see you at two then. Oh and it's Jake."

It is from this inauspicious meeting that my career in the States takes off and I've never forgotten it was all down to Velma.

After touring the country, singing in Jazz clubs, on stage and in radio studios, Josh and I travel to New York. By this time I'm a star and it is here I meet someone who will change my life completely.

It is a cold December night and snow is in the air. I leave the restaurant with Josh and head for a waiting taxi but before we can reach it a woman, holding the hand of a young boy, rushes up to us.

The woman's face is deathly pale and she is shivering uncontrollably as she coughs into a grubby handkerchief. Josh starts to push her away but the hopeless expression on her face strikes a chord deep within me. I've seen it before, etched into my own mother's features.

"Please help, take him." She thrusts the young boy at me. "Please."

A Tangled Web

I reach out to touch the child just as the woman rushes away and into the road. The screech of brakes and screams of the passers-by are appalling. A crowd gathers at the side of the road as I take the boy's hand and follow Josh into the anonymity of a waiting taxicab.

When we reach our hotel room, Josh explodes. "What are you going to do with it? You should have left it behind."

"*It* is a young boy, Josh, not a commodity."

"Yeah, yeah, but he's not ours."

There is a moment's silence as I pick up the boy, who hadn't cried or uttered a word since his mother thrust him at me.

"He is now," I say, picking up the phone and ordering room service. "And he's starving."

Extract from Olivia Maitland's Journal

Chapter 29

"You should ring someone. Get him taken into care. You can't keep him. He's American for God's sake."

I ignore most of Josh's tirade but the part, about him being an American citizen, strikes home.

"I'm going to ring Velma," I reply. "She'll know what to do. In the meantime I'm going to call him Ross."

"Ross?"

"Yeah, It suits him don't you think?" The little boy is asleep on the large sofa, only his face showing beneath the coverlet I'd tucked around him once he'd fallen asleep in my arms. "I wonder how old he is?" An image of my brother Terry leaps into my mind. "I'd say six or thereabouts."

"Liv, you're getting into deep water here." Josh paces the floor.

"Why don't you go for a run? It's frosty but clear; it will do you good. I'm going to give Velma a ring."

Josh grunts, picks up a thick sweater from the back of a chair and leaves the room, saying, "When I come back, I expect him to be gone." He nods in the direction of the sofa.

The elevator stops at our floor, I hear the doors open then close and the sound of my husband being transported to the foyer. Then I pick up the phone and ring Velma.

"I'll get Bill on to it right away. Yeah, no problem, money talks here. I'll ring as soon as I have some news." Velma sighs. "You do know what you're getting yourself into I suppose?"

"You know me – in for a penny."

"Rather more than that I should imagine." Velma's laugh rasps down the phone line.

"I'll be forever in your debt, I can't thank you and Bill enough."

"Well, what are big brothers for, Especially if they're an attorney?"

Watching the boy sleeping, I feel as though his future is secured. I have no doubt Bill will sort it out so I can legally adopt the boy without too much fuss. The war in Europe has focussed most people's attention. The world has far greater problems to worry about than the adoption of a destitute child.

Two weeks later, during which I buy clothes for Ross, cosset him, feed him and rock him to sleep at night when he's missing his mother, I hear from Velma.

"It's fixed. Bill has the papers for you to sign. Once you've a decent photograph sorted, your son can be added to your passport."

I can't help smiling; I like the sound of it – my son. I've been desperate to have a child of my own for years, with no joy; a readymade child is more than I can ever have wished.

Josh, however, is not happy. He spends most of the day elsewhere. I never ask him what he's been doing. I don't really care; all I care about is the young child who had started to call me Mom.

It is no real surprise to me when Josh appears, stoned out of his mind, one morning after a three-day bender. I know he is back on drugs, rehab was always a dirty word to him, it never lasted more than a month or two and this time I know he feels aggrieved by my insistence on the matter of adoption. I've not even asked him to sign the papers; Bill has managed to make sure it's me who has adopted the child, which is just fine.

But the situation with Josh goes from bad to worse over the forthcoming weeks, until the phone call I dread comes.

It is all over the papers the next day. Josh Maitland's death from an overdose of a cocktail of drugs makes headline news.

"Might be time for me to take Ross back to England," I tell Velma, "The war is over. The trouble is there are sure to be reporters at the airport here and in London and I don't want Ross subjected to it all."

"No problem. I'll come with you. The child can travel with me, after we've checked him in on your passport of course. When we reach England we can split up and I'll take him to your place."

"No. Not in London. They'll be waiting at the door like a pack of wolves. You must take him to Longacres; I'll let you have the address. They won't find us there. It's in the back of beyond."

As I suspected, reporters thrust their microphones at me as I try to leave the airport building and the air is rent by flash blubs popping like popcorn. Managing to force my way though the throng, I catch sight of a young child holding the hand of a woman wearing a thick winter coat and fur hat, as they step into a taxi. I breathe a sigh of relief and instruct my driver to take me to my London house.

A Tangled Web

I spend the night in London and wait until the reporters decide to call it a day. At half past five the following morning I leave and drive down to Longacres. A local couple Joe and Esther Travers have been looking after the place for a month or two, after my previous caretaker became too old to care for the place. He'd recommended his cousin and his wife and, although I had yet to meet them in person, I had no doubt his recommendation would prove to be satisfactory.

Driving towards the house, I marvel at the fact I've managed to keep the purchase of Longacres out of the public eye. It is partly due to Grant Fairfax, my second husband. His solicitor had fixed up the sale in the name of Olive Grant, which at the time had seemed ridiculous.

"Will I ever be famous enough to want to escape by anonymity – I should be so lucky," I remember saying at the time.

Grant's foresight, together with his penchant for secrecy, has enabled me to keep Longacres well away from prying eyes. Being secluded on the Devonshire coast helped and Grant's honourable nature, in not revealing my ownership to anyone, makes me realise, what I'd known all the while, that I'd been a fool to divorce him in favour of Josh Maitland.

I'm singing softly to myself as I drive towards the house. A cold wind is sweeping through the bare branches of the trees and there are flakes of snow drifting down from a leaden sky. But no amount of grey skies will dampen my spirits. I'm looking forward to seeing my son again; my career, my fortune, nothing compare to the feeling of wanting to see his little face light up at the sight of me and hear him calling me

A Tangled Web

Mom. I am truly in love and I know it's for the first time.

Extract from Olivia Maitland's Journal

Chapter 30

We've been living at Longacres for nearly a month when Velma announces that she has to go back to New York. Her sister-in-law is ill and Bill is finding it difficult to cope with his young family, as the nanny he's employed is no better than useless.

"I have to go sort him out, for a while. Will you be OK here, Liv?"

"Of course. Give Bill by love. We'll pop over once things settle down here. I know I can't hide Ross away forever. It will just be until he gets used to things. He'll need to go to school and I've found just the place. In fact I'm going to see the headmistress the day after tomorrow."

The village school is not what I have in mind for my son. Oaklands is a private school set up by Miss Nora Blunt and the fees she charges have encouraged exclusivity. The school is situated in a former country house, two miles away from Longacres in the opposite direction to the village of Little Minnock. It takes boarders, but I have no intention of leaving Ross there overnight, he will become a day pupil.

As I've anticipated Ross settles into school life without any problem. He is a good-natured child and whether or not he remembers his early life and his birth mother, he never refers to either. And as the years pass he grows into a handsome young man.

A Tangled Web

Since the day I moved into Longacres with my young son, I haven't looked at another man. I have everything I've ever wanted, a successful career, Ross, and a future I have no intention of sharing with anyone.

There are a few minor hic-cups along the way. When Ross is ten he comes home from school one day in floods of tears; Erin Trelawney has told him he is a bastard and laughs at him. It is obvious neither child knows the meaning of the word or its unpleasant connotations. But for a child with no father on the scene, Ross has been hurt, as much by her unkind laughter as by the word, which had preceded it.

I comfort him. Then, as it is near his birthday, or the date I have created as his birthday. I decide a lavish party will be held for him at Longacres. Invitations are sent out to all his classmates, with one notable exception – Erin Trelawney.

When the day arrives there is a children's entertainer and a magician to astound them all. Hide and seek is played in the rooms on the ground floor and outhouses and there is enough food to feed a small army, complete with an enormous birthday cake. Ross never mentions Erin again and by the time he's started Public school, with a view to studying music, he is so engrossed in his studies he has other things on his mind besides girls. At least that is what I assume to be the case.

Ross is thirteen when I take him to the villa in the south of France. Larry bought it years ago and after he died on the Monte Carlo racing circuit, I couldn't face holidaying there. A French couple, Pierre Marmerat and his mother Louise maintained the place throughout my long absences during which a succession of my friends have taken advantage of my generosity in allowing them to stay there.

Ross is as excited as any thirteen-year-old can be to anticipate spending the whole of the summer holidays on the Riviera. He's seen photos of a young starlet called Brigitte Bardot and has cut one out of a magazine. He's stopped short of pasting it on his bedroom wall but keeps it under his mattress where he can dream she is lying close to him. He thinks I don't know.

However, I'm unaware of his budding development where the opposite sex is concerned, never having been in the situation before and without a husband's input, I bury my head in the sand and wait for him to tell me.

Weeks pass at the villa; we sunbathe on the terrace, swim in the pool and spend the afternoons at the cove or wandering around Monte Carlo and Beaulieu Sur Mer. It is on one such afternoon, when the sun is at its highest, that I feel a hand on my shoulder and turn to see Jacky Norman.

"Liv, darling. I thought it was you." Jacky stands aside as a tall fair-haired man and a young girl with curly blonde hair step forward. "This is my husband Nick Ferris and my daughter Avril. It's so good to see you again."

I remember Jacky from our days touring the London clubs together. "Pleased to meet you," I say, shaking the hands that are thrust in my direction. I introduce Ross as my son and I'm ready to move away when Jacky stops me.

"We've just bought a villa along the coast. It belonged to Ned Bright, the comedian. It's great, the

A Tangled Web

views are magnificent; I do hope we'll see more of each other, it will be good to catch up on the old days."

"It will. Nice to see you again, Jacky" This time I manage to steer Ross across the road to my car. I have no doubt we will see more of Jacky and Nick Ferris. Ned Bright used to own the villa adjacent to mine and, although the properties aren't exactly on top of each other, they are near enough to be called neighbours.

"You OK, mother?" Ross asks, as I switch on the ignition.

"Of course, dear. Why wouldn't I be?"

"Oh, nothing really. I just thought perhaps you didn't want to meet the Ferris's again in a hurry."

"Nonsense, they seem like nice people and they are going to be our neighbours."

"Great!"

So I haven't mistaken the look Ross gave Avril Ferris and the thought of it sends a shiver down my spine.

Extract from Olivia Maitland's Journal

Chapter 31

It's the height of summer and Ross wants me to take him to Monaco to see the Tour De France. He begged me to buy him a bicycle in Beaulieu, not long after we arrived, and he's ridden it around the estate and through the woods bordering the Ferris's property for weeks.

"OK, OK I give in," I say.

"Can Avril come too?"

"Avril?"

"Yeah, Avril Ferris, she lives next door." He looks down at his feet.

"I didn't know you and she were friends." Although the Ferris's live in the bordering property, I haven't seen them since the day we met in Beaulieu weeks ago. But I remember how Ross had looked at the young girl with the golden curls. I must monitor the situation.

"Er, she rides her bike around her place and into the woods. We've met up a couple of times. I know she wants to go to see the race too." He reddens.

"Of course, dear. Tell her to ask her mother and we'll arrange it."

Watching the look of pure delight on his face I wonder whether it's the thought of seeing the Tour de France or having Avril spend the day with us, which is responsible for producing such a reaction in my son.

As it turns out Jacky Ferris insists on driving us all over to Monaco, saying, "One young person to keep an eye on is enough, two is madness."

131

A Tangled Web

To some extent I am relieved and the day turns out to be better than I'd expected. Jacky is good company and Avril appears to be a pleasant child with no other thought in her head than watching the cyclists as they speed past.

It is a day which, to some extent, sets the pattern for years to come. Ross and I spend our summers at the villa and Nick and Jacky Ferris, accompanied by their young daughter, become our friends.

*

Ross is seventeen and it's the year before he is due to start a graduate course in business studies. We begin our summer holiday at the villa, as usual. I have the strong feeling it might be one of the last occasions I will have him to myself before he became a man.

"I think we should invite the Ferrises to come to a party tomorrow night. Velma is coming over and she's bringing Bill's son Lance with her."

Ross looks up from his book and smiles, "Great."

"I thought we could try out the arrangement of Blue Moon – the one you've been working on."

"Not sure."

"It's fine. I love it."

"OK. If you think I'm up to accompanying you."

"You're the best, Ross darling."

"Yes, OK, no need to go overboard, Ma."

Velma and Lance arrive later that day. I must admit to being shocked to seeing the change in Lance. When I'd last seen him he was a spotty fourteen-year-old, more than a little on the plump side. The young man carrying Velma's case up to her room is tall and tanned with a mop of fair hair worn rather longer than is usual. There isn't an ounce of puppy fat on his muscular frame and he has an easy, relaxed manner, which I have to admit is appealing.

It's the night of the party, Pierre has arranged for caterers to provide the food and to serve my guests. The night is warm and moonlight strokes the sea, with delicate fingers. A selection of jazz music drifts out from the music room where the new radiogram is kept and fairy lights twinkle in the trees.

Our neighbours arrive and are introduced to Velma and her nephew and conversation flows easily. I am certain it will be a perfect night, except for one thing. I see it at once. Avril Ferris can't take her eyes off Lance.

Partly as a means of focusing Avril's attention on Ross, I say, "And now everyone, I hope you'll enjoy a little number I'm going to sing for you, expertly arranged and accompanied by my talented son.

Everyone shows their enthusiasm as they follow us into the music room. Ross sits down at the piano and plays the introduction. But to my dismay Lance picks up a guitar from the corner of the room and begins to strum an accompaniment.

Even I have to grudgingly admit the boy has talent but the whole point of the exercise has been lost. Although Ross is complimented on his expertise, it is Lance who has captivated Avril to such an extent I am sure Ross has noticed it.

A sliver of ice pierces my heart at the thought of my son's disappointment. I know he's hoped the friendship with Avril, which has grown since they were children, would turn into something more. For weeks I've had the feeling he's anticipated that this holiday would be

A Tangled Web

the start of it and it might have been so, were it not for
Lance Houston.

Extract from Olivia Maitland's Journal

Chapter 32

I'm heartbroken to see how pitifully he watches the two of them. Avril takes every opportunity to call at the house and Ross follows her and Lance around like a lost dog. I've tried to think of ways to resolve the situation. I've invited the glamorous daughter of an acquaintance to the house in the hope of diverting Lance's attention away from Avril or maybe getting Ross interested but to no avail. And as the heat increases, the intensity of the budding relationship seems to rise with the temperature. They can't keep their hands off each other.

It is with a sense of relief, on waking up one morning at the beginning of August, that I hear the sound of activity from below followed by Velma knocking on my bedroom door.

"Liv, darling. I've had a call from Bill. I'm so sorry not to stay for the rest of the month but Lance and I are needed at home. I hope you don't mind."

"Not at all. It's been great to see you both. Have a safe journey. Pierre will arrange transport to take you to Nice."

Velma kisses me. "I'll be in touch. Give my love to Ross. Lance tried to find him but I think he's gone out walking."

"I will, goodbye, my dear."

It is nearly lunchtime when Avril makes an appearance on the terrace.

"Is Ross or Lance about?" she asks, twirling a strand of golden hair around her finger.

I can see she's made a special effort and has dressed in a figure hugging cotton dress and white leather high heels.

"Lance has gone back to the States and Ross is spending the day with some friends in Beaulieu. I'll tell him you called."

If Avril detects the icy tone in my voice, she is trying hard not to show it or her disappointment at hearing about Lance's departure. I watch the young girl making her way down the garden towards the woods and smile with satisfaction. Those shoes are going to take a hammering on the rough ground.

"Did I hear Avril?" Ross says, walking up from the terrace.

"No, I don't think so, dear. I feel like a drive. Why don't we make for Saint Tropez? You never know your luck, Brigitte Bardot may be sunning herself on the promenade."

"I should be so lucky," Ross replies with a grin.

The next two weeks pass without incident. Avril Ferris decides to cut short her summer holiday and return to London. Shortly afterwards Nick and Jacky follow, leaving us the sole occupants of the hill on which the villas are situated.

"I'm going to miss you so much," I say, at the end of August. "In a couple of weeks you'll be off to University making new friends, new experiences."

"Of course but don't forget at the end of it, I'll be qualified to look after your estates and finances. A couple of years study is small price to pay for a son who'll be taking care of your future business interests.

After all, there's nothing like keeping it in the family, eh?" He kisses my cheek and I try to hide the tears.

"As long as you don't forget about your dear old Ma."

"Not a chance, besides you're nothing like old."

The years during which Ross studies at the London School of Economics are difficult ones. I miss him more than I'd thought possible and although I spend most of the time at my London house, Ross is busy with friends and has rented a shared flat on the other side of town. In addition to which my manager, Danny Bailey, is keen for me to do a round Britain tour, as young bands are flooding the market with rock and roll and jazz is not as popular as it was in the thirties, forties and early fifties.

I agree to a couple of dates to placate him and I'm booked for a television appearance, on a show being filmed at Shepherd's Bush, for the BBC but my heart isn't in it. I have enough money not to have to work. My records sell well amongst aficionados and I have a loyal fan base. OK they aren't as young as I would have liked, but then neither am I.

Once Ross finishes his studies I will think about retiring and maybe writing a biography. Griff Blake, the publisher, is a personal friend and has often made the suggestion that I should do so.

There is the slight problem of not having a clue how to write a book of course, as the only writing I've ever done is in my journals. However, Griff made a throw away remark at a party recently about getting a ghost-writer to do all the work and it has sort of stuck in my mind like a splinter.

Chapter 33

I replaced the journal and began searching through Olivia's papers in an attempt to discover more about her final days. Underneath a folder I found a bundle of letters at the back of a drawer. It felt like prying but, as I was mistress of Longacres now, I had no one to ask for permission to do so. Spreading them out in front of me I began reading them.

Most of the letters were from the States. Velma and Olivia had been friends for years and their correspondence was fairly prolific during the periods they were separated by the Atlantic.

I spent the next few days reading through some of the letters but they weren't particularly interesting that was until I found one written by Velma during the time Ross had insisted I leave Longacres. It read;-

My dear Livia,

I'm so sorry to hear about your troubles. I wish I could be with you but Bill has childcare problems and I can't justify rushing to your side. There has to be an answer to this. Please do as I suggested on the telephone and seek another professional opinion; do it before it's too late."

My thoughts are with you, my dear friend.

Velma

Without Olivia's letters to Velma, I was in the position of having to imagine her reply. My imagination, fruitful at the best of times, ran away with me. Most of the thoughts assailing my consciousness were fanciful rubbish and I pushed them away with a metaphorical hand. I was left with trying to discover what type of professional opinion Velma was urging her friend to seek and for whom, Olivia, Ross, one of her close friends?

I sat back in the chair and picked up Olivia's desk diary for the previous year. Flicking through the pages I stopped at August and traced her appointments for the following month. She'd returned from the south of France after Ruby's death. There was a hair appointment in Little Minnock, a visit to the dentist, a meeting with her agent and a coffee morning in aid of orphans held at the Parish Hall. I smiled. Ross had no doubt encouraged Olivia to get involved with local charities. I could imagine him making the suggestion. But there appeared to be nothing out of the ordinary.

Esther was knocking at the study door. "Shall I bring up a cup of tea, Mrs Maitland?"

I'd tried insisting she call me Anna but it was one step too far for Esther.

"Yes, thank-you," I replied.

When she returned with a pot of tea and a plate of biscuits on a tray, I said, "Has Joe managed to find someone to help Tom in the garden yet?"

"He's got someone coming up to the house today, a young man, who saw the advertisement. He sounded OK on the telephone, evidently. Will you want to see him with Joe?"

"Oh no, Esther, nothing like that. It's up to Joe to appoint him. I was just curious. This is all so new to me."

She seemed to unbend a little then, "Aye, I expect it is. There've been a lot of changes around here lately. Will you be carrying on with writing her book now?" She inclined her head towards the journal.

"I'm not sure. It depends on what Ross thinks about it."

A Tangled Web

She nodded then sighed. "He's taken it better than I thought. But perhaps that's down to you."

"I hope so, Esther. I know how much Olivia meant to him."

"Aye, well I better be getting along now."

Picking up my cup, I sat back in the chair and ran my eyes over the bookshelf above the desk. There were a couple of coffee table books focussing on the jazz scene. I'd seen most of them before. But there was one, which stood out as being unfamiliar. It lay on its side underneath a stack of paperbacks.

When I'd finished drinking, I leaned across the desk and prised the book out from the others. The title in dark purple letters read;- *Olivia Maitland, My Life in Pictures.* It was a badly produced book, sensationalising every twist and turn in Olivia's early appearances on the jazz scene. It looked to me, as though it had been hastily put together, as soon as she began to make a name for herself.

Idly turning the pages, I flicked though a succession of photographs, a young Olivia, impossibly stick thin, her large eyes sparkling with vitality, others of her in the company of film stars and singers who had made their names in the States.

I was about to place it back on the shelf when I saw a photograph of Olivia holding the hand of a young child. It was a black and white print and the child was facing the camera.

The date underneath the photo coincided with a year after she'd adopted Ross. Holding the book closer, I inspected the photograph in more detail. The child looked serious, he was holding on to Olivia's hand for grim death, his eyes wide, as the flashlights popped. Studying the face, I tried to find one identifying

A Tangled Web

feature, one trait, which would point me in the direction of my husband but failed to find either.

Chapter 34

The following day I awoke to the pattering of raindrops sliding down my bedroom window. It would be a good day to work without any distractions, I decided.

It was nearly midday before I looked up from the typewriter in order to take a break and a quick walk in the grounds before lunch. The rain had stopped and the air smelled fresh and clean.

Tom was in the potting shed and I could see him talking to someone through the window. The young man was wearing a knitted hat and glasses. His head was half turned away from me so I couldn't see him clearly as he seemed engrossed in whatever Tom was saying. I thought about introducing myself but decided to leave it for the present, no doubt Tom would inform me of his progress, or lack of it, later.

In spite of the earlier rain, I could feel summer eager to begin and felt Ross's absence as acutely as ever. I couldn't wait to see him again and perhaps we could begin to plan our honeymoon at last.

When I arrived back at the house, Esther greeted me. "You've just missed him, Mrs Maitland. He rang a moment ago."

"Ross?"

She nodded and tucked a stray curl of grey hair behind her ear. "He said to tell you something's come up and he'll be delayed a further week."

My face must have showed my disappointment.

"He said that he'd ring you tonight at nine o'clock our time."

"Oh, right, thank-you Esther. I wonder, would it be too much trouble for me to have a tray brought up to the study? I don't want much lunch, just a sandwich will do." I'd lost any appetite I'd acquired during my walk and couldn't wait to speak to my husband later that evening.

As the afternoon lengthened into dusk, a fog sprang up, covering the lawn and enveloping the house in an impenetrable cloud.

After dinner I sat in the study and waited for the phone to ring. Nine o'clock came, ten, and still I sat waiting for the call from my husband. At half past ten I decided to ring his hotel as I was getting concerned. Ross was a man of his word and it was most unlike him not to ring.

It took me a while to make the operator understand my request. I suspected the local exchange had very few requests for international calls. Finally I heard a voice say, "New York Plaza, how may I help?"

"Hello, I'd like to speak with my husband, please; Mr Ross Maitland."

"Do you have his room number, Mrs Maitland?"

"Er, not to hand, I'm afraid."

"No problem. Just hold the line for a moment."

Whilst I was left waiting, I searched the top of the desk for my diary where I'd written the details of Ross's hotel but couldn't find the number of his room. He'd always rung me before and I'd had no reason to require it.

The phone line clicked. "Mrs Maitland? I'm afraid your husband checked out earlier today."

"He did? Did he leave a message for me?"

"No. No message." The words sounded clipped and slightly impatient.

"I see. Thank.." The connection was cut and I was left holding the phone as if my life depended on it.

143

Where was he? My heart was pounding in my chest. Something was wrong; I knew it. What on earth could I do? My eyes fell on Olivia's journal and it sparked an idea.

Velma's telephone number was listed under her name on the back page of Olivia's journal. This time the exchange put me through in a relatively short time.

Velma answered and I was reassured by hearing a voice I recognised in New York. I explained the reason for my phone call and asked if she knew of the whereabouts of my husband, quite forgetting that she may not have been informed of our marriage. To be fair, she composed herself very well on hearing the news.

"Congratulations honey, I had no idea. But what's this about Ross going missing. Doesn't sound like him at all."

"I suppose I might be making a fuss about nothing. He did say he'd ring and well..." I tailed off beginning to think I was jumping the gun. "I expect he'll ring tomorrow."

"I'm sure he will. Tell me how has he been bearing up lately. Olivia and he were *very* close."

There was something in Velma's tone that made it sound like a criticism. I answered as truthfully as I could, eager now to cut the connection.

"Just ring again, if you're bothered, won't you, Anna?" she said.

I couldn't sleep. I kept tossing and turning, certain that something had happened to prevent Ross from ringing. Finally, I got out of bed. It was half past five. Early morning mist shrouded the countryside but in the east the sun was starting to rise turning the sky to the colour of coral.

A Tangled Web

Pulling on a pair of loose cotton trousers, a tee shirt and cardigan, I left the house by the back door and strode across the field to the stile. The trees in the wood dripped moisture on the dew coated grass as I trod the path leading to the creek.

I'd always felt closer to Ross here and longed to see him emerging from the cruiser, which was still moored to the jetty, as if he'd never been away. I walked towards it and jumped aboard. It was simply my intention to go below and inhale any scents of him, which might have lingered. A fanciful thought but all I had to cling on to in order to stop me from thinking that something dreadful had happened. I couldn't think what could have stopped him from ringing me the previous evening.

The inside of the cabin was neat and tidy. Everything had been stowed away for the winter as until a week or two ago the cruiser had remained in the boathouse. I shivered remembering my incarceration at the hands of burglars then went back on deck.

Emerging from the trees was the new gardener, I recognised his knitted hat. He'd been running.

"Caught you at last," he panted. The voice belonged to Red.

I grinned. "OK, the disguise is a good one but why bother? And what are you doing here?"

"Shall we?" He indicated the cabin. "I'd rather sit inside to explain." He caught his breath. "Do you always get up this early?"

Holding the cabin door open for me, he stood aside as I descended the stairs ahead of him.

"That's better." Red pulled off his hat and I had my second shock of the morning.

"Your hair!"

"Well, it's a bit obvious. Your husband might not recognise me as being your saviour in Saint Tropez under normal circumstances as it was such a brief meeting but the red hair might be a bit of a give away."

"What difference would it make if Ross recognised you?"

He hesitated. "The point of my being here at all is because of Ross Maitland. Remember I told you Nick Ferris had employed my services to keep an eye on his daughter?"

I nodded.

"Well Avril Ferris is in New York."

I gasped.

"She's expected home today. I have no doubt your husband will arrive at Longacres later in the day."

"I don't understand."

"My investigation is on-going. In addition to which, once I'd heard you were married, I thought it wise to come down to Little Minnock, stay at my friend's place and keep an eye on you. The advertisement was a bonus."

"But do you know anything about gardening?"

"Not a thing. But I'm willing to learn and the rest of it, I'll blag."

The full importance of Red's conversation began to sink in. I trusted my husband and was sure he was mistaken where Avril Ferris was concerned. But, somewhere inside, a small voice was telling me otherwise.

Chapter 35

Later, working in the study, I heard a commotion coming from the driveway. I reached the window in time to see a taxi being driven away from the house. My heart began to pound. It was Ross, I was sure of it. He was on his way home, that's why he left the hotel and didn't ring last night. I descended the stairs two at a time and skidded to a halt in the hallway, right in front of Velma.

"Anna, darling. I came right away. I could tell you needed some support."

By the size of the luggage accompanying Velma, I could tell this visit was going to be a long one. I covered my disappointment, as she hugged me, by saying, "Velma, it's so good to see you. I didn't expect you to race over here, really I didn't."

"Nonsense; besides summer in Longacres is far more preferable to sweltering in New York. Now tell me what that husband of yours thinks he's up to." She took my arm and led me towards the drawing room.

"Just a mo., you go on in and sit down, Velma. I'll get Esther to bring in coffee and something to eat. You must be exhausted. Joe will see to your cases and put them in your room."

"Thank-you, hon. I wouldn't turn my nose up at some refreshment. Oh, it's so sad to be here without Olivia." She raised a lace-trimmed handkerchief to wipe away non-existent tears, as I went in search of Esther.

The day following Velma's arrival, the landscape was once more shrouded in fog; thicker this time, it seemed almost impenetrable. The view from the study was limited to the tree outside the window.

Velma was having a lazy day. Tired after her journey, and suffering from the time difference, between England and New York, she slept until midday. I'd been writing all morning and felt I was making some headway when the phone on the desk rang.

"Listen. I haven't much time." It was Ross. "I'm OK. You mustn't worry but I'll be staying here for another week, possibly longer."

"You're not at the Plaza?"

"No. I can't explain. It's complicated." I heard the sound of laughter in the background and my husband whispering, "I love you. Trust me,." And the connection was cut and I was left staring at the phone wondering if I'd dreamt the last few minutes.

Velma was heading for the dining room when I finally recovered enough to go downstairs.

"I've just heard from Ross," I said.

"Good. I told you it would be nothing, didn't I? Now let's have lunch. I'm famished."

We were drinking coffee in the morning room when I broached the subject I'd been thinking about ever since the phone call.

"I've been ploughing through Olivia's journals this morning and I've reached the part where she adopted Ross. You remember how it was at the time? Could you fill me in on some details, it's all a bit sketchy."

Velma stretched out her legs and sighed. "It was a long time ago, darling." She opened her cigarette case. "You mind?"

I shook my head.

"Livia was desperate to have a child." She inhaled the smoke and blew it back around her head like a halo. "It was fortunate that she was in the position whereby money was no object. It always talks in such situations."

"Who were his parents?" I asked. "Did she know his mother?"

Velma frowned. "Er, no, not exactly. She heard that a friend of a friend had found herself in the unfortunate position of having had another unwanted child. Someone in the business, I understand – it would have ruined a budding career - something of the sort. It was all handled very discretely." As she talked I had the distinct feeling that she was repeating a story, it sounded as if she'd recounted it many times before. It was as if she was reading a prepared account.

"Has he ever asked about his birth mother?"

"Not that I'm aware. He was, as I said, *very* close to Livia."

"You know I've started to work on Olivia's memoirs again."

"She would have been so pleased." Velma sniffed

"The thing is, she wrote about Ross being thrust at her by a woman who later rushed into the traffic and died. I can show you. It's nothing like you've described. It happened so suddenly and she went on to explain how you and your brother Bill helped her with the legalities so she could bring him over to this country."

Velma lit another cigarette. "Did she now? Well that's Livia for you."

"I'm sorry?"

"Won't let the truth get in the way of a good story. I bet at the time she wrote up her journal she had in mind

149

the possibility of a future book deal. You have to bear in mind she was at the peak of her popularity, and you have to admit, it's a much juicier story than mine."

I was more confused than ever. Was Velma's version the truth? However much I doubted it to be the case, I saw no reason why she should lie about it and was well aware of the fact that celebrities often coloured the truth with invention where their lives were concerned. As Velma had pointed out, it made a much better story. Even so, I wanted to write a truthful account of Olivia Maitland's life, if only for Ross. Nevertheless, the more I thought about it, I wondered whether he would thank me for it and perhaps I should let sleeping dogs lie.

Chapter 36

Velma and I rubbed along quite well. She was an avid reader of paperback novels with lurid covers and whenever I had a break from working on Olivia's book, I saw her lounging in the drawing room or on brighter days, wrapped in a fur coat on the terrace.

The weather was improving as April showers gave way to May blossom. I'd not heard from Ross again after his frantic phone call and he'd been in the States for nearly a month. I was desperate to know what was going on. He'd asked me to trust him but trust was wearing thin as my imagination kicked in. What if Red was right and he and Avril were having an affair?

As the weeks passed, I'd begun to meet Red on a regular basis, after our first encounter on the banks of the creek. I assumed he'd learned enough about gardening from Tom not to raise alarm bells. Our meetings took the shape of a walk along the riverbank, usually at sunset and occasionally we'd have a drink at the pub in Little Minnock in the evenings. If anyone noticed the frequency of our 'chance' meetings, I wasn't aware of it.

I'd like to think we'd become friends and had no doubt that he had my welfare at heart. It was comforting to know, especially as I was feeling abandoned by Ross.

On one such evening, having met in the pub, we walked back to his place. The moon shone out of a clear sky as he turned the key in the lock. "A nightcap before you drive back to Longacres," he said.

There was no such thing as the breathalyser in those days, besides there was very little traffic to worry about, especially on country roads. I wasn't in the least bit concerned about Red handing me a glass of brandy mixed with Babycham. It was the accepted mixture of the day and I'd consumed a couple in the pub earlier.

Reading this you might think otherwise, but I was not a drinker. Alcohol, then as now, has an unwanted effect on me, my cheeks become inflamed, I feel lightheaded and the hangovers are just not worth the bother.

I don't think Red took advantage of the fact that I was getting drunk, or why would he have offered me such a nightcap? Nevertheless, it was more than obvious that I was in no state to drive as I got up to leave.

"I'll drive you back to the house," he said as I tried unsuccessfully to find my keys in my handbag.

I tried to say, "Nonsense, I'm OK" but the words thickened on my tongue and I couldn't rely on what I actually said. All I remember now is closing my eyes and sinking into oblivion.

I awoke the following day with a pounding headache, a coated tongue and feeling like I wanted to vomit. The morning sunlight hurt my eyes as I looked around the unfamiliar bedroom. Realisation began to dawn as I heard Red singing the chorus of *Love Me Do* from somewhere below and the smell of bacon frying. I staggered out of the bedroom and into the bathroom just in time to rid myself of the alcoholic excesses of the previous evening.

"You OK?" He was standing in the doorway.

"Slightly less fragile," I replied. "What happened?"

"You passed out. I thought it best to let you sleep it off."

"How did I get up here?"

"In the arms of a strong man." He grinned and I noticed the roots of his hair were emerging like fiery stalks of corn through the brown hair dye.

I felt my cheeks burning at the thought of last night. "God, I must get back. They'll be wondering what's happened to me."

"No, they won't. I rang the house last night and told Joe you'd met a friend and had asked me to ring to say you were staying the night. It wasn't a lie now was it?"

In spite of feeling like something the cat had thrown up, I smiled and agreed.

"Right then, bacon and eggs will put some hair on your chest."

I heaved at the thought. "Just a slice of toast and a mug of black coffee for me, please. Then I really must get back."

"Coming up."

My absence was not commented upon other than by Velma who said, "Have a good time, honey?"

To which I replied, "Fine thanks." But somehow I was aware that things had changed between Red and me; it was as if we were conspirators, each with our own secrets, most of which centred on Ross Maitland. What was he up to and with whom? It was a question, which, however much I trusted him, refused to go away.

Chapter 37

The letter arrived at the end of the week. It was the warmest May on record and I'd already begun to discard my winter clothes in spite of the hawthorn struggling to blossom after the cold days of winter.

The envelope was resting on the hall table and it was addressed to me. Neither Joe nor Esther had thought to tell me of its arrival and I wondered at their lack of foresight, especially as the envelope bore a foreign stamp and the name and address were written in Ross's unmistakable hand.

I picked it up and ran up the stairs like a two year old, determined to read it in my bedroom, far away from prying eyes. The room, which I now shared with Ross, was the master bedroom and had previously been occupied by Olivia. However, soon after we got married, Ross had insisted that the room be redecorated and as I opened the French doors leading to the balcony overlooking the coast, I was aware that no trace of its former occupant remained. No lingering aroma of Channel Number Five, no ghosts hiding in the closets.

I sat near the windows and looked out over the lawn towards the sea. There was a warm breeze blowing towards the coast and I felt it thread through my hair as I slit open the envelope.

Inside the envelope was a single sheet of paper, folded once and typewritten. It read, :-

My darling Anna,

I'm so, so, sorry that my work here has taken so long and has delayed our much longed for honeymoon. All I can do is apologise and hope you will forgive me.

154

A Tangled Web

*If everything goes to plan, and I see no reason for it not
to do so, I should be home early next week.*

*I am desperate to hold you in my arms once more
and determined to make it up to you.*

Please stay safe.

I love you. R x

I held the note to my cheek hoping I would feel or
smell part of him but there was nothing just a faint
odour of print. After a while, I opened the bedside table
drawer and placed the note inside. Then I walked on to
the balcony and inhaled the salt-tinged air.

In the garden I could see Tom planting begonias in
pots ready for the summer. He looked up and raised his
hand. Remembering his words when I first arrived at
Longacres, I left my room and went into the garden. I
caught up with him as he was finishing the last pot and
starting to clear away the spilled earth.

"How's the new guy shaping up?" I asked.

"He'll be OK. Doesn't know much but he's willing
to learn."

I tried to hide a smirk by turning away from him but
his head was bent to his task.

"Tom? I've been thinking."

He straightened up. "Yes, Mrs Maitland?"

"How many more times? It's Anna."

"Aye, if you say so." He smiled. "Though Joe
Travers wouldn't be too pleased to hear me being so
familiar with the mistress of the house."

"Yes, well, Joe's of another age. Anyway, when I
first arrived at Longacres you warned me to be careful.
Why was that, Tom?"

He shifted from one foot to the other. "It were
nothing."

"Tom?"

"OK, well, if you must know, it was because of Diana."

"Diana Huntley?"

"Aye. She and I had become close, when she first came to work here. You could say a bit more than close and we rubbed along together really well. Until.." He hesitated as if unsure how to continue.

"Go on, " I urged.

"Until she fell for someone else." He ground his heel into the gravel on the driveway. "And now she's dead." He spat on the ground.

"You don't think her death was murder do you?"

"Who knows?"

"So that's why you were warning me?"

He nodded.

"I see."

Neither of us continued with the conversation as Red appeared with a wheelbarrow full of seedlings. "Where d'you want these, Boss," he asked, winking at me behind Tom's back.

I watched them walking towards the newly turned earth bordering the lawn then went back to the house.

Clouds gathered overhead and blotted out the sun as I pondered over Tom's words. It was ridiculous. He'd been jealous that Diana had transferred her affection to Ross, although he hadn't actually said his name, the implication was plain to see. It was simply jealousy, nothing more. However, if only it was as easy to forget the implication of Ross being involved in her death. It spun around in my head like a whirlwind gathering force with each spin, picking up blurred images of him with Diana – Ruby and Ross – Ross and Avril until I began to doubt my own judgement.

By the time, I reached the house I was full of uncertainly. Who could I trust? The answer was plain – no one but myself.

Chapter 38

Velma was in bed. She'd been complaining about a sore throat for days and had finally succumbed to a heavy cold. I knocked at her door and she croaked, "Come in."

She was sitting up in bed, her cheeks and nose fiery red.

"Can I get you anything?" I asked.

"Yeah, sure, a new body would be a start."

I patted the blanket covering her legs. "Summer colds are the pits. Do you want me to call the doctor in Little Minnock?"

She shook her head. "I'll be fine in a day or two. Just pick up a pile of trashy magazines for me, when you're next in the village, there's a luv and I'll stick it out until I feel better."

"Will do. I was thinking of walking into the village in a while, actually."

"Walking!"

"It's only two miles. I could do with the exercise."

"Makes me feel tired just to think of it."

"I'll pick up some throat lozenges from the pharmacy."

"You are a saviour."

"I'll tell Esther to look in on you later. Bye." I shut her bedroom door and could hear her coughing, a dry rasping sound, as I went downstairs.

Outside, it was pleasantly warm and I strode down the driveway at a steady pace. The road to Little Minnock was little more than a country lane but I knew of a shortcut across the fields, which on such a morning would be far more pleasurable than dodging the traffic.

158

A Tangled Web

The grass was dry, the sun on my back and the air smelling of summer. Dandelions, celandines and daisies littered my path, whilst butterflies hovered near the hedgerows. I'd spent too much time in my car, I decided. I'd missed a stroll through the countryside. At least it had the effect of focusing my mind on something other than Ross and the inhabitants of Longacres. I began to relax and enjoy the morning thinking of nothing but the pleasure of walking in the fine weather.

Avoiding the cows lining up near a hedge, I made for the stile leading into the lane. I could see the steeple of St Martins a short way ahead, which was on the outskirts of the village. A small rabbit shot across my path and into the hedge; I imagined it lost, parted from its loved ones and frightened. Determined not to draw analogies, I left the field, by climbing over the stile and headed down the lane toward Little Minnock.

However, again my thoughts strayed to Ross, who was never far from them and I began to feel the longing that only sight of him would appease. Lost in thought, I was faintly aware of the sound of a car approaching behind me. I kept into the hedge to allow it to pass but as it drew nearer it picked up speed. I could hear the engine revving up a while before I saw it. Someone was driving straight at me as I tried to flatten my body into the hedge. Realising that if I didn't move, I'd most certainly be killed, I reached into the thicket and hauled myself up and over it into the field then ran as fast as I could towards the river thankful that I'd kept myself relatively fit.

Once I was sure I was safe, I risked looking back and saw the car reversing back into the lane and racing towards the village at speed. It was all over in minutes but it took a while longer for my heart rate to stabilise.

It happened so quickly. I later told the police I couldn't be sure whether the driver was male or female and had no idea of the make and model of the car. The only thing of which I was certain was it was a large, dark coloured saloon either black, navy blue or dark green. Obviously nothing I could tell them would be of any help in discovering who had tried to kill me.

The police took the incident seriously, made their reports but I had the distinct impression that Sergeant Lodge at Little Minnock thought I might have been over reacting by insisting the car had been aimed at me and perhaps a more likely explanation was that the vehicle had simply spun out of control after being driven at speed on a narrow lane.

I was driven back to Longacres in a police car and spent the rest of the day trying to forget the whole incident.

I had no appetite for dinner and Esther suggested a plate of cold cuts and salad as Velma was still in her room and couldn't face a hot meal. Afterwards, I sat on the terrace looking up at the stars and wondering if Tom's warning could be given any credence. Of course I didn't think for one moment Ross would do anything to hurt me but I was starting to think someone, most definitely, was.

"Hey, Anna, over here," The voice was coming from behind the hedge bordering the terrace. It was dark now, the garden silvered by moonlight. I recognised the voice immediately. It was Red.

I walked towards the hedge and smiled. He was crouching down on the other side; the glow from his cigarette visible in dim light.

"What on earth are you doing down there?" I asked.

"I didn't want anyone at the house to see me."

"Why ever not?"

"I'm worried about you. Tom told me you'd come home in a police car earlier today. He didn't know why exactly but had some cock and bull story about someone trying to kill you."

"Look, I don't intend to talk to a hedge, why don't you come over to the terrace?"

"I think it might be better if you and I take a walk, as far away from the house as possible."

Rather than argue and beginning to feel he might have a point, I followed Red into the woodland. "Where are we going?" I asked.

"The boat. At least we won't be overheard."

"I'll need to pick up the key to the cabin."

"No need. I'm a P.I. remember."

"You can pick locks?"

"Part of my stock in trade," he chuckled.

The cruiser shone like polished glass in the moonlight as we climbed aboard. Red was true to his word and in a matter of a few minutes had managed to open the lock on the cabin door. We climbed down inside and Red found the oil lamp and some matches in a cupboard and lit the wick. It cast an orange light over the interior and gave our faces an ethereal glow as we sat like conspirators discussing the events of the day.

He listened as I told him about the car in the lane and when I'd finished he took my hand in his,

"I don't want to worry you but this is serious. I don't buy the police's version. Surely the driver would have stopped to see if you were OK."

A Tangled Web

"Exactly. So you think someone's out to cause me harm? I'm in danger?"

"Absolutely," he replied, and the word echoed around the walls of the cabin and came back to me like a slap in the face.

Chapter 39

Red assured me he'd do his best to make sure I was safe. He told me not to leave Longacres, unless I Okayed it with him first. At least Tom's suspicions about Ross being involved in Diana Huntley's death couldn't be linked in any way with whoever had driven at me in the lane. Ross was on the other side of the Atlantic Ocean.

I wracked my brains to think who could possibly want to kill me and why. To some extent I was reassured by Red's words, however the threat still existed and I became very uneasy and wished my husband would keep to his promise and come home soon.

Velma appeared the following day having assured me she was quite recovered and desperate to go into the village for some retail therapy.

"Come with me, honey, you've been working in that study for days; you need a break."

But I made some excuse and told her to ask Joe to run her into the village.

"If you speak nicely to him he'll pop in the pub and wait for you to finish shopping," I said, hoping she wouldn't see the fear in my eyes. I was beginning to distrust everyone, even Velma.

"Well, if you're sure. Can I get you anything?"

"Er a magazine would be nice. Don't mind which sort – you choose."

"No problem, see you later alligator."

I smiled; Velma was in her early sixties and was determined to stay young. I'd often heard her praising some of the emerging pop groups, even though her true love was Jazz. She used words like *fab,* and dressed in cotton shift dresses, the hems of which were way above the knee, whilst her *blue jeans* fitted like a second skin.

After Velma left the house, I couldn't settle. My conversation with Red on the boat had unnerved me. I clung to the fact that Ross couldn't be involved, by squeezing out every drop of trust I could muster; I believed in him and to think otherwise would be inconceivable.

Opening the study door, I felt the presence of Olivia seeping into the atmosphere for the first time since her death. The cream painted walls wrapped around me like one of her chiffon shawls. I imagined her sitting at her desk, her reading glasses perched on the end of her nose, her journal in her hands. Was she trying to tell me something or was I being fanciful? I'd never experienced anything like it before. Even when I sat down at the typewriter I sensed her looking over my shoulder. I shivered. Perhaps there was something I was missing in her journal. If Velma was to be believed, it was only a version of the truth anyway, so I doubted it. Nevertheless I opened the top drawer and lifted out the volume dated the year after Ross graduated.

Extract from Olivia Maitland's Journal

Chapter 40

I'm in London. The party is in full swing when I see Nicky and Jacky arrive but I am unprepared for who is with them. The last I'd heard was that Avril was touring in Europe.

"Liv, sweetheart, so good of you to invite us to Ross's graduation party. He's more handsome than ever, I see."

I kiss Jacky's cheek and then see Avril making a beeline for my son.

"We hoped you wouldn't mind if we brought Avril? They were such good friends when they were young," Jacky says.

I have no choice but to mutter, "Of course not, the more the merrier."

The evening grinds on, I sing, Ross plays the piano, and the jazz quartet from Benny's in Soho has arrived late but is now making up for lost time. I'd like to bet the neighbours are pleased they've been invited for more reasons than one.

It is a quarter to three and the guests are drifting away.

"Fab party."

"Thanks – great night."

I stand at the door, smile and air kiss until my jaws begin to ache. Nick and Jacky Ferris left hours ago but there is no sign of Avril and to my dismay Ross seems to have disappeared into thin air.

A Tangled Web

Heading for my bedroom I see the door is open and I hear the sound of voices coming from within. My heart misses a beat at the thought of Ross and Avril together on my bed. I contemplate creeping away but anger takes over. Marching into the room, I begin, "What on earth do you think you're doing?

The young couple break apart, "Sorry, so sorry."

They pick up their clothes and hurry out of the door, giggling. Their faces are vaguely familiar but at least they don't belong to Ross and Avril.

I hear him coming in at ten past six. I am wide-awake. He creeps along the landing to his bedroom and I hear him close his door. My son has grown up and I have to adapt. Determined not to be an over-protective mother, I shower, have breakfast and make an appointment at the beauty parlour in town. The day stretches before me. I won't go back to Belgrave Square until this evening. Perhaps then I'll be able to look him in the eye without crying.

Dressing for dinner, I take care not to look too overdone. I am getting older, every line on my face a testament to the fact. However, the beauty parlour has helped, so has my visit to Bond Street that afternoon. Lounging Pyjamas they called them, lilac silk with a chiffon wrap; I could look worse, I decide, glancing at my reflection in the hall mirror. The image is one he can be proud of, surely? If only I can hide my disappointment at his renewal of the acquaintance with Avril Ferris. I'm sure she will break his heart.

Ross is already seated when I enter the dining room. "Ma, you look great; new hair-do?" He stands up, kisses my cheek and waits for me to sit down. "Thanks a bunch for last night. I had a great time."

"No thanks necessary, my darling boy." I give a benevolent smile. At least I think it is such, it feels like a tight grimace to me. "Did you and Avril have a good time?"

"Avril?"

"Avril Ferris." Is he being deliberately obtuse, I wonder?

"Yeah, she's a nice kid." He picks up his knife and fork and tucks into the duck liver pâté as if he hadn't eaten for months.

"Where did you get to after the party?" I ask, as casually as I can.

"Benny's Bar."

"With the band?"

"Yeah."

I frown. It isn't like Ross to be deceitful. But then what did I know of his life? He's been in University for three years and I've been travelling.

After dinner, we relax in the music room. I offer him a cigarette, which he declines and we drink black coffee. I've become an addict since touring the States and apparently Ross has also developed a fondness for it. I can thank my lucky stars he is addicted to coffee and not anything stronger. I've seen the effects of the emerging drug scene, in San Francisco and at first hand with Josh, and hope he'll never get involved in anything so sordid.

Velma telephones the following day to find out how the party went and to congratulate Ross on his graduation. She sounds distracted. "Everything OK with you?" I ask and hear a sharp intake of breath from the other end.

"Not really. Just some bad news; I won't bother you with it now but we do need to talk at some point."

A Tangled Web

The phone call bothers me and I am troubled all day. I have the distinct feeling I'm not going to like what Velma has to say. Ross is everything to me; she must know that by now.

Around teatime Ross drops the bombshell.

"Ma, I'm taking some time out before I start working in the business."

He always referred to my financial matters as 'the business' and of course it is, in a way. It is why I need him to take charge of my investments and manage my affairs. I imagined by 'taking time out' he meant a short holiday.

"I intend to take a year travelling. I've had a word with Velma. I'll be staying with Bill for a month and then touring the States. I need to see a bit of the world before I settle down to some serious work."

"Of course, my sweet. But why don't I come with you. I could introduce you to all the right people. It would be great fun," I suggest, but his face falls a yard.

"I…" he begins.

"Don't worry, I was joking. Take as long as you like," I say through gritted teeth.

He breathes a sigh of relief and kisses my cheek. I want to hold him and stroke his hair as I did when he was a child. But my child is a young boy no longer.

He won't allow me to go to the airport with him and insists on saying goodbye at the station. I watch as he disappears and feel the loss like a knife between the shoulder blades.

If only he'd decided to travel elsewhere, anywhere but America. I am terrified that old sins cast long shadows and one might reach up from the past to devour him.

Extract from Olivia Maitland's Journal

Chapter 41

I meet Velma at Heathrow. She looks older, jaded. There's something in her face, which strikes terror into my soul.

We embrace, I help put her luggage in the boot of my car and drive towards Longacres.

"Lance bumped into Ross in New York. He said he was going to spend a week or two there and then come down to Bill's ranch."

"Right."

"I thought it wise to see you first in view of the circumstances."

So, I thought, it is true - the bit about old sins. I find it impossible to write about, too near the knuckle, too difficult to explain on paper.

In the event, Velma stays a month at Longacres, which is enough time for us to decide what to do. I can't let this change our lives. Ross is too important to me.

When she leaves, I call Ellis Cohen, my solicitor. Ellis was a good friend of Larry's and I trust him. We make an appointment for him to call at Longacres the following afternoon.

It's difficult; I pace the floor until he arrives. Joe shows him into my study where I have been waiting for over an hour. He's not late, I just can't settle.

"Good to see you again," Ellis says, and sits down opposite me, the desk separating us like a bridge. I hope we can cross it and reach each other.

He listens to my tale, sighs and reaches across the desk to take my hand. "My dear, you do realise this is an almost impossible situation to rectify. Are you sure it's what you want?"

I nod, unwilling to allow the words to come in case they are the wrong ones. He senses my distress and pats my hand.

"However, I'll do my very best. Give me a week or two to think about it, make some enquiries and then we'll meet again. I'll ring you."

When he leaves, I watch his car until it disappears down the drive then go back into the house. Joe is waiting for me in the hallway. "Esther wonders if it's just you for dinner, Mrs Maitland."

"Tell her not to bother with dinner tonight Joe. I have little appetite. A sandwich will do."

"Right, if you're sure missus," he says.

It's three weeks later, during which time I have had little communication from Ross, other than a hurried telephone call from Bill's ranch. He seems to be enjoying himself but says he must move on in a week or two, he has a lot of ground to cover. I urge him to keep in touch and am left holding the telephone receiver long after he's cut the connection.

The week following the phone call I receive the news that Ellis would like me to make an appointment to see him at his office in London. So I arrange to spend a couple of nights in Belgrave Square.

The house, although looked after by an efficient staff, seems cold and unused. A fire is burning in my bedroom and in spite of the room being warm, I start shivering; the reason is my reluctance to hear Ellis's summary of the situation I now face. I can only hope it's a positive one.

The trees in Belgrave Square shiver and shake in the breeze, leaves rustling together in a cacophony, which assails my heightened senses, as I return from my meeting with Ellis Cohen.

For now, it appears the situation is stable. For that I can only be thankful. Our lives will return to normal in spite of Velma's news, at least for the present. How I am going to survive the year is anyone's guess but to ease my conscience it had to be done. I could go and stay with Velma but it seems disingenuous to do so.

I decide to stay in London for a while and maybe when winter descends I'll go to Gstaad. I haven't been skiing for a while. Plans made, however insubstantial, can have the effect of raising ones spirits, I find.

As it turns out, I never do travel to Gstaad. Ross returns unexpectedly from the States, with an excuse about missing me that even I can see is contrived.

"I suggest I talk to Danny and Ellis and begin making arrangements about taking over the reins as soon as possible," he says, over breakfast, the morning after his return.

"Of course, if you're sure, but there's no hurry."

There is nothing in his demeanour to indicate a cause for concern, but I know my son and fear he is hiding something.

The year passes and another, Ross is doing a good job and he seems to like the work. I decide to begin work on my memoirs. I leave the hiring of a ghost-writer in the hands of Diana Huntley, my new secretary, and travel to Beaulieu for the summer.

The telephone call telling me an Anna Fairfax has been hired comes as I decide Diana must come out to the villa; I can't exist without a secretary. Life has moved on and I have no intention of looking back.

Chapter 42

Before I had time to think about the implications of the 'secret' Olivia was hiding in the pages of her journal, Velma returned from her shopping trip. Using the opportunity to take a break from my research, I went downstairs to see what she'd been buying.

However, prior to me being treated to the contents of her cardboard carriers, Velma said, "Do you know the strangest thing happened in the village? I was waiting for Joe to pick me up when I could have sworn I saw Ross."

"Surely not."

"You're right, of course, I must have been quite mistaken." She looked doubtful.

"What was he doing? This person, who looked liked Ross," I asked.

"He was getting into a car, parked on the opposite side of the street."

"What type of car?"

"Type, honey?"

"I mean, what colour, size: was it a sports car?"

Velma looked thoughtful. "Well, it was either dark blue, or black I think and it was a saloon. Is it important?"

I thought back to the car in the lane.

"No, it's not important," I said. "It couldn't be Ross anyway, he's still in the States."

Velma's expression changed. She became defensive. "I'm sure you're right. My old eyes deceiving me I expect. Well now, let me show you the darling little number, I bought in the quaintest store next to the church."

A Tangled Web

The rest of the day was unremarkable; Velma rested before dinner then joined me in the dining room. Our conversation steered well away from Ross and concentrated on Bill's son Lance, who was due to get married in a couple of weeks.

Afterwards, I decided to have an early night and left Velma reading in the drawing room. I'd opened the French windows in my bedroom before going downstairs earlier. The air was warm and I decided to sit on the balcony for a while and watch the stars. My conversation with Velma on her return from Little Minnock that afternoon had disturbed me. Could it have been Ross? And if so why hadn't he been in touch?

Yawning, the answers to my questions still buzzing like mosquitoes in my brain and making no sense, I stood up and looked out over the lawn. Not a creature stirred in the still evening air. There was a faint glow coming from the light in the drawing room below my window but, as I watched, it faded. Velma must have called it a day, I thought. But before I could turn back inside, I heard the distinct sound of heels on the terrace and saw Velma's unmistakeable chiffon skirt floating around her in the moonlight. She walked over to the hedge as a man approached her from the direction of the oak tree. Stepping back into the shadows, I watched them, their heads bent deep in conversation, but their voices were indistinct, whispers in the quiet night. The conversation lasted merely a minute or two before I saw Velma retracing her steps and the man disappearing like a figment of my imagination.

At the end of the next week Ross would be home. I clung on to his promise like a drowning man to a life raft. In the meantime I would seek out Red as soon as I could in the morning and ask him if he'd heard any more about Avril. I might even tell him of my conversation with Velma. It felt a bit like being disloyal to Ross to do so, but I felt the situation required openness if it was to be resolved satisfactorily.

Red was late for work,

"Haven't seen him, Mrs Maitland," Tom said. "He's not much good to be honest, so I won't miss him."

"I thought you said he was keen to learn, and it's Anna."

"I did, but I was mistaken." Tom sighed, "Happens sometimes, they think it's a walk in the park – gardening but after a while they become disillusioned."

It struck me then that Tom was very articulate and began to wonder about his past.

"Have you always been keen on gardening, Tom?"

"Yeah, you could say that. Originally I started a university course studying mathematics but I dropped out. It wasn't really my thing."

I couldn't hide my surprise. "Maths?"

"Didn't need it. This is much more to my liking. And life's too short to bury yourself in books when the outdoor life calls."

"Very philosophical, Tom. Anyway, if Paul turns up ask him to come up to the house. I'd like a word with him."

"Will do," he said, turning back to a large standard rose and attacking it with a pair of secateurs.

As the blades clicked together, I pondered over the fact that no one appeared to be what they seemed at Longacres and I wondered where I fitted into the scheme of things.

Chapter 43

Whatever had delayed Red, long enough to absent himself from his job at Longacres, he didn't say when I bumped into him in the grocers in Little Minnock.

"I need to talk to you," I said, catching up with him at the till.

"Meet me at my place in ten minutes," he said, then hurried out of the shop leaving me feeling like an actor in a second rate melodrama.

After placing my groceries in the boot of my car, I walked the short distance to the cottage where Red was staying. He was waiting for me anxiously looking out of the window and opened the door before I could knock.

"Come in, sit down, what's the problem?" he said, his usual cheery smile no longer in evidence.

I shifted uncomfortably in my seat before recounting the events of the last few weeks, finishing with Velma saying she'd thought she'd seen my husband in the village, and adding the bit about me seeing her with her night-time visitor.

He stroked his chin, sat beside me and took my hand in his.

"I'm afraid the time has come to get you away from this place."

I thought he was overreacting and told him so. But he stood up and walked over to the window resting his elbows on the sill. Then as if coming to a decision he said, "You have no idea. I didn't want to tell you this but your husband is definitely in this country and I believe you are in great danger."

A Tangled Web

"What makes you think Ross is a danger to me? It's ridiculous. You shouldn't make such accusations unless you can back them up." I was indignant; he had no right. I stood up.

"OK, sit down. As I said I didn't want to do this but you have to know." He turned away from the window and came to sit at my side.

"I told you I've been hired by Nick Ferris in my capacity as a private investigator, to keep an eye on his daughter Avril. Well the trail led me to her involvement with Ross Maitland, which was why I was travelling down to the south of France when I met you on the train last summer." He sat forward, tapping his forefinger on the coffee table then continued, "To cut a very long story short, I discovered your husband was deeply involved with Avril Ferris just as her father suspected. My investigations also led me to believe that your husband had affairs both with Diana Huntley and also Ruby Dent." He frowned and hesitated.

I said, "Go on." My tone was icy.

"There is no hard evidence to prove he's been involved in their deaths but my instinct tells me otherwise. Now it seems Avril Ferris is pregnant and has been seeing your husband frequently during his recent visit to New York."

"How do you know? You've been here all the time. And may I ask why, if that is the case, you're not looking out for Avril, as you've been instructed to do?"

The reason I know he's been seeing her is I have a contact working on my behalf in the States. And the reason I'm here is, I fear you are next on Ross Maitland's list."

I gasped and my hand flew to my mouth to stifle my response.

177

Red stood up, walked into the kitchen and came back with a glass of brandy, which he thrust into my hand. "Here, drink this. It will help you to get over the shock."

The brandy hit the back of my throat and made me cough. The warm liquid flowed into my body and my hands stopped shaking. "This is ridiculous. I can't accept it." A vision of a dark colour saloon car, slid into my mind, approaching at speed as I'd walked down the lane. Then there was Velma's comment about seeing my husband in Little Minnock.

"You're beginning to put two and two together?" Red took the glass from me and put it on the table.

"I can't believe it, not Ross."

"I suggest you ring the house and tell them you'll be spending some time in London, in Belgrave Square. Where is your car?"

"It's parked outside the grocers."

"Right, we'll put it in the garage here, where no one will find it. Then I drive us to my flat."

"In London? Surely it's the first place he'll look." I couldn't believe I was saying it, that I was willing to think the unthinkable.

"He won't look where I live, it's the wrong end of town. Don't worry. It will only be for a while. Just until I've got some hard evidence I can take to the police. We must make sure you are safe."

The next few hours passed in a haze of indecision on my part. I let Red take over; he took my keys and drove my car into the garage at the side of the cottage. His grey VW Beetle was parked in the lane and he quickly packed a case for himself, promising we would buy clothes for me once we were in London. "Look on it as

178

an adventure," he said, patting my hand, as he took the road leading out of the village.

"Won't they think it odd that you and I have disappeared at the same time?" I asked.

Red grinned. "Tom will tell them I've been taking time off for weeks and he isn't a bit surprised I've left."

Remembering my conversation with Tom Trevellyn, I nodded. "I'm sure you're right. You seem to have thought of everything."

"Part of the job. You have to be one step ahead of the game."

Chapter 44

Red was right. There was certainly no way Ross would think of looking for me here. His flat was on the top floor of a block of old terraced houses on the edge of town. Each building as dismal as its neighbour.

He parked in a side street and I followed him through the front door past a bicycle without its front wheel, and up three flights of badly carpeted stairs to his flat. Once inside I could see it was little more than a bed-sit with one main room, which had been divided into a seating area and kitchenette. There was a couch, upholstered in a green greasy looking material and a small table and two chairs. Grey and green patterned curtains covered the window through which I could see the rooftops of London, and a factory on the edge of town belching smoke into the air.

"It's not Belgravia, I'm afraid," he apologised. "But at least it's safe. There's only one bedroom but I can sleep on the couch."

Red looked at his watch. "We should eat, you must be famished. What if I get us some fish and chips from the chippy on the corner?"

"I don't think I can eat a thing," I said, beginning to feel the enormity of my hasty flight from Devon.

"Must eat something, old thing. Got to keep your strength up. I'll unpack my things and get the food. You might fancy it when you smell it. And tomorrow we'll get you a change of clothes."

When Red had left the flat, I put my head in my hands and let the tears fall uninterruptedly. What on earth was I doing here? I should be with my husband. But the fear, that staying with Ross could mean the end of my life, floated in the musty air like a spectre, haunting my waking moments and sliding into my dreams.

I picked up my handbag from the floor and opened the door to the bedroom. It was dark, the curtains were closed; I switched on the light and wished I hadn't bothered. In the dim glow from the overhead bulb I saw a single bed, untidily made, blankets hastily pulled up to cover sheets that could do with a wash. The top of the chest of drawers was littered with books, papers, a packet of cigarettes, a box of matches and a black and white photo in a tarnished silver frame.

I picked up the photo. It was of a woman holding the hands of two young boys, one on either side of her. She looked serious, as did the boy on her right but the young boy to her left was smiling into the camera lens. There was something vaguely familiar about the smile until I realised that, of course, it must be Red.

Determined not to feel sorry for myself any longer, I pulled back the blankets, stripped the bed and was waiting for Red when he returned with our supper.

"I've decided not to fight it any more," I said. "Thanks for the fish and chips. Where's the nearest Laundrette? After we've eaten, I'll get these done and any washing you have, then get to bed. I'm exhausted."

"Good for you, " Red grinned. "But there are clean sheets in the airing cupboard. You obviously haven't found my bijou bathroom yet."

There was a door leading off the main room that I'd thought, at first sight, was a cupboard. It led to a tiny bathroom, which contained a lavatory, sink, airing cupboard and the tiniest bath I'd ever seen.

A Tangled Web

"Time enough in the morning to get the washing done, " Red said, handing me my supper wrapped in newspaper. "Tomorrow is another day."

I awoke to the sound of rain drumming on the roof. For a fraction of a second I was disorientated, until I realised where I was and became aware of my surroundings. The sound of gentle snoring coming from the main room was confirmation of my whereabouts. I slid my feet out of bed to rest on the cold linoleum floor then went to look out of the window. The view from here was over the back yard. It couldn't be called a garden. Several floors below was a long straight strip of concrete bordered by an overgrown hedge and littered with the ribs of a broken bicycle, two car tyres, a stack of orange boxes, a pushchair lacking a seat and, from my elevated view, what looked like a settee with the stuffing spilling out from its upholstery like a dog with a bad case of the mange.

I closed my eyes and thought about the view from the bedroom window I'd shared with Ross, the grounds of the estate looking at their best during the summer months. The results of Tom Trevellyn's artistry blossoming along the driveway, spilling out from oversized pots and borders, carefully tended during the spring, becoming a riot of colour, the lush green lawns, and well tended hedges trimmed to perfection and the sound of the wind whispering through the leaves of the oak tree outside our window.

I sighed, wondering if I'd ever stand there again with Ross's arm draped about my shoulders and his warm breath on my cheek and decided, once this nightmare was over, I'd make it happen. Whatever Red discovered to the contrary, deep down, I was certain Ross was innocent. And it was up to me to prove it.

Chapter 45

It was nearly nine-thirty when I eventually dragged myself out of that tiny bedroom. I thought by now Red would be awake, not having liked to disturb him earlier. However, the flat was empty, the bed settee cleared of bedding and folded back into a couch. On the table was a note.

Anna, Didn't want to wake you. I've taken the washing to the laundrette and gone to do some shopping. Make yourself at home. Will be back soon.

Taking the opportunity of being alone to have a bath, I lay back in the water and closed my eyes. The rain still drummed on the roof but now competed with the sound of a baby crying from the floor below. "I can do this," I whispered. "There's no reason why I can't adapt to my surroundings – it will only be for a short while."

Afterwards, I dressed in a pair of clean cotton men's pyjamas, which I found in the airing cupboard, promising myself a visit to the shops at the earliest opportunity. At least I had some money in my handbag.

It was nearly mid-day, when I heard the sound of Red whistling as he turned the key in the lock and opened the door to the flat.

"You look good," he said, putting a couple of carrier bags on the table. "My pyjamas suit you."

"Needs must," I said. "What have you been up to?"

He thrust one of the carriers into my lap. "Take a look, I guessed the sizes."

To my surprise the bag contained a sprigged cotton dress in shades of blue and white, a pale blue cardigan, a bra, two petticoats and five pairs of pants. I found my cheeks glowing red with embarrassment.

"Don't worry, I said they were for my sister who had chicken pox and needed a change of clothes. I hope they are OK?" He looked so anxious to please that I found myself smiling at him.

"They are fine. But I could have bought them later; there was no need for you to go to all the trouble. I'll get my bag. How much do I owe you?"

"Nothing. My pleasure," he said. "Besides, you don't want to go out in this, it's raining cats and dogs, to coin a phrase. Have a gander in that bag, I bought you a couple of fashion magazines and a few paperbacks, so you won't be bored and there's always the radio, of course."

He took the third carrier over to the kitchenette area and unpacked some groceries. "We won't starve, either," he said, as he filled the small fridge then stacked tinned food in a cupboard.

"Looks like you're planning for a long stay." I hoped he'd say no, but he didn't answer.

Much as I would like to say I was bored, I had to admit, I'd be lying. The day passed in a relaxed manner. I changed into my new clothes and sat reading for most of the afternoon. Red prepared a meal of smoked salmon and scrambled eggs followed by tinned peaches and we opened a bottle of chilled Chablis and chatted companionably. He was good company and when I eventually went to bed, it was to spend the night undisturbed by the dreams which had plagued me the previous night.

I awoke to sunlight shining through the gap in the ill-fitting curtains and the birds singing an early dawn chorus. I crossed the floor and drew back the curtains. There was no trace of the rain clouds, which had caused the previous day's relentless showers. The sky was ice blue, the sun piercing in its intensity, although it was still early. It was Friday morning and I could hear the street cleaners in the road, although I had no sight of them as the strip of garden led down to a narrow lane bordering the backs of the terrace.

Inhaling, what passed for fresh city air into my lungs, I heard a door slam below me and shortly afterwards saw a young woman, wearing jeans and a tee shirt, walk along the concrete yard pushing a pram, she passed the broken bicycle and edged her way around the pushchair until she reached the gate to the lane

"You awake?" Red knocked at my door.

"Yes, come in."

"Great morning."

"For a walk?"

He frowned. "I wish. Look I'm sorry to disappoint you but I've had a letter this morning from Nick Ferris. He wants to meet me in town." He glanced at his watch. "In fact I've only time for a quick slice of toast and a mug of coffee and I must be away."

"No problem. You go. I'll take a walk later."

"I wouldn't advise it. Not around here anyway, at the very least you'd get your bag stolen. And besides, I've only one key and I'm taking that with me in order to get another cut for you, after I've seen Ferris. Don't look so downhearted. It will only be for today. We'll sort something out tomorrow, maybe a stroll around Hyde Park, how does that grab you?"

"OK, no problem, I'll finish the Agatha Christie I started yesterday."

"That's the stuff. Toast OK for you?"

"No, thanks. You go ahead. I'll see to myself, when you've gone. After all I've got the whole day, haven't I?"

When Red left the flat, I heard his footsteps on the stairs and waited at the window to see him leaving the house. Before too long I was rewarded with the sight of him, his hair gleaming fiery red in the sunshine.

He walked down the short overgrown path to the gate just as the postman was arriving at the house, with the morning mail.

Chapter 46

Alone in the flat, I had time to think. Red had lied about receiving a letter from Nick Ferris, as the post hadn't arrived before he'd left the house. Why? It made no sense - unless he was going somewhere he didn't want me to know about.

At mid-day, I opened another tin of peaches and ate them from the tin. This, together with a mug of strong black coffee, was my lunch. Looking out of the window into the street, I wondered what else Red had lied about. I was a fool. What did I know about this man who had led me to place my trust in him in preference to my husband?

The day wore on and I became more and more convinced that I'd made a massive mistake in trusting Red so implicitly.

Daylight began to fade and I saw that it was nearly half past eight. Red hadn't returned to the flat and I was virtually a prisoner. The front door had two locks, a Yale lock, which I could open from the inside by sliding the catch and a Mortice lock for which Red had the one and only key. Fruitlessly pacing the floor, I started to contemplate what would happen if he didn't return tomorrow. I had plenty of food, I wouldn't starve and there was always the possibility I could make someone downstairs hear my cries for help, maybe the woman with the baby.

After listening to the wireless tuned to Radio Luxembourg until my eyes started to close, I went to bed and surprisingly, under the circumstances, slept until dawn.

A Tangled Web

It was another beautiful day but like a caged bird I could only view it through the windows of the small flat. After breakfast, I decided to search the two main rooms for anything which might shed some light on my captor, as I had now begun to think of Red.

In the main room I found little of interest, most of the surfaces were littered with everyday objects, an atlas, which had seen better days, a half-smoked packet of cigarettes and a lighter, a thriller with a lurid cover written by an American author and the novels and magazines he had bought for me soon after we arrived.

In the bedroom I searched through the chest of drawers. Red had emptied the contents of the top drawer into one lower down, in order for me to have somewhere to put the underclothes he'd bought for me. I shivered at the thought of him choosing such personal items alone, believing he would be too embarrassed

The second drawer held Red's socks, pants and a couple of tie-dyed tee shirts. It occurred to me that he didn't seem to have many clothes and I wondered how often he spent time at the flat, considering if what he'd told me was true and the cottage in Little Minnock really did belong to a friend. Although, I now realised I'd been a fool to believe everything he'd said without question, however plausible.

In the bottom drawer was an electric shaver, unused and still in its box. An empty leather wallet, a business card similar to the one he'd given me, and a college scarf under which I found his passport.

I sat back on my heels on the dusty linoleum and opened the passport. His photo stared back at me. Red held an American passport in the name of Steven Carter. I leant forward and removed the business card from the drawer. So who was he, Paul Weston of

A Tangled Web

Weston Investigations or Steven Carter, an American citizen?

The rest of the day passed with still no sign of Red and that night I slept fitfully, determined that as soon as it was light I would make an attempt to escape from my prison. For although I had no doubt he would return at some point, I had no intention of staying around to find out.

After washing and dressing in the clothes I arrived in, I opened the window, facing the front of the house, to the half and leaned out. It was still early, a paperboy was cycling down the middle of the road, whistling and showing off by not holding on to the handlebars. Shortly afterwards I saw the postman. He was, I estimated, as near retirement age as it was possible to be. His postbag hung from his hunched shoulders as he slowly made his way down the street. I shouted, as loudly as I could, "Hello, up here, please, look up." But he just continued like an automaton, up one path and down the other, never raising his head from the stack of letters in his hand.

I knelt on the floor, my chin resting on the windowsill whilst keeping my eyes trained on the street. At half past nine I saw her – the woman with baby. She was pushing the pram through the gate and on to the pavement.

"Hello, hello, please look up," I shouted but the baby was crying so loudly that my cries drifted away from me as she walked quickly towards the end of the terrace.

I sat at the window for hours with no further opportunity to attract anyone's attention. It was as if ghosts had suddenly inhabited the street and I was the last person alive. Later in the afternoon I'd still had no luck, other than to get the odd wave from a young man who thought I was trying to do the same to him, and a wolf whistle from a couple of builders who were driving down the road in a white van. After further futile attempts to attract someone's attention, until I became hoarse, I banged my fist against the glass in frustration and, to my surprise, saw a glimpse of red hair from behind a hedge at the end of the street, soon followed by the rest of him, as I shrank back away from the window in case he saw me.

During the time it took for him to walk the length of the terrace to the house, I'd decided how I was going to respond, without showing him that I was afraid it was he who meant me harm and not my husband.

I heard the key in the lock and ran to the door.

"Where have you been?" I demanded with what I hoped was the right amount of indignation.

"Yeah, look, sorry about that. I hope you didn't worry too much. It's my job you see. That's how it goes. I had to leave the city for a few days in a hurry and there was no way I could contact you to let you know." He sat down and I saw dark circles around his eyes. I wondered how much sleep he'd had in the interim. "You were OK though? I knew you had plenty to eat and read."

"I was locked in!" I spat at him, unable to hide my fury any longer.

"Locked in?" He looked up. "Oh yeah, I forgot, I had the key didn't I?"

How much of this was artifice I found difficult to decide but was aware I would have to play a cunning game if I was to escape without him following me.

"Yes, well, I suppose I should have realised you'd be OK," I said, grudgingly. I was getting to be quite a competent actress, I thought.

"Hey, you were actually worried about me?" he sounded surprised.

"Of course."

"I see, right, well I'm here now and I suggest we have something to eat and open one of the bottles of wine, in celebration."

"I've got a better idea," I said. "As we are celebrating, let's go out to dine. I've some money – my treat. I could do with getting out into the fresh air."

He was silent for a moment and I believed it was because he was trying to think of a valid reason why this would not be possible.

"Red?" I prompted.

"Yeah, OK. Why not? I was just trying to think of somewhere locally that wouldn't be populated by deadbeats. Yeah, there's the Black Bear Club at the top of the street and down a bit. It's a Jazz club but it's great music and the food not's bad. I'll just take a quick bath and we'll be off."

Later, as Red locked the door of the flat behind us, I wondered how I was going to pull off my escape successfully and as he closed the outer door to the street, I realised I had the answer.

Chapter 47

The atmosphere inside the Black Bear Club was smoky, dark, intense and vibrant, all of which I'd seen in many similar clubs prior to starting work at Longacres. We sat at a table in an alcove and inspected the menu before deciding what to eat. A jazz quartet was playing and a young black guy with an incredible voice accompanied them for the occasional number. Just before I gauged the meal was due to arrive, I said, "Must pop to the Ladies. Won't be a moment."

In the passageway leading to the lavatories I'd previously noticed a public telephone attached to a wall under a soundproofed hood. I picked up the receiver and rang Lyn's number, which I knew by heart having lived with her for a while. Crossing my fingers I waited for her to pick up.

Afterwards, I went back to the table and joined Red. We'd finished eating when I saw Lyn and Mike arriving. They looked around then walked over to our table. Red had his back to them.

"Fancy seeing you again, Anna," Lyn said, sitting down at my side. "You know Mike, of course and this is?" She smiled at Red.

"Paul."

"Nice to meet you," he said, standing up and pulling out another seat for Mike.

We chatted about old times and Red appeared friendly and ordered a bottle of red wine, which he shared between the four of us. It was gone midnight when Lyn said, "Anna and I are off to powder our noses before Mike and I call it a night. See you in a mo."

The excuse worked as I'd hoped it would. As arranged on the telephone earlier, a taxi was waiting outside the club. I thanked Lyn, kissed her and said I'd be in touch. Through the back window of the cab, I saw her waiting until the taxi turned the corner before going back into the club. Driving towards the Belgrave Square house, I breathed a sigh of relief. Thanks to Lyn, I'd escaped. This time I was determined to go with my instinct and trust my husband.

My key was in my bag, on a ring, which held my car keys, the Longacres keys and of course the Belgrave Square house, although I hadn't used it for some time.

I paid the taxi driver and unlocked the front door. The middle-aged couple looking after the place were Jean and Len Rivers and they lived in a self-contained flat at the back of the house. It was late and their flat was in darkness. I saw no reason to disturb them but wrote a hasty note telling them I'd arrived late, in case they saw a light and were worried. The house smelled of furniture polish, the rooms immaculately maintained. I took a deep breath and inhaled the scented air in an attempt to rid myself of the cloying atmosphere in the attic flat, which had been my prison for the past week.

I spent the rest of the night under silk sheets in a large comfortable bed in a room decorated with pale yellow drapes and bed linen and in the morning I explained to Len Rivers and his wife that, although I'd spent the night, I would be travelling down to Longacres in the Bentley later that morning.

A Tangled Web

Len assured me that he'd make sure the car had a full tank of petrol before I left later that morning. So after a delicious breakfast, cooked by Jean, I lingered in the bath, dressed in clean clothes and set off for Devon. I'd not rung the house to let them know I was coming because I wanted to see exactly what the situation was with my own eyes first. I'd had plenty of time to think during the last couple of days and I'd come to the conclusion that there had to be a perfectly reasonable explanation for Ross's behaviour. It was important to me to hear it from him and not second hand via Velma. I also hoped to gauge his reaction when I arrived – was he frantic with worry – had he tried looking for me and would he be delighted that I had returned to him unharmed? This time I was determined to give him the opportunity to allay my fears instead of listening to a relative stranger's accusations.

The nearer I drove to Longacres the more excited I became at the prospect of seeing my husband again. The sky was blue, the birds were singing, and the horror of being locked in Red's flat was beginning to recede. I was humming to myself as I entered the driveway. The gardens spilled colour into the afternoon. The distant sound of a lawn mower completed the idyllic scene but, as in the Garden of Eden, there was a serpent lingering in the undergrowth waiting to pounce.

Chapter 48

I turned off the engine of the Bentley and stepped out just as a taxi drew up behind me. My husband paid the driver and walked towards me carrying the case I'd helped him pack what seemed like an eternity ago.

"Ross?"

"Anna, I was getting worried. I've been trying to ring you for days. Where on earth have you been?" He put his case on the ground, wrapped me in his arms and kissed me.

"It's a long story," I said, when I'd got my breath back.

"One I can't wait to hear but first let's get inside out of this heat. I could do with a long bath and a cool beer."

Incredulously, considering the circumstances, I managed to stammer, "You've only just arrived back from the States?"

He frowned. "Didn't you get my telegram?"

"No. I've been in London. I've only just arrived myself."

"I can see we have a lot of catching up to do."

Joe opened the front door, Esther hovering behind. There was no sign of Velma. "Mrs Maitland and I would like to take a late lunch in our room, please Esther. Oh and we don't want to be disturbed for the rest of the afternoon."

With his arm around my shoulder, we walked up the wide staircase and I felt as though the previous weeks had been a dream. As we reached the top of the stairs, I turned around.

"Esther? Is Mrs Houston about?"

"No. Mrs Maitland. Mrs Houston left soon after you went to London. She said she'd be in touch."

I sighed with relief, so we had the house to ourselves and I couldn't be more relieved.

Whilst my husband bathed, I stood at the window and marvelled at the scenery. My recent experience had somehow made me appreciate how fortunate I was, something I was afraid I'd taken for granted.

"Why don't you come and join me, my love?" Ross called from the bathroom. And unwilling to disobey my husband so soon after our reunion, I agreed.

Later, wrapped in each other's arms we lay on the coverlet and slept until the daylight faded and turned into night. Esther had left a tray of cold cuts and salad outside our bedroom door not wishing to disturb us for dinner. Ross, wearing nothing but a cotton dressing gown, carried the empty dishes back to the kitchen and returned with a chilled bottle of white wine and two glasses.

We sat on the balcony and watched the stars appearing in a cloudless sky and I felt my body relax for the first time in ages.

"Now then, tell me what you've been up to," Ross said.

Not knowing exactly where to begin, especially as there was just the faintest possibility that Red had been telling the truth, I skirted around the truth like a skater avoiding thin ice. I didn't mention Red's accusation and ended up by saying I'd stayed with Lyn for a while before spending the night in Belgravia. I'm still not sure why I didn't blurt it all out as had been my initial intention. Perhaps I wanted to hear his story first because to my mind there were many unanswered questions as to his reasons for prolonging his stay in the States, and one of them was his involvement with Avril Ferris.

"Now your turn," I said, once he seemed satisfied by my explanation.

"Business, all very boring, I'm afraid."

There was no way I was going to let him get away with that. "Someone told me they'd seen you with Avril."

"Did they? Who?"

"Not sure, it may have been something Velma mentioned."

He hesitated, but only for a fraction of a second. "Trust Velma. I'd hoped I could avoid mentioning Avril."

I bet you did, I thought. "Well?" I said.

There was obviously something in my tone that made him stop in his tracks. He leaned forward in his seat. "You don't think....?"

I waited, without commenting.

"My darling girl, Avril Ferris and I are friends. We have been since we were in school. Friends, nothing more." He took my hand in his, raised it to his lips and kissed it. "I don't know what you've been imagining."

"Tell me, Ross, is Avril Ferris pregnant?"

There was silence. Somewhere in the night an owl hooted as I waited for my husband to reply.

"How did you find out? We were keeping it a secret, and as far, as I know no one knows but us. Is there something you're not telling me?"

"So it's true then."

He sighed, a sound that spoke volumes and told me nothing. My imagination, over active at the best of times, ran away with me, I could hardly speak and as

A Tangled Web

the night closed in, I waited to hear the words that
would surely end my brief marriage

Chapter 49

"I'll go and raid the fridge for another bottle. We need to talk." Ross stood up and went inside.

I remained seated and thought how little I trusted my judgement. Red had told me Ross and Avril were involved and that she was pregnant and I'd refused to accept it. A tear of self-pity slid down my cheek and I let it fall. I was twenty-three and should have known better. I should have stayed in London with Lyn and never have answered the advertisement, which had transported me to Longacres in the first place.

Ross returned just when I'd made up my mind to hear the worst. He filled my glass to the brim. "I think you're going to need this," he said wryly.

"You think?"

He sat alongside me. I could smell his shampoo and feel his body heat as his arm brushed against mine. Our recent lovemaking still inflamed my senses and I wished this night had never begun.

"I told you a lie, Anna, when I said I was going to the States on business, but it was a white lie. It was a business trip but it had nothing to do with Maitland Enterprises. I'd found a document in Ma's papers, which held details of my birth mother, father and brother. I'd always believe I'd been adopted from a nursing home in Surrey along with my brother Harry but I'd been told Harry had died a while later. I didn't want to discuss it with you before I went to the States, as I wasn't sure what I would find and it was something I needed to do alone."

This wasn't quite how I'd anticipated the course his explanation would take. To say I was surprised would be an understatement so I sat, sipped my wine and listened.

"I contacted Bill, Velma's brother and showed him the document. At first he denied knowledge of what it contained but something in his demeanour told me otherwise. I rang Velma, who had decided to come to Longacres before I had time to meet up with her."

I remembered Velma's meeting with someone on the terrace, just before I went to London with Red.

"But she was evasive, unwilling to betray the confidences of her friend," Ross said.

"Olivia and Velma were very close," I added. "I could imagine them having secrets."

Ross raised his glass to his lips and his eyes locked on mine. I couldn't read his expression but then that was no surprise. If I'd learnt one thing recently it was that I could no longer trust my own judgement.

"Bill was more forthcoming. He could see I meant business and took me into his study; removing a folder from his filing cabinet he handed it to me."

"So you learned about how your mother begged Olivia to take you and then ran into the traffic?" I exclaimed.

"I what!" he spluttered.

"Your birth mother – how she died soon after handing you to Olivia."

"Where did you get such an idea?"

I hesitated. "It's in your mother's journal. I've been continuing with her memoir – at least I had before…"

"Before?"

"Never mind."

"I don't know what rubbish Ma's written in her journal or why. Although perhaps the why is clearer to understand, she obviously thought it made a better story."

I shivered and Ross reached over and handed me a rug from the back of his chair. "We can go inside, if you're getting cold."

"No, really. I'm fine, please go on, I interrupted you."

"The story is not as theatrical as the one Ma concocted but in its own way perhaps just as dramatic, at least for the people involved." He sighed and I realised how difficult it must have been for him to make his recent journey of discovery.

"Apparently, Ma was desperately unhappy with Josh Maitland. Bill told me he was back on drugs and the older she became the more she wanted a child but definitely not his. She feared another marriage, another scandal, would irreparably damage her career, when fate suddenly took her by the hand. Both Velma and her brother knew of Ma's situation when a colleague told Bill of the case of a destitute young mother and her children. The woman fearing her children would starve had taken to the streets as a pickpocket in order to feed her children. The woman was facing a jail sentence and the children, two boys, were to be placed in a home."

As the night breezes rustled through the trees my husband's voice held me spellbound. "But the woman, who must have been at the end of her tether, was found hanging in a police cell soon after the trial."

"What happened to the children? I asked, my voice barely above a whisper."

"Bill contacted his colleague about the case and arranged for Ma to take the older child. "But both children were inseparable it seemed and she had to agree to take both of us."

"Oh Ross. I'm so sorry you've had to go through this alone."

He leaned across and kissed my cheek. "I couldn't involve you; not until I knew the details first. I wasn't sure what can of worms I'd be opening, for a start."

He sat back and stared into the garden as if he was seeing none of it but the sight of two young boys having to cope with the loss of their mother and being thrust into an alien lifestyle with a stranger.

"What happened to your brother?"

"I was told he'd died. But I later learned this was not true. During my stay in the States I tried to trace my older brother, which was the initial reason why I delayed my return. But every lead proved fruitless. All I know is he was fostered by a family in New Jersey, and disappeared when he was sixteen. I don't even know his name; he was born Harry but the family changed his name – that's all I know."

Tears slid down my cheeks and I wiped them away with the back of my hand.

"I'd planned to return to Longacres, at the end of the week, as I told you on the phone but then I bumped into Avril Ferris. She'd heard I'd been staying with Velma's brother and had rung Bill to tell me she was coming over that evening as she needed to speak to me urgently."

I waited; was this the part of his story I was dreading?

"We went to a bar where we could talk. I could see she was distressed. She looked pale and as if she'd been crying. After a while she told me she'd been having an affair with someone, who she suspected was married and was now pregnant with his child."

I gasped. "Did her parents know?"

"Not then. She was sure the father of her baby wouldn't marry her and she didn't know what to do. I advised her to tell Nick and Jacky straight away. But she couldn't think clearly. She was tired, she'd been living in a flat downtown; it was all she could afford, without having to ask her parents for help. At this point she began to cry, thinking how shocked they would be when they heard the news."

"Did she think of arranging to terminate the pregnancy – perhaps the father could have paid privately to have it done?"

"She was too far gone for that, besides terminations are against the law as you know. So she was in a predicament. You can see I couldn't just leave her to cope alone, can't you, darling?"

"Of course, but I do wish you'd told me."

"In hindsight so do I but it wasn't my secret to tell. Anyway as it turned out Bill spilled the beans to Nick Ferris. Avril, truly spooked by now, begged me to take her away from New York so she could think it out without her father putting on pressure."

"Where did you go?"

"Ma used to take me to Key West sometimes when she was touring. I arranged for Avril to stay there for a while and told her to I'd speak to Nick and once I'd sorted things out, I'd come down to Key West and bring her home."

"Home?"

"To London. Nick and Jacky have a place in Kensington."

"So you were in London before coming here?"

He nodded. "Just overnight."

"And Avril?"

"She's OK. Her parents are supporting her, at least until the baby is born."

"She's fortunate her family are wealthy, unlike the situation that faced your poor birth mother."

Although the story was painful, I could see he was relieved at having told it to me at last. He couldn't have known my own feelings of relief were mixed with guilt at realising Ross hadn't been responsible for Avril's predicament. Tomorrow, I would ask him about his brother again. The picture, in a discoloured silver frame of a mother holding the hands of two young boys, refused to let me rest. I was sure there was a connection of some kind but for the moment had to be content to leave things alone and enjoy my time with my husband.

Chapter 50

Ross was singing in the bath when I awoke. I think we both believed this to be a new chapter in our lives and in some ways it turned out to be such but perhaps not in the way we'd anticipated.

After breakfast, we took a stroll around the grounds. I don't think it was my imagination but I noticed a change in my husband as if a great burden had been lifted from his shoulders. When we reached the creek he said, "Let's take her out into the bay. It's a beautiful morning and there's no wind, the sea will be as calm as a millpond."

I jumped aboard remembering that the last time had been with Red when he'd warned me about Ross and the danger I was facing. "Luckily Tom knows a bit about boats and he's seen that she's in tip-top condition, just as I anticipated," Ross said, starting up the engine.

"Tom's quite an enigma," I said, "he's not your usual run of the mill gardener."

Ross was whistling in the wheelhouse as I sat in the stern and watched him competently steering the boat out of the creek and into open water. It was as he'd said, the surface of the sea was calm and sun-speckled. I closed my eyes against the glare, wishing I'd brought sunglasses with me.

Seeing me squinting, Ross said, "Slip down to the cabin, there should be a couple of pairs in the cupboard. Don't want you getting wrinkles before your time, do we?"

I descended the ladder into the cabin uncomfortably aware that I could still see Red's face and hear his warning as I opened the cupboard to find a pair of Olivia's sunglasses and another, which I guessed belonged to Ross. Something caught my attention, it was a business card wedged into the upholstery of the seat. I lifted it out and saw it was the one Red had given to me, at least, it was its twin, as mine was still in my handbag. It must have fallen out of his pocket whilst we were talking.

I picked it up and slipped it into the pocket of my shorts then went back on deck. Ross was making for the coast. "Where are we going?" I asked

"Smuggler's cove."

"Sounds exciting."

"I could make it exciting, if that's what you want." He smiled and took his hand off the wheel to circle my waist.

"Excellent," I said, reaching across and kissing him.

We spent an idyllic day and I was sorry when the sun dipped on the horizon and we made our way back to the creek and moored the cruiser for the night. It occurred to me that at some point I would have to tell my husband about Red but I was putting it off, partly because of the guilt I felt in doubting him and partly because I didn't want anything to spoil my new found happiness. But there was the question of how I was going to get my car back to consider. I'd have to contact Red before long, much as I disliked the idea.

Ross was in the bathroom getting reading for dinner when I removed the business card from my handbag and went into the study to make the call I'd been dreading.

I picked up the receiver and dialled the London number of Red's 'supposed' investigation office. To my surprise a woman answered the telephone.

"Weston's investigations, how may I help you."

"Hello, I'd like to speak to Mr Paul Weston, please."

"Hold the line and I'll connect you."

So he hadn't been lying about his occupation.

"Paul Weston speaking."

"It's Anna Maitland."

I heard a sharp intake of breath from the end of the line. "Hello Mrs Maitland and what can I do for you?" It was then I realised that I wasn't speaking to Red.

"Is that Mr Paul Weston?" I asked.

"It is."

"Look, I'm sorry to have bothered you but I think I may have the wrong number."

"I see. Very well, but do pass on my regards to your husband, Mrs Maitland."

I muttered some sort of reply before replacing the phone and stared again at the business card. Turning it over I saw another number written in biro on the reverse. I recognised the Longacres exchange number and rang it immediately. As I'd anticipated Red answered.

"It's Anna."

"Good Lord. Are you OK?"

"I'm fine. I'm sorry I took off without letting you know, Paul." I needed my car; I had to be careful not to upset him. "I had to get away. I should have explained."

He sighed. "No need. It was wrong of me to expect you to stay in that miserable apology for a flat. I should

208

have realised you wouldn't be able to stick it for long. Where are you now?"

I thought about lying but it wouldn't take him long to discover my whereabouts. "I'm at Longacres at present but I need my car."

"Oh, Lord, I'd forgotten all about your car."

Yeah, right, of course you did, I thought.

"Will you meet me in the pub, later?"

"I can't tonight, Paul, but I'll be in the village tomorrow morning about eleven. I could call at the cottage then, if that's convenient." There was no way I was going to meet him in the dark.

I thought he hesitated just a fraction too long. "I, er, OK. I'll see you tomorrow morning at eleven," he replied.

Again I know I should have told Ross all about Red, over dinner that evening, I should have explained. But somehow, I missed the opportunity. In hindsight, it might have been better if I had. It couldn't have made matters any worse.

Chapter 51

The following day, Ross said he had phone calls to make and he was waiting for a visit from Miles Cohen, the family's solicitor, who had taken over the business from his father Ellis.

"Don't worry about me, I've shopping to do in the village. I'll see you at dinner this evening," I said, kissing him on the cheek.

Luckily it was another dry sunny day so I left the house, walked across the fields and soon reached the lane leading to the village. Uncomfortably aware of my previous near miss in the lane, I kept close to the hedge and this time reached my destination without mishap.

It was a quarter to eleven and the street was busy with shoppers and tourists. The village had become a popular holiday destination and many locals had rented out their properties for the summer. It occurred to me that Red's friend had been very accommodating where he was concerned and I wondered if he'd ever return. I also began to consider who the 'invisible friend' might be and whether this might be another fabrication on his part.

As it happened, Red was standing near the gate as I walked towards the cottage. He was nervously puffing away at his cigarette and when he saw me he took it from his lips and ground it under his heel.

"Great to see you again," he said, opening the gate for me. "Fancy a cuppa?"

"Sorry, no time, just the car." I tried to smile but the memory of him leaving me locked in that flat wouldn't allow me to do so with any conviction.

"Pity. Your husband's returned then?" he said, opening the garage door. "Avril said he'd run home like a scalded cat."

He was starting to annoy me. I took my keys out of my handbag and opened the car door. He put his hand on my shoulder. "You do realise, it could be very dangerous for you now. He thinks he's invincible."

I wanted to reply; to spit out the words that were begging me to say them, to ask him why he'd lied about being Paul Weston, but my need to get away from him was the greater force.

"Goodbye, Paul," I said, closing the car door and starting the engine.

My hands stopped shaking once I'd left the village and was driving towards Longacres. At least that was an end to my association with Paul, or whatever he decided to call himself. But I didn't feel like going home, Ross would be busy and I needed to think. Passing a signpost for Smuggler's cove, I headed in that direction knowing I'd have the peace and quiet I needed.

The road wound downhill passing fields of corn waving in the breeze until I reached a small gravelled parking area. Two cars were parked side by side and a small van stood in the clearing out of which a young man was selling ice cream.

Remembering the groceries I'd left in the boot of my car, before I'd left the cottage with Red to flee to London, I parked up and opened the boot. The smell knocked me backwards. Rotting cauliflower has an odour all of its own and when added to over-ripened fruit, it's unimaginable. Reaching in to the carrier bag,

I lifted it out of the boot and dropped it into a nearby waste bin.

Deciding to leave the boot open for a while to disperse the smell, I strolled over to the ice-cream seller.

"A small vanilla cone, please."

"Another nice day; shouldn't wonder if this keeps up," he commented amiably. "There you are Miss, fancy a 99?"

I looked at the flake hovering over the filled cone and at his face, obviously expecting to make it a more lucrative sale, and smiled. "Yeah, why not?"

"Why not indeed. On holiday are you?"

There was no guile behind the question so why did I lie? "That's right."

"Well, have a good time and if it's night life you're after my cousin owns a bar in Bridgemouth, just around the coast."

I thanked him, closed the boot of my car and walked down the rocky track to the beach as the sun beat down from a cloudless sky.

The only other occupants of the cove were a young family, the father building sandcastles with his small son and the mother feeding a baby. There were two swimmers making for the rocks to one side of the cove and a young man, lying on his back on the sand, reading.

Finding a shaded spot near a rocky overhang, I sat down and for the first time in ages relished the chance to be alone with my thoughts. Ignoring Red's warnings, I decided to trust my husband implicitly, unless I was proved to be mistaken and to enjoy the trappings of wealth, which fate had placed in my path. It was time Ross and I had the honeymoon we'd been

A Tangled Web

promising ourselves, time to forget Red, Avril, Velma
and the lot of them; time to get away.
    If only it had been that simple.

Chapter 52

Ross was still in the study with Miles when I drew up, so I parked my car in the drive and went inside. The phone in the hall was ringing. I picked it up. It was Velma.

"Anna honey. So glad you've come back. I wanted to say goodbye in person but I couldn't get hold of you."

"I'm sorry, I was staying with a friend. I should have rung you."

"No reason why you should. You're young; enjoying yourself is what young people do. Is everything OK your end?" It seemed an innocent enough question but could I be sure of anything?

"Fine, we hope to start our honeymoon at last. You?"

"Sure thing. Well, give my best to Ross, take care; I'll be in touch."

I liked Velma but wasn't sorry to know she wouldn't be dropping in on us anytime soon. We needed to be alone to start building our marriage.

It was nearly six o'clock when I heard Ross saying goodbye to Miles. I was in the kitchen chatting to Esther, who was busy baking. He came to find me a short while later.

"Ah, here you are. Fancy a walk around the grounds before dinner?"

"Great," I said. "It's such a lovely evening why don't we eat on the terrace later?"

"Good idea. But don't go to a lot of trouble Esther. Salad will do; what d'you say, darling."

"Salad's fine."

I followed him into the hallway and he took my hand in his and led me into the garden.

We walked into the rose garden and sat down on a bench above which Tom had build a wooden frame covered in trailing wild roses. The scent from the roses was intoxicating as I heard the words I was longing Ross say, "I know it's time we started our honeymoon and this time I've done something about it. I've arranged with Miles to see that the business is looked after and I'm taking six months off. I thought we'd start in Beaulieu at the villa and as winter approaches we could go to Italy for the skiing, how does that grab you?" He was desperately trying to move into sixties-speak but however hard he tried, it sounded forced.

I leaned against him and stroked his cheek. "I don't think I could be any happier if I tried," I replied before he kissed me.

The next day, Ross and I went to stay at the Belgrave Square house, as he suggested I might need a couple of days shopping in town before we left on our travels. There had been no further mention of his brother and I decided to forget my previous intention of questioning him on the matter.

Ross proved to be willing to help me shop, which was a surprise. He waited, whilst I was shown items suitable for a summer wardrobe, only commenting when I was indecisive. In the winter sports department, he advised me on what I should wear, as I had no idea what I would need, never having been in the fortunate position of having to acquire such items before.

A Tangled Web

Afterwards, we had lunch in the Savoy and headed back to Belgrave Square to prepare for our flight to the south of France the following day.

To say the first week we spent in the villa was idyllic would be about right. We swam, sunbathed, cruised around the south coast and drove to Monte Carlo, Nice, and the surrounding countryside, without a care in the world.

It was during the second week that Nicky and Jacky Ferris arrived at the neighbouring villa, accompanied by Avril. We were both larking about in our pool when Pierre announced that we had visitors. Ross was towelling himself dry and I was stepping out of the pool when they arrived on the terrace.

I knew so much about Avril Ferris and yet had never met her. She was taller than I'd imagined, broad shouldered, with blonde hair which was cut very short like a soft cap. I thought it suited her. Her pregnancy was showing and she was blooming. However, there was something niggling away at me, I was sure I'd seen her somewhere before but for the life of me couldn't place where.

"Hiya," Avril said, making a beeline for Ross and kissing his cheek. He was still wet from the pool and I noticed a damp patch spreading over her bump when she drew away from him.

"So you two tied the knot, I hear, congratulations." Nick Ferris pumped Ross's hand and Jacky stepped forward to hug me.

"Such good news," she said, but I detected a lack of genuine enthusiasm behind her words. Had she perhaps been hoping Ross and Avril would have made it to the altar?

"Good to see you all, isn't it Anna?" Ross said, pulling out a chair for Avril. "I don't think you've met Avril, darling."

"Hello, nice to meet you at last," I said, hoping it sounded genuine. But she just smiled then turned her attention back to my husband.

"Pierre," Ross called. "Some drinks and a bucket of ice please.

The afternoon wore on. Jacky commented on how sad she was to hear of Olivia's passing and how they would miss her during their summer visits. Nick talked to Ross about the Stock Market and Avril was uncommunicative. I caught her casting sidelong glances at my husband from time to time but tried to ignore them.

It was approaching dinnertime and there was still no sign of the Ferris's departing when Ross suddenly said,

"It's been lovely seeing you all but I'm afraid I'm taking my wife to the casino this evening so we must call it a day. I'm sorry to rush away but we have to get moving." He stood up and held out his hand to me. "Do feel free to call, anytime, providing of course we're at home. It's our honeymoon you see, so we could be anywhere."

Nick Ferris coughed, "Erm, yes, of course old man. No need to explain. Come along Jacx, must leave the young ones to their play. I don't suppose you'd mind if Avril tagged along with you two tonight? She's desperate for some company of her own age."

What could we say? A crease appeared between Ross's eyes and I sensed his fury at being put in such an awkward position. "Avril's welcome to join us," I said, with what I hoped was a gracious smile.

A Tangled Web

So I was partly to blame for what happened, I suppose.

Chapter 53

The lights of Monte Carlo twinkled in the warm night air as we drove past the harbour.   A party was in full swing; we could hear the sound of laughter, conversation and the clink of glasses coming from one of the cruisers. Avril sat silently in the back of the car and after a while conversation faltered, even between Ross and myself, so what should have been a romantic evening became a duty visit with an uncommunicative passenger.

When we arrived at the casino, Ross helped Avril up the steps and I saw her smile knowingly at him as if they shared a secret.   Jealousy reared its ugly head as I walked disconsolately behind them.

Under other circumstances spending an evening in such surroundings would have thrilled me. I could feel the buzz drifting around the room and the expectation of winning a fortune, which was written on the faces of those sitting at the gaming tables. But Avril was like a spectre at the feast. I could see Ross was concerned about her welfare and tried to get her interested in a game of roulette but after an initial loss of money she became eager to follow my husband, who was now sitting at the black jack table. Even my beginner's luck at roulette didn't thrill me as much as it might have done had I not been aware of Avril's hand on Ross's shoulder.

The evening dragged on.   I left the roulette table, cashed in my winnings then searched for Ross. Unable to find either him or Avril, I went to stand outside on the terrace. A warm breeze, drifting in from the coast, wafted through the palm trees, their leaves sliding seductively together. I went to stand near a rail and looked out into the night. Then I heard the sound of voices close by.

"I've hardly had a chance to speak to you. What are we going to say?"

"Please don't worry, it's not good for you. I'll tell them it's my baby."

"What will your wife say?"

"I haven't told her yet. I'll explain when the time comes."

I shivered in the warm night air, as the voices drifted away. Closing my eyes I tried to blot out the last five minutes. I didn't want to think about any of it.

"Here you are." Ross slid his arm around my shoulders. "I think it's time we called it a night; Avril is tired."

I followed them back to the car and insisted on sitting in the back seat as we drove to Beaulieu.

We dropped Avril off at the Ferris's and then drove the short distance to the villa in silence. When we reached our bedroom, I told Ross that I had a headache and thought it might be better to sleep in my old room in case I disturbed him.

Sleep was the last thing I did; I tossed and turned and when I did close my eyes it was to see Red and my husband, each of them cradling a baby in their arms.

At half past five, I washed, put on a pair of shorts and a tee shirt and left the villa by the door leading to the pool area. Although it was early, the sun had coloured the sky in shades of pink and gold. It was another beautiful day and one, which I could not appreciate. As far as I was concerned it might just as well be raining.

A Tangled Web

I'd left a note for Ross telling him I was unable to sleep and was taking an early morning drive around the coast and would see him later. It wasn't until I reached the costal drive at Beaulieu that I decided I would have to sit down with Ross upon my return and explain how I felt. I'd learned from experience it was a mistake not to talk it out.

After parking my car, I walked towards the seafront. Early morning dog walkers, a woman wearing running pants and a vest, and an old man sitting on a seat, were the only people mad enough to be out of their beds so early.

I sat down on a bench a short way off from the old man and inhaled the salt-tinged air. I closed my eyes and felt hands on my shoulders, which were rapidly transferred to my eyelids before I could open them.

"Guess who?" a familiar voice said.

"Red?"

"Got it in one," he replied removing his hands and sitting down at my side.

"What are you doing here?"

"Working, my dear, always working."

"What a coincidence." I wondered, was it really?

"Not such a coincidence considering Avril Ferris is in residence."

"You don't mean to say you are still working for Nick?"

"I am indeed."

I didn't reply, wondering if I'd been mistaken and he really was a private investigator. By this time I didn't trust my own judgement about anyone.

"Anyway, what are you doing out so early without your loving husband in tow."

"I couldn't sleep."

It sounded a hollow excuse and I knew he thought as much and probably imagined a quarrel would be nearer the truth.

"Right. Why don't we hook up then? I fancy going to Saint Tropez and let Avril Ferris off the leash for today."

I should have said no. But then I wasn't feeling well disposed to anyone right then, especially Avril and Ross so I accepted his offer on the proviso that I drove. At least I could escape, I thought, the threads of my last experience with Red still clinging to me like an annoying child.

Saint Tropez in the early morning was delightful. Before the crowds of people-watcher-tourists descended and the starlets were still getting their beauty sleep, the promenade was ours. Red was good company and made me laugh. However, one of the reasons I'd accepted his offer of spending some time with him lay in the memory of the photograph in the silver frame. I had to find out who the woman was for a start, the identities of the children, I was sure, would be a different story altogether.

Chapter 54

We were sitting outside a café watching the ever-changing parade of tourists when I said, "So who is the father of Avril's baby then, did you find out?"

"I know who she told me it is."

"But you're doubtful?"

"Well put it this way. Avril knows which way her bread is buttered and Daddy is very wealthy." He screwed up his eyes and lit a cigarette. "Want one?"

"No thanks."

"You led me to believe it was Ross."

"What? Did I?" He blew the smoke high into the air then inhaled.

I nodded.

"Well there we are then."

"Look! "I felt anger surfacing and tried to keep calm. Losing my temper would get me nowhere. "It's my husband's name you're trying to blacken and as far as I can see without any real evidence."

He actually laughed out loud. I could have slapped his face but the twinkle in his eye stayed my hand.

"If only I had someone like you to fight my corner I'd be a happy man." He placed a hand on my arm. "Once again, I'm sorry if I've said or done anything to cause you pain. I was only looking out for a friend."

"So you agree, you made a mistake."

"Let's say, I hope you'll be very happy. I can't say fairer than that now, can I?"

There was no answer to his question. So I decided to change tactics. "Let's walk for a while, I'm getting bored by the scenery."

He chuckled and gave me his hand. "If you please; Madam, will you walk and talk, with me?"

I matched his good humour and accepting his hand, rose to my feet and walked alongside him in the direction of the town. "I'd like to take a look at a small art gallery I noticed when I was last here. I think it's this way," I said, leading the way across the cobbles towards a narrow street.

All the time we were walking, I was thinking of a way to bring up the subject of the photograph. Eventually, after browsing the lower floor of the gallery, the opportunity arose. On the stairs, leading to the upper gallery was a painting of a woman holding the hand of a young boy. We stopped for a while, admiring the brush strokes and the depths of colour in the picture.

"I've been meaning to ask you, when I was incarcerated at your flat, and was looking for something to do, I noticed a photograph in a silver frame in your bedroom." So far so good, he hadn't accused me of snooping. "I wondered if it was of your mother."

"Yeah; though I never knew her. I was adopted when I just a kid."

"I see. How sad that you never got to meet her and what about your brother?"

He hesitated just a fraction of a second before answering, "Haven't got a clue," he said, just a little too quickly.

There was little more I could say without sounding as if I were prying so I said. "How long do you intend staying in the south of France?"

"As long as it takes," he answered. "Depends on Nick Ferris, I suppose."

"So you're still working for him?"

"Yeah, you could say that."

For the first time, I noticed a slight trace of an American accent and realised I had another far more pressing question to ask him.

We left the gallery and walked towards a bar tucked away in a side street. It was approaching midday, the sun at its highest; I couldn't believe how quickly the morning had flown.

"Looks cool inside. I don't know about you but I could do with a beer." Red looked at me for approval.

"I notice you've forgotten you're teetotal, now. Why not? But I'll skip the beer in favour of a chilled white."

"Excellent. I thought you'd be more interested in my tale about a drunken relative, when we first met. My fault, I've a habit of embroidering the truth as no doubt you've realised."

"Yeah, I had noticed."

The interior of the bar was typically French. Two men stood drinking beer at the bar whilst an elderly woman sat at a table drinking coffee, a poodle was curled up on the wooden floor at her feet.

We sat at a table in a small alcove where it was cooler but more dimly lit. As Red quenched his thirst I began to think how I could approach the subject of his passport, without it sounding as if I'd been prying but came to the conclusion there was nothing for it but to be blunt.

"I found an American passport in the name of Steven Carter at your flat." I blurted out. His reaction was not the one I'd anticipated. He started to grin.

"You don't beat around the bush, my dear girl, do you? It's one of the things I first noticed about you."

225

"Well?"

"Yeah, rumbled, I've dual nationality. It's no big deal."

"It is if you're using dual identities, Mr Carter or should I say Weston, Harrison, whatever?"

"Touché. OK, so I embroidered my story a bit. I'm Steven Carter, born in New York, where I lived until I was seventeen and then travelled to the UK to further my studies. I took over the failing Weston Investigation Agency a couple of years back. I'm known as Weston for business purposes. If you don't believe me, I can show you my British passport in the name of Steven Carter. How does that grab you?"

"You are a very plausible young man, Mr Carter. However, once I've been lied to, I find it very difficult to trust anything that person might say in the future, especially as I rang the Weston agency and asked to speak to Paul Weston and guess what – it wasn't you."

"You're beginning to sound sanctimonious, Anna dear, and far too old for your years." His face clouded over. "You probably spoke to Nigel; I tell all my male employees to answer to Paul Weston on the telephone – it makes the client feel important when they think the boss is dealing with them personally."

"Again, plausible, I suppose." I frowned at him.

"Perhaps you can simply believe that I'm enjoying your company, and in spite of us getting off on the wrong foot occasionally, I have nothing but good intentions where you are concerned."

In spite of my better judgement, I found myself smiling at him and wondered if this was how it would always be between us. Instinctively I was drawn to his easy-going manner and desperately wanted to believe

A Tangled Web

I'd found a friend in Red but I'd been wrong so many times before that I hesitated to fall into yet another trap.

Chapter 55

After I left Red, I headed back to the villa and arrived to find my husband and Avril Ferris deep in conversation on the pool loungers. My stomach flipped as jealousy raised its ugly head once more.

"Anna! I've been looking all over for you?"

"Not far enough, it would seem," even my voice sounded spiteful. In an attempt to mitigate the effect, I added, " You're looking good, Avril. How long now?"

"Two months exactly."

"I expect you're keen to get it over with and then you'll have your little baby to make up for the months of waiting." I honestly thought this was a reasonable remark but she burst into tears and, to my horror, was swiftly comforted by Ross, who glared in my direction.

Avril stood up. "Will you walk back with me, Ross?" she asked, dabbing her eyes with his handkerchief.

"Of course," he replied, and I was left wondering what I'd said to produce such a reaction.

Deciding I'd had enough of puzzles for a while, I went upstairs, ran a bath and tipped enough bubble oil in to drown a whale then stripped off and slid beneath the surface of the bathwater.

Wiping away the worst of the foam from my face with the back of my hand, I heard the bedroom door close, followed by Ross entering the bathroom.

"You are the limit." He was fuming.

"What? What did I say?"

He sat down on the stool at the far end of the bath and faced me. "You really don't know?"

"I really don't."

"Do you honestly think Avril is going to keep the baby?"

I sat up, bubble foam dripping over the sides of the bath and sticking to my breasts making me look like an exotic dancer in the *Follies Bergere*. "She's not?"

"Of course not. Her parents wouldn't hear of it especially as there's no sign of the baby's father who might be willing to make an honest woman of her."

"It's the sixties, for heaven sake. Let them make up a story for form sake, if they must. If Avril wants to keep her child she should be allowed to do so. It's barbaric to think otherwise."

My indignant attitude produced the sort of reaction in my husband, which surprised me. He stood up then, bent over the bath and kissed me. "You're adorable, frustrating, and I love you very much, Mrs Maitland," he said.

I was beginning to think that at last I could put aside jealousy, suspicion, and intrigue and enjoy my honeymoon. Anticipating a languorous few weeks until summer waned and we could transfer our idyll to an Italian ski resort, I lazed near the pool with Ross in the mornings and followed him like an eager puppy to our bedroom each afternoon.

When we could be bothered to move, we took the cruiser out of the creek and into the bay where we made for secluded coves or when the fancy took us, further afield. It seemed as if, during those weeks, the sun always shone. There was only one black cloud on the horizon in the shape of Avril Ferris and as her pregnancy progressed, Ross became more solicitous of her wellbeing.

I kept telling myself it was one of the reasons I loved him. He cared about his friends and wouldn't abandon them when they were in trouble. But if I was honest my words went unheeded; the green-eyed monster would not be stilled.

One afternoon, when we were sunbathing near the pool, thoughts of the lovemaking we were soon to enjoy teasing our bodies, our peace was shattered by the arrival of Avril struggling to squeeze through the gap in the hedge. She'd been taking the short cut from her parents' villa for a week or two and I felt unaccountably exposed at the thought of her being able to pop over unannounced whenever the fancy took her.

She was in the advanced stages of her pregnancy and to me her stomach looked enormous. Ross hastily stood up and went to help her.

"Sit here, is there anything I can get you – another pillow, lemonade?"

I felt my lips drawing into a tight line. I didn't like how I felt. I was immature and desperate not to show it.

"Sit here, under the sun shade," I said, getting up and making room.

"Are you sure you should be walking about in this heat?" Ross asked and I wanted to shout –'she's pregnant not ill' but managed to keep my mouth firmly shut for once.

"I'm so fed up," Avril replied. "Pa's making my life a misery; he keeps asking me how I'm feeling and then I hear him on the phone to the adoption agency and I can't bear it."

"Is there no way you can keep the baby?" I asked.

She sighed. "He won't hear of it – says he'll not give me a penny."

"Your mother?"

"Mother's under his thumb, always has been."

I wanted to ask her about the baby's father but could see the warning look in Ross's eyes and again kept silent.

Later that evening after we'd dined, the telephone rang. Ross went to answer it and when he returned his suntanned face has lost most of its colour.

"It's Avril. She's in labour. The doctor has been called and he's at the villa now. Nick wants me to go over; he says Avril's calling for me."

Is she indeed, I thought, right. "Of course she is Ross, she needs her friends when she's frightened. I'll come with you."

"There's no need; it could be hours yet." He was pacing the floor.

"Nonsense, of course I'll come. We'll take the short cut."

Jacky Ferris greeted us at the door. "Come in, Avril's in the bedroom on the ground floor, the doctor and midwife are with her." She turned to me. "Anna dear, perhaps we should let Ross see her first. Nick and I are waiting for news in the conservatory, why don't you join us?"

Feeling like an unwanted guest, I had no option but to follow Jacky and wait for my husband to return. No doubt Avril required some hand holding although why it had to be my husband's was a mystery.

When we entered the conservatory, Nick was in deep conversation with a thickset man who was wearing a shirt patterned with palm trees. They stopped talking and Nick walked towards me. "Anna, so good of you to come in Avril's hour of need." He turned towards the man in the pattered shirt. "Paul, come and meet our neighbour, Mrs Maitland, Ross's wife. Anna this is Paul Weston, of Weston's Investigations, a business colleague."

I gasped. This man was a perfect stranger. I could hardly believe this was one of Red's employees, Nick would have insisted on the top man. So who was the man calling himself Paul Weston, amongst other things, and why had he being lying to me from the minute we'd met on the Blue Train?

Chapter 56

Avril gave birth to a baby boy an hour later. Ross and I stood alongside Jacky and Nick at her bedside after the doctor had left. Nurse Lefevre, the midwife, had cleaned the baby and shown him to us all in turn. Avril lay back, propped up on pillows, her face red and her eyes tearful.

Surely, now that he could see his grandson, Nick Ferris would have a change of heart, I thought. But the set of his shoulders told a different story and I felt desperately sorry for the young girl who would soon be parted from her son.

Nurse Lefevre smiled and stood at our side. I glanced once more at the puckered face with the fringe of spiky fair hair as the sun filtered through the blinds and turned it fiery red.

There was no mistaking the resemblance. I blinked; the nurse moved away from the beam of sunlight and the baby's face resumed is former characterless expression. I was becoming paranoid, I decided.

Ross and I walked back to our villa, hand in hand.

"It's up to Nick and Jacky now. I can do no more," he said.

"You've been such a good friend to Avril."

"Not good enough it would seem. I believe Nick is adamant and the baby will go for adoption."

"Maybe they'll change their minds; he's such a cute little thing.

"Who knows? I'm shattered."

"Me too. Bed?"

He hugged me close to him and I began to believe that at last it was over. His commitment to Avril, whatever he considered it to be, was finished. She was out of our lives.

Complacency is a dangerous emotion; it lets you drop your guard. I've lived long enough to know that now but my immature self wasn't so enlightened.

The gardens at the villa were in full bloom. I don't think I'd ever seen them looking so beautiful. The sun was warm on my back as I took my early morning walk around the grounds, leaving Ross to sleep off a slight hangover. He'd called it 'wetting the baby's head' last night.

The grounds of the villa stretched on the one side to the Ferris's property and on the other to woodland. The lawns spread out in front of the house and dipped towards the rocky coastline where Diana Huntley had met her death. I loved walking along the cliff top, watching the ever-changing view, the sun sparkling on the water, the blues and greens of the sea, which in the morning turned orange as the sun rose higher in the sky. I sat down on a stone bench and stretched my legs out in front of me, closing my eyes and inhaling the fresh salty air.

The voices were indistinct; at first I thought I'd imagined them. They drifted on the breeze from the direction of the Ferris's place, which lay behind me.

"I won't let them take him. You'll have to do something soon," It was Avril speaking.

The answering voice was less clear. "What can I do? I've tried everything. I told you there's nothing more I can do to help. You'll have to go along with it, you have no choice." I wished I could move nearer but they were too far away. I thought I recognised my husband's voice but couldn't be sure. Struggling to make out the rest of the conversation I heard Avril becoming almost hysterical. "You promised!" Sobbing followed this outburst and the rest of the conversation was indistinct.

Aware that I'd eavesdropped on Avril and her baby's father discussing the proposed adoption of their son, I desperately wanted to know to whom Avril had been speaking. But fearing the answer would mean the end of my marriage, I decided to forget the encounter, and bury my head in the sand.

Later that day, Ross took a telephone call in the study and emerged looking harassed.

"That was Velma. She's in a state and has asked me to come over. I told her it was impossible." He wrung his hands together and bit his lip.

Aware that Velma, his mother's best friend, was the only connection he had left with Olivia, I said, "Perhaps we could both go. I've never been to New York."

"You wouldn't mind?"

"Of course not, as long as we are together it doesn't really matter where, and if Velma needs you I'm sure it must be important otherwise she wouldn't have rung."

Preparations for us to travel to New York were undertaken immediately. Ross was on the telephone for the rest of the afternoon, whilst I packed a suitcase for us both. Always travel light was Ross's maxim and I suppose, having never had to worry about money and being able to buy anything you required when you arrived, it seemed the sensible thing to do.

Deciding to think of the journey as another leg of honeymoon, I sat back and enjoyed the flight and the prospect of seeing New York. Obviously Velma had been upset or she wouldn't have asked Ross to make the journey, which was fine by me.

It was dark when we arrived at Velma's apartment in Manhattan. I'd managed to sleep on the plane and was refreshed but Ross had dark circles under his eyes.

Lance answered the door to us and I was amazed at how he'd changed from the photograph, which Olivia had on her desk, showing Velma, Bill and Lance together at a party.

"Come in, Mom's in the lounge-room. Here let me take your valise. Nice to meet you at last, Anna, sorry it's in such circumstances."

He obviously thought I knew the reason for our visit. Perhaps I wasn't the only one in my marriage to be less than expansive with the truth, I thought.

Velma had been crying. Her eyes were red, her cheeks blotchy. Ross crossed the floor, hugged her and sat at her side; I air-kissed her cheek and sat with Velma sandwiched between us.

"It's so good of you both to come. I really don't know what Bill is going to make of all this. As if he hasn't enough to cope with, Marcie having passed on only a year back." She sniffed loudly.

"Mom, we'll sort it out." Lance was pacing the floor."

"I'm still baffled by your phone call," Ross said, and I thought, you and me both chum.

"Sit down, Lance. Explain to Ross, I'm all talked out." Velma lay back, her thin body, like a feather at my side.

"It's Avril. Her folks are playing up and well you know the story there, better than I. The thing is - I thought this was all settled between us. I like Avril, don't get me wrong but I'm getting married – there's no way I could agree to it. I guess she wanted me to take the rap during her pregnancy so they wouldn't insist she sought a termination, then when the baby was born, they'd marry."

"Who?" I asked, the word slipping out even though I'd decided not to get involved and to just listen.

"Pardon me?"

"Who was going to marry Avril?"

"The baby's father, of course."

"And who is that?"

"You mean you don't know, Anna. He's kept you in the dark too."

I looked from one to the other of them. Velma, clutching her chest, Lance looking at Ross and my husband looking at his hands as if the answer lay at his fingertips, and then I knew, the answer had been staring me in the face all the time.

Chapter 57

Velma, having recovered from her attack of palpitations, stood up and took my hand. "I think it's time you learned the truth my dear." She led me along the hallway to a room at the far end of a corridor. It was a small room without windows, a tiny office space with boxes on shelves and a desk against one wall.

She lifted the lid of a metal box and removed a key ring. The keys jangled as she lifted them up and selected the key which opened the top drawer of the desk, from which she removed a black leather-covered journal.

"Olivia gave me this shortly before she died. She trusted me to keep her secret until I thought it time to show you the true version. It was her intention that you should write her official biography, the one she'd spent years devising."

"It was fiction?"

Velma gave a wry smile. "Most of it, at least the bits she couldn't reveal to the world."

"I see."

"I don't think you do. It's quite a tale I don't mind telling you, honey, and it's one you must read, if nothing else for the sake of your marriage." She handed me the journal. "But not now. You're exhausted. Leave it until the morning."

"I don't think I can stay here," I said.

"Of course you can. Lance and Ross will stay at Bill's tonight. Ross wants to give you some space."

"He knows about this?"

"He's known for months. I showed it to him when he was last over, just before he came back to start your honeymoon. He agreed you should not be made aware of it in order to protect his mother's memory. But now circumstances have changed. He feels there should be no secrets between you."

A tear slid down my cheek and I angrily wiped it away. I wasn't sure I wanted to know. It seemed to me as if I'd been surrounded by secrets and lies ever since I first arrived at Longacres. Could I stand to hear any more, I wondered.

"There, there, you're bushed. It'll all come clear in the morning. Your things are in the bedroom. Get a good night's sleep and we'll talk again tomorrow.

She patted my arm and kissed my cheek as if comforting a young child so I became one, a young child afraid of the adult world and what it might hold.

As I slid beneath Velma's silk sheets in a bedroom smelling of lavender, I doubted if I'd sleep a wink but exhaustion took over and I drifted into a night undisturbed by dreams. When I awoke and remembered the journal, my first thought was of Ross and our future together – was there one, or was this the end of the road for us? This was the day I was about to find out one way or another.

Velma's daily maid, Carla, had laid breakfast for us both in a room overlooking Park Avenue. Velma's father had been in the real estate businessman and had divided his extensive fortune equally between his two children upon his death.

As I toyed with my food, I watched the hustle and bustle of a busy morning unfolding in the street below.

"I've an appointment in the beauty parlour in an hour, then I'm off to see Bill, so you'll be left in peace. Carla will keep you fed and watered and I'll be back this evening. Don't look so sad, honey. We'll work this out. "

After I'd showered, I took the journal into the lounge-room with its wall of plate glass windows and after a brief hesitation, opened the black leather cover and began to read.

Extract from Olivia Maitland's Journal

Chapter 58

For anyone reading this, be sure it is a true account of what happened on the night I first saw my son and the subsequent events following it.

I was with Velma, we'd been to see a show on Broadway, a small group of photographers and reporters had hounded us as we left the theatre and Velma suggested we head them off by cutting through an alleyway and jumping into a taxi a block away.

At first I was apprehensive, it seemed a rash suggestion, it was New York after all. But the flashlights were popping and it was only a shortcut, what could happen to us?

We were giggling when the man approached holding the hands of two scruffy, snivelling, little boys.

"Spare a dime, missus, my wife's sick."

He thrust a grubby hand towards us and Velma told him to get lost. But something in the little boys' faces made me stop. I been desperate to start a family for some time but Mother Nature wasn't listening.

I opened my purse. It was all so sudden; he grabbed my purse and ran off down the alleyway leaving the two little boys looking up at us. Thankfully they'd stopped crying, but Velma was keen to get out of the alley and was pulling at my sleeve. "Come on, Liv, leave them, they're probably street kids, nothing to do with us."

But I couldn't just leave them. I took their hands in mine and walked them back to the main street where we picked up a taxi and drove back to Velma's apartment.

After we'd bathed them and put them to bed for the night, we intended to see what Bill could suggest as we were reluctant to drop them off at the precinct's headquarters, knowing what their fate would be.

I picked up their clothes from the floor and as I did so a photograph fell from one of the pockets. It was of a young woman holding each of their hands and looking soulfully into the camera lens. Putting the grubby clothes into the garbage bins, we had Gloria, Velma's maid, go out and buy clothes for the young boys. They were roughly the same size and could have been twins but they were not identical, not by a long chalk, one was dark haired with bright blue eyes and the other had fair almost red hair with eyes the colour of hazelnuts.

When Bill, who had just graduated in law, saw them, he sighed. "You don't have many options, in my opinion. You either hand them over to the authorities or you try and trace the mother, an impossible task in my opinion."

The country was still suffering from the after effects of the war in Europe, nothing was as it had been before. Lives had been lost on both sides of the Atlantic and if you were poor in New York then you had very little future. I remember thinking that I could make so much difference to these little boys. They were bright and after their initial cautiousness they became more talkative and interested in exploring their surroundings.

Bill said he'd make enquiries in the area and had taken the photograph with him. But he had little hope of finding anyone who could recognise the woman or her children. He combed the area near to the alleyway and beyond but no one appeared interested in the fate of the children. They had far too many worries of their own to care about a couple of lost street kids.

Days turned into weeks and at the end of a month of fruitless searching, I'd become attached to the children, one in particular. I decided to call him Ross, the other we called Harry.

I doubted whether I could take the two of them back to England with me but Velma said she'd help. I was still too recognisable by the press so Velma arranged the legal documents with Bill's assistance in order that the boys could travel with her. He'd already managed to arrange adoption papers for the two of them so now I had two children and I couldn't have been happier.

However, Harry was trouble; whereas Ross was even-tempered and quiet, his brother was disruptive and voluble. He was difficult to manage. I'd known from the start I couldn't keep him. He kept causing trouble for Ross.

Velma and I decided that we'd concoct a story to explain that I'd adopted a child after the mother had pleaded with me to take him and had then rushed into traffic and been killed. It was the sort of story, which would appeal to the press, it was publicity and it worked.

Velma looked after Harry for a while and when she could see how difficult he was, decided to take him back to the States with her and have him fostered over there. Bill knew of a woman who was desperate for a child; it seemed the best course of action all round. I agreed to pay for his welfare, of course, and arranged with Bill to see that money was transferred each month. It was a salve to my conscience for a child who'd been effectively abandoned twice during his short life.

Life continued in the manner I've previously written about, in the journal, which will become my official memoir but the secrets hidden within these pages will never see the light of day. I'll show Velma, my closest and dearest friend, once I know my days are numbered, with the strict instruction that after she's read it, this book is to be destroyed.

As I said before, I loved Ross dearly. He was an easy child to love and I feared for him in this world where you had to have a tough hide to survive. His nature was gentle and kind and he had none of the wilfulness displayed by his brother.

I was a watchful mother, careful to protect him from harm, possessive to the point of obsession. I can write this down now; it's something I knew but would never admit, even to myself, a flaw in my character, if you like. And as the years passed I watched him grow into a handsome, intelligent, young man.

My obsession with him took on a new level when I saw with horror the effect he had on the opposite sex. Once he left to study at the LSE I knew I no longer had any control over his wellbeing. The years during which he studied for his degree were the worst imaginable. I moved to the Belgrave Square house to be near him but he preferred his shared flat in Notting Hill, untidy and smelly though it was. I tried not to make it too obvious that I was missing him but it was with a gigantic sense of relief I saw him graduate and after a year of travelling finally settle down with me at Longacres.

Diana Huntley was my secretary and personal assistant. She was more beautiful than I would have liked but she was competent and I was too busy to look for another to take her place. She'd been working with me for a short while when I noticed that she'd grown close to Ross and as the weeks passed my fears grew.

We were holidaying at my villa near Beaulieu and I desperately required her assistance with some secretarial work. So naturally I asked her to come out to the villa. It was the worst thing I could have done and I regretted it almost as soon as the arrangements were made.

All I can say is that the situation between my son and my secretary intensified to such an extent I had to step in and make sure it didn't develop any further. I spoke to Diana about it but she was adamant that there was nothing in it and she didn't know what I was talking about. I could tell she was lying.

So you see, I had no option other than to see to it that she was removed, permanently.

Chapter 59

I placed the journal face down on the chair and closed my eyes. Unable or unwilling to properly assimilate the full impact of the passage I'd just read, I began to think how awful this must have been for Velma. I didn't want to think of how Ross would have felt, not then, it was too soon to think clearly about my husband and his actions.

Red, the photograph, the passport, swirled around in my brain threatening to drag me under; I had recently developed a strong suspicion that Red was more involved in my husband's life than he'd let on but had yet to discover what that connection might be as my suspicions were merely supposition; I had no real evidence to the contrary.

As for Olivia's revelation that she was responsible for getting rid of Diana, it didn't bear thinking about. The implication that she was involved in Diana's death was plain to see; there could be no doubt in the mind of anyone reading the journal.

Carla was singing in the kitchen area. It was a song Olivia had made famous in the early fifties. It brought tears to my eyes. I left my bedroom in the need of a hot black coffee.

"Mrs Maitland, you're up early. Breakfast?" she stopped wiping over the surfaces and gave me a cheery smile.

"Just toast and black coffee, Carla, please."

She picked up a notepad from the counter. "Mr Maitland phoned and said he'd come over when you feel up to it. He said to phone him; the number's on the pad. And Miss Velma told me to tell you she'd be staying at Mr Bill's ...." She looked uncomfortable. "Until you two sort it out. If that makes sense?"

"It does, thank-you. I'll be in the lounge room, please don't bother to lay a space at the table."

"Tray, do you?"

"Fine."

I knew I was delaying the moment when I would have to pick up the journal again, as I watched the early morning traffic building up on Park Avenue. The commuters like miniature figures, moving about below me, each with their own purpose in life, most of their thoughts and dreams unrelated to each other, struck a chord and I wished I could change places with them.

It seemed to me that ever since I'd started working for Olivia my life had revolved around the inhabitants of Longacres, to the exclusion of all else. I'd become involved with them so quickly, entrenched and entangled with the Maitlands until I'd entered their ranks by marrying the heir.

In the cold light of day the thought that Olivia was a murderer seemed ridiculous. I'd finished reading the journal the previous night to the point where she had suggested she had to put a stop to Diana's involvement with her son. But that could mean anything. The police report stated that Diana Huntley's death was an accident. It was Red who had led me to believe it was nothing of the kind.

The coffee was making me think more clearly. Sure that I'd been too willing to jump to the wrong conclusion, and that exhaustion had played its part, I decided to take a walk to clear my head.

"Carla? Can I walk to Central Park from here?" I asked.

"Sure, take you about five minutes."

"Good, then that's what I'll do. I won't be long."

"You take care now. Don't go wearing any expensive jewellery, and keep an eye out for pickpockets."

"I'll be OK."

"Yeah, young girl like you, you can always run."

She was smiling, which put the warning into perspective. So I pulled on a pair of blue jeans and a sweater and left the apartment.

As I'd anticipated I needed the sweater until the sun made an appearance, as I headed down the four blocks to Central Park. There were plenty of people about, no one taking a speck of notice of me. Carla's warning didn't sit too heavily on my shoulders as I entered the park and inhaled the fresh morning air.

An old woman, feeding the birds from a carrier bag, shuffled along at a snail's pace and two young women were taking a run, whilst chatting and laughing together. For the first time in ages, I temporarily forgot I was a Maitland and joined the human race unencumbered by the past.

When I reached the avenue of trees, I marvelled at the multitude of green leaves forming a tunnel above my head. Sunshine filtered through the foliage creating patterns on the wide avenue beneath and touching the heads of the commuters hurrying towards their various destinations. A young couple, pushing a toddler in a pushchair covered by a white sunshade that bobbed and twisted as they walked, passed me. The young woman smiled and nodded a greeting. Her partner had his arm around her shoulders and I saw him plant a kiss on the top of her head as they walked towards a street seller, who had sited his stall selling cookies, a short distance away. I blinked away tears, wishing desperately that I

A Tangled Web

could forget the last few days and remember the
happiness Ross and I had shared. But the shadow of the
journal separated us and it was no use putting off the
hour when I would discover the truth.

The pleasure of the morning and my brief escape
from reality evaporated, as I walked back to the
apartment, a feeling of approaching dread in every
step.

Olivia Maitland's 'Hidden' Journal

Chapter 60

Once the thought had entered my head I found it became a distinct possibility and the closer Ross and Diana became the more it occupied my mind. Even so, I recognised it as a fantasy, there was no way I was going to commit a murder - it was just too preposterous to consider.

Diana continued to deal with my correspondence and to keep me up to date with how things were progressing at Longacres. She had developed a good relationship with Joe and Esther Travers, primarily because she was distantly related to them. It was how she'd ended up being employed by me in the first place.

I'd agreed to the position being filled by Joe's relative as I was far too busy at the time to bother with interviewing candidates and besides I trusted his judgement. I hadn't been prepared for how attractive she was though, otherwise I might not have agreed so readily.

It was Diana who arranged for the ghost-writer and as far as I could see she was fitting in nicely. She was young and I couldn't see her being a threat where Ross was concerned.

Diana was a different matter. I'm not a snob, it's not as if I want Ross to lead a celibate life either but it's not time yet. I need him so much. I can't let him go – not yet.

A Tangled Web

As fate would have it Ross was called away to London on business and was likely to be staying in our Belgrave Square property for a week or two. Diana mooned about the place for the first week, there were endless telephone conversations and I was certain there would be a tearful reunion when he returned.

During the second week I suggested she take some time to herself, go for a walk, enjoy the sunshine; I insisted I could do without her for a few hours every afternoon. Reluctantly she agreed.

It was on one particularly hot afternoon that I saw her walking in the direction of the coastal path. I followed at a safe distance knowing she was headed for the cove. I lost the opportunity to call out to her, to explain she was better off following the path to Beaulieu and still I followed behind.

She reached the place where, a while back, there had been a landslip and hesitated. The earth was damp after overnight rain, she slipped and I watched her slide towards the sea. Her dress caught on a ledge and she reached up and held on trying to pull herself up. I could have knelt over, given her my hand; I could have saved her.

Diana was wearing a yellow cotton frock that billowed around her legs, her long hair flowed behind her in a shiny brown wave, as she slid into the water. I could have called out before she fell; she hadn't noticed the warning sign, which was partly obscured by an overhanging branch. If by doing nothing to save her I was culpable then that's what I was, I had murdered her by my reluctance to act. I dispassionately watched her hair flowing in the current and her head sinking beneath the surface of the water then walked back to the house to await the news.

251

A Tangled Web

Ross was distraught, of course, but I knew it would be short lived. It was an accident, everyone said so, even the police. And, after a week of sadness during which Ross ambled around the place looking lost, I decided we should take a well-earned holiday in Italy.

It did the trick; the sun-drenched Amalfi coast was the necessary panacea for a broken heart. We spent three weeks during which I was subjected to an unwanted analysis of Diana Huntley's numerous virtues. I played a waiting game and when I saw that a beautiful Italian girl had diverted his attention as we strolled through the gardens at Ravello, I knew he was over her.

When we returned to Beaulieu, Ross was occupied by work. Soon afterwards, he left for Longacres where he was to have a meeting with Miles about an infringement of copyright issue regarding one of my recordings.

When he returned, he was thoughtful and a while later suggested, as I needed some secretarial help, why not arrange for Anna to come over to the villa, as she could work on my memoir at the same time, thus killing two birds with one stone.

It was during the time Anna spent at the villa that we had the party. Ruby Dent had been staying in Monte Carlo and Ross and I had met her a few days before. I suggested she come to the party and stay over, as the hotel she was staying in was extremely expensive.

She was great fun. I'd met her before, of course and she livened up the party no end. But for some reason, I hadn't counted on her clinging to my son like a limpet. In addition to which she showed no sign of leaving the villa.

252

A Tangled Web

Ruby was a different proposition to Diana. This I definitely had to stop. I couldn't have Ross marrying someone who was at the start of her career in show business – I'd travelled that road, you see, I knew what it entailed, the long days on the road, the late nights, the broken marriages.

It was the sixties, drugs were freely taken by the young and not so young. She was young. It was easy. I have no regrets about Ruby.

Chapter 61

The journal slid from my hands. My heart began to race. There was no lapse of judgement this time. Olivia had murdered Ruby. I remembered the party and how I had liked her, even though she'd clung to Ross. I'd thought it was a game to her, she was a girl who liked to have fun; there was nothing more to it than that.

A thought suddenly occurred to me. Had I been next in line? Ross had married me, without Olivia's prior knowledge. Was it too much of a leap of the imagination to think that she would have found an occasion whereby I would meet with an accident too? And where did Red fit in – for I was sure he did. My meeting with him on the Blue Train, him suddenly 'saving' me in the harbour at Saint Tropez, not to mention his insistence that Ross was responsible for my accident and possibly worse. Then there was my foolish flight to London – what had I been thinking about to allow myself to be whisked away in such a manner? The answer to the question, how was he involved with the Maitlands, still eluded me. He had lied about being Paul Weston, so why was he supposedly following Avril Ferris around? Had he lied about the person he was following – was it Ross or was it me?

At least he wasn't likely to be staying in Manhattan so I wasn't in danger of bumping into him in Central Park. I considered whether I should phone Ross but decided against it. I needed some space, to think about the implications of Olivia's revelations and how they affected us all.

A Tangled Web

Velma rang and asked if I wanted to meet her in Bloomingdales for lunch. At first I hesitated, knowing she would want to quiz me about the journal but then I decided I could probably head her off the subject by saying I needed more time to read and think about it.

Part of me wanted to find out how Ross was feeling but I just couldn't get the idea out of my head, that he was more involved with Avril than he'd let on. Was he the father of her baby? Why had she involved Lance in the deception? Did anyone know the meaning of the word 'truth'?

Velma was seated in the restaurant when I arrived a little later than planned. I apologised for keeping her waiting, ordered lunch, and once we'd finished eating she hit on the reason for asking me to meet her.

"It's Ross, hon; he's missing you desperately. He thinks that after you finish reading the journal you won't want to see him."

"It's not his fault," I said, but there was still the question of Avril's baby to consider and the only way I could cope with it all was to take small steps towards the truth.

"No, that's right, I keep telling him so but he's always been such a sensitive child. Ring him, put him out of his misery."

I turned away from her. Other diners, oblivious of the traumatic revelations in Olivia Maitland's secret journal, chatted away unconcerned with my problems. I wished, I could join in their laughter and conversation and not be Anna Maitland, wife of Ross, son of a murderer.

"Anna?"

"Sorry, yes, I can't ring him just now, Velma. Please tell him I need time to work this through and that obviously I don't blame him in any way for Olivia's revelations."

"It would come better from you, you know."

"Yes, of course, and I will, I promise but not at the moment."

"Well, he'll just have to be grateful for that." She finished her coffee and leaned forward. "How about we take a look at the dress department? I always find buying something extravagant puts things into perspective."

I smiled and as we stood up and walked out of the restaurant, I tucked my arm in hers and for an hour or two tried to forget all about the Maitlands.

I was putting off the moment when I would finish Olivia's journal, fearing it would be about me. Afterwards I'd ring Ross, arrange to meet him and try to make sense of it all. But for now, I'd follow Velma, like a puppy, around the store.

Olivia Maitland's 'Hidden' Journal

Chapter 62

I was still not sure about her, she seemed competent and I quite liked her but I had to decide whether she was a threat. Ross seemed preoccupied; he didn't appear to look on her as anything other than my employee, which was satisfying. For now I'll play a waiting game.

She seemed upset about Ruby. I can't think why. She didn't really know her; she'd only met her a few times. But I still couldn't decide whether Ross was interested in her. They walked around the grounds together and I pondered whether they might be friends, nothing more.

She was no threat. My memoirs proceeded at a good pace, at least some of it's true, most of it in fact. There was no reason why anyone should know the rest. But it helped to write it down. I've always kept a journal and this one is special, it's the absolute truth.

Then I began to think Avril Ferris and Ross were seeing each other, just when I'd thought they'd done with all that and Avril had moved on. I knew I'd have to watch her. I didn't want her hurting him again.

I was confused by the news. Velma told me Ross's brother was still alive. How can that be? I thought he'd died. I asked her where he is and she hesitated, she was unwilling to tell me. She thought perhaps it was for the best. But time has changed things and I have to make amends.

A Tangled Web

I couldn't believe it. Ross told me yesterday – they are married. He was so happy, it swelled my love for him to new heights. I supposed if I had to have a daughter-in-law it might just as well be Anna. She wasn't like the others, full of themselves, likely to cheat on him. I hoped he'd found his true love and we could forget about the past.

It did bother me that Avril Ferris was still hanging around the place though, making sheep's eyes at him, chatting with him like a co-conspirator. I was sure that Anna was jealous even though she made a valiant attempt to hide it. I was on her side, at least until she did anything to hurt my boy. I decided to play a waiting game.

Chapter 63

In Velma's flat I read the last page and sighed. It was beginning to look as though I'd had a lucky escape. I could hardly believe what I'd been reading. I ran my eyes over the last chapter once more and was struck by the difference between this journal and the others I'd been working on. This time Olivia had chosen to use the past tense, in the others she'd always written in the present tense. I wondered if it was because this was a retrospective account and decided it was nothing more than that. I was starting to look for trouble where none existed, so confused was I by the thought that Olivia Maitland had been a murderer.

Picking up the phone I rang Bill's number. Lance answered.

"It's me, Anna, is Ross there please?"

"Hold the line, Anna, he's on his way."

"Ross. I think we need to talk. Will you come over?"

"Of course."

He looked older. His face creased with worry. I stepped aside and followed him into the lounge room. The shoppers on Park Avenue below us hurried along without any idea of the traumatic conversation we were about to have; I wished I could have changed placed with them to avoid the inevitable.

"You've read it?"

"Yes." We sat opposite each other, he wringing his hands in despair." I'm sorry, Ross. It must have such a shock for you."

"It's no excuse."

"No, it's not. Perhaps now you can tell me the truth."

He sighed and I saw him desperately trying to explain the inexplicable, wrestling with the truth as if it were a serpent.

"I found this in her things before Ma died. Believe me, I'd fallen in love with you but had no idea how I could make it work, especially in view of the revelation that by doing so I could be putting your life in danger. Avril comforted me at a time when I was distraught."

"She knew about this?" I indicated the journal on the coffee table.

"No, no, of course not. She just knew I was sad." He looked up from his hands as if trying to make me believe him. His blue eyes sought mine and I wavered. "I've been trying to help her, that's all."

"An understatement," I commented bitterly.

"When Avril knew she was pregnant she expected the father to marry her. But it didn't turn out that way. She was desperate. I'm not proud of my actions but I wanted to help her. I tried to persuade her to think of a termination but she wouldn't hear of it, she wanted this baby. I told her I was sure Nick would hit the roof when he heard and she started to cry and plead with me to help."

"So that was when you hatched the plan to involve Lance?"

"No that was Avril's idea. I told her not to even think about it. Eventually I agreed to let Lance off the hook and say the baby was mine. It was a ridiculously stupid thing to do. I don't blame you for hating me." His eyes met mine again and I knew I was lost. "I'm so sorry Anna, I wouldn't hurt you for the world. You must know that?"

I started to cry. I wished I hadn't but the tears fell in spite of my resolve to stay cool and detached. He came to me then and cradled me in his arms. There was nothing I could do. I loved him and was willing to believe him.

The journal lay open at the last page; it sat between us on the table like a ghost from the past. I stood up, closed the cover and placed it in Velma's bureau.

I knew I would use it, with or without Ross's agreement. Olivia Maitland's memoir would be finished and the truth would be told. Even after her death, her poisonous tentacles, reaching from the grave, could so easily have been the catalyst for the break up of our marriage. I owed it to our future life together, which I was determined should not be founded on lies, to publish a truthful account of her life.

However, determination alone sometimes is not enough and we can have no control over what fate has in store for us.

Chapter 64

Velma waved to us as we left her flat in a yellow cab bound for the airport. The atmosphere between us was frosty, admittedly more on my part than his. Ross tried to hold my hand but I was still annoyed at his duplicity where Avril Ferris was concerned and knew it would take a while for me to come to terms with it.

We both slept on the flight to London, the trauma of the past few days having drained us of energy. When I awoke the aircraft was making preparations for our descent. I stretched and saw that my husband was watching me with a slow, sad, smile on his face.

"You had a good sleep. How do you feel?"

"I'm fine, thank you."

"Good. I've arranged for Tom to pick us up and drive us back to Longacres."

"So he's a chauffeur now?"

Ross didn't answer.

It wasn't long before we were sitting in the back seat of the car and driving towards Devon. Tom Trevellyn appeared to be wary of me and spoke little throughout the journey. It seemed an age since I'd slept in our bed at Longacres, so much had happened in the meantime.

I slept in my own room that night, feigning a headache. Ross sympathised and kissed my cheek before making for the master bedroom. In spite of, or perhaps because of, the long flight, I couldn't sleep, tossing and turning until the sky lightened with the approach of dawn.

At breakfast Ross sat opposite me, asked if I'd slept well then buried his head in the morning paper. There were questions that needed answers and neither of us could break down the dam which we'd built between us fearing the outcome.

It was much later in the afternoon, when I was working in the study and Ross had been out walking, that he returned and I heard his footsteps on the stairs.

"Anna," he said, rushing towards me and taking my hand. "We need to talk. I hate this atmosphere; it's not like us to be so cold with each other. I know I'm to blame but please forgive my stupidity and believe I want to make amends."

His plea weakened my resolve and I let him lead me over to the couch where we sat, holding hands as he tried to explain how he'd become involved with Avril.

"You know we'd been friends since childhood?" I nodded. "There was a time when I hoped we could be more but was aware it was Lance she wanted, not me." He hung his head then shrugged. "As fate would have it we met up again in London, when I was studying for my degree. She stayed at my shared flat for a while, had a brief fling with my friend, I finished my degree and didn't see her again until much later."

"Go on," I said.

"When you told Esther you'd seen two Diana's, I nearly had a fit. You see, whilst Ma was in Beaulieu, Avril wanted me to agree to her staying at Longacres because her boyfriend was living nearby. It had to be top secret in case her parents found out but she let Joe and Esther in on her plan. When you arrived she said she was Diana, in a panic, not wanting to be discovered as having stayed at the house."

"I see"

"The next time I saw her she was holidaying at her parents' villa in the south of France and Ma invited them over for drinks one evening. It was after Diana died, and before I could tell you how I felt about you. By the way, Ma got it quite wrong, Diana and I weren't in love; she had a thing going with Tom for a while but broke it off when she fell for someone else, some guy she'd met in London before she starting working for Ma."

He shifted uncomfortably in his seat but held my hands in his as if fearing to let them go.

"Anyway, to get back to that night. It was when Avril first told me she was pregnant and that it happened during the time I allowed her to stay at Longacres incognito."

I sighed, "So that's the full story?"

"Well the rest is history. Obviously I felt in part to blame as if I hadn't allowed her to stay at Longacres in order to meet her 'boyfriend' perhaps none of this would have happened."

"What a mess."

"You can say that again. I'd met you by this time and desperately wanted it all to go away. Needless to say, Nick and Jacky Ferris think I'm a rat and are sure I'm the father of their daughter's baby. I'll have to cope with that, it's you I'm concerned about - do you forgive me?"

What could I say? No one is perfect, myself included. "I suggest we put the past behind us and start again," I said.

He was like an excited child, he kissed me, stroked my hair and I began to feel that surge of excitement at his touch.

We were climbing the stairs to our bedroom when Ross said, "Are you sure it's wise to write up Ma's memoirs using the volume she gave to Velma? There's bound to be an almighty stink when it's published."

He held me close and kissed me again.

"I believe it's what she wanted, Ross, otherwise why would she have given it to Velma in the first place. She knew her friend and that she was unlikely to destroy it. Besides we owe it to Diana and Ruby."

"Well in that case, we have to go ahead – what is the expression – *publish and be damned?*

Chapter 65

For the next few months, I spent every day working on Olivia's memoir. Ross met with the publisher in London and arranged a suitable deadline, which would coincide with what would have been his mother's seventieth birthday and I watched spring turn into summer and the approach of autumn from the study window.

When I was satisfied that the book was finally finished, Ross and I left for London. We spent a month at the house in Belgrave Square and when the proofs came through we sat in the elegant lounge and read them.

"What do you think?" I asked, when we'd finished reading.

Ross raised his empty wine glass in my direction. "Congratulations, my clever, beautiful, wife; you do realise our lives aren't going to be worth living for a while, once this reaches the shops."

"Mmm, it all seems so much worse now it's printed. The press with have a field day."

"Which is why I suggest we spend the winter in Italy and continue our interrupted honeymoon. There's a place near the Dolomites that is excellent. I went there once, a long time ago." He looked sad. "It was with Ma, when she was the life and soul of the party. It's high up in the mountains, and exclusive. No one will find us there, I'm sure."

"Excellent idea. I'll start shopping right away."

"Then I suggest, we celebrate, first; I'll be back in a sec.,"

A Tangled Web

True to his word, Ross appeared soon after with a bottle of champagne, two glasses and a smile that turned my legs to water.

The following days were spent planning our holiday. We were to be staying in the Grand Hotel in a place called Cortina d'Ampezzo, Ross explained that an exclusive clientele favoured it, so we wouldn't be bothered by tourists with their intrusive cameras.

It was this sort of remark that separated us – he was still stuck in the nineteen forties, whereas I was a sixties child with no such entrenched ideas. However, it wouldn't be possible for anyone to be a carbon copy of their partner, I decided, and embraced our differences with good humour.

Our flight was short in comparison to the one to New York and uneventful as was the journey to our hotel. The amazing scenery entranced me as we drove higher into the Italian countryside. Snow capped mountains rose like an army of soldiers protecting us as we reached the sanctuary of our hotel.

The inside of the building was in every way majestic. We were transported to an earlier time; luxurious décor, attentive staff and an atmosphere of elegance permeated the building, cocooning us in its grandeur.

As the deadline for the book launch approached, I felt in need of anonymity. The publishers had wanted Ross and me to be present at the launch but Ross insisted it wouldn't be wise to do so and for that I'd been grateful. After all it was his mother's story, I had merely been the mechanic, the translator of her journals. I hoped I had completed the task to her satisfaction but was sad that I would never know. I still found it difficult to assimilate, that the woman I'd worked so closely with, was a murderer and knew there would be a furore when the book hit the streets. Even in the darkest hours of the night, I'd become haunted by the idea and couldn't reconcile the inconsistencies in the story with reality.

During the week prior to the launch, every morning we'd make for the ski slopes. I'd spend the morning with an instructor on the nursery slopes, whilst Ross, a competent skier, would make for the more advanced runs. Afterwards, we'd meet up for drinks and a light lunch, then make our way back to the hotel for an afternoon of leisurely lovemaking, all thoughts of our recent problems placed firmly behind us.

"It's as I feared," Ross announced on the morning following the book launch in London. He held up the newspaper. Although it was in Italian, the photographs of Olivia and lurid headlines left me in no doubt as to their meaning.

"What do we do now?" I asked

"Sit it out. They won't disturb us here. I've had a chat with the manager and crossed his palm with silver, if you get my drift. Don't worry, as far as anyone is concerned we are just Mr and Mrs Smith from London."

"Really?"

"Of course, you don't think I'd sign in as Ross Maitland, do you, my love?"

So he'd been one step ahead of the game once more, my clever resourceful husband.

Chapter 66

The Italian news on the T.V reported the story. I didn't need a translation to get the gist of the report. Photographs of Olivia in her heyday, even photos of Ross and myself, were shown together with the book, which had now been launched successfully.

We stayed in our room that day and the next hoping to avoid the sidelong glances of our fellow guests. On the third day, a scandal involving a starlet and a member of the Italian government conveniently placed Olivia's story in the past and we felt able to resume the rest of our holiday. In Britain it was a similar story, we knew it would soon be yesterday's news, if we stayed in Italy long enough.

Heavy snow began to fall at the beginning of December. Although spectacularly transforming the countryside, it meant that our skiing was curtailed as it was considered to be too dangerous, especially for novice skiers.

"You go, I don't want to spoil your fun," I coaxed but Ross simply kissed the top of my head and went back to reading his book.

"I thought we'd take a sleigh ride later. I understand the hotel has arranged for one, which will take us through the woods to a chalet where we can sample the local brew. I gather it's good fun and we'll be well wrapped up in blankets on the ride. What d'you say?"

"I say, yes please, it sounds just the thing."

We were dressed for the weather in our warmest clothes. I remember wearing a hat and mittens made from reindeer skin and a fur coat that reached the top of my boots. Ross, as always, looked immaculate and as handsome as ever. I caught a few admiring glances thrown in his direction from some of our fellow passengers in the sleigh and smiled with satisfaction that he was mine.

When we left the hotel the snow showers were light, feathery flakes dusting our clothes like sprinkles of icing sugar. We were well into the woods before the weather changed. The wind speed increased bringing with it a snowstorm. The horses pulling the sleigh whinnied and raised their heads but the sleigh-driver managed to control them, telling us that we were nearly at the hostelry.

"Am I glad we made it," Ross said, taking my hand and leading me into the building where a log fire was burning in a large room overlooking the forest.

The rest of the party soon joined us and assembled near the bar where jugs of mulled wine and sweetmeats were waiting. My cheeks were glowing in the heat from the fire and I removed my hat shaking a shower of snowflakes around me like confetti.

"Here," Ross handed me a beaker of mulled wine and clinked it against his. "Cheers, my love."

"To us," I said.

Entertainment of a sort was laid on. A group of musicians of indeterminate age played a selection of festive music and I was suddenly struck by the fact that Christmas was just a few weeks away.

Outside, the wind strengthened and the snow fell continuously. As the evening drew to a close, I followed our party out into the cold night air in order to make our way back to our hotel and became aware that we were now snowbound. There was no way we could make it back to our hotel that night through drifts, which were piled across our path.

"Please, do not worry, ladies and gentlemen. This is not an unusual occurrence at this time of the year. We have plenty of accommodation, food and drink. It will be fun to spend the night in such a manner, no?" The manager announced.

His optimism wasn't reflected by the older members of the party who complained about not having brought nightclothes, toothbrushes etc., to which Ross and I giggled like schoolchildren. It seemed to us a great adventure, snowbound and loving every minute, we made our way towards the room where we were to spend the night, relishing the fact that we would be naked and unencumbered.

Our room was typical of most chalet-style dwellings; wooden walls smelling of pine, shuttered windows and a bed covered by a bright patchwork eiderdown. It was nothing like the Grand Hotel but it was comfortable and cosy.

We settled down for the night wrapped in each other's arms, oblivious of the weather. I woke just once during the night. The wind was howling like a banshee as I stretched across the bed to seek the comfort of my husband's arms but found I was alone.

"Ross?" I whispered, but there was no reply.

In the darkness, I waited, wondering where he could be. He returned over an hour later saying he couldn't sleep and had gone for a walk.

"A walk! In this?"

"Steady on, I didn't say outside. I took a stroll around the covered terrace. You should see the snow it's feet deep; we're stranded, like an island, in the middle of it. I don't fancy our chances of getting away tomorrow, unless this clears up."

I shivered. "Come back to bed, darling. I need a cuddle."

The following morning, Ross's warning about the weather was clear to see. Although it was picture-postcard scenery, made even more beautiful by the snow, the reality of the situation in which we now found ourselves was less than appealing.

The dissenters of the previous evening were still in full voice.

"I'm not staying here a moment longer than necessary."

"We've paid for a holiday in the Grand, not a hostelry in the middle of the nowhere."

"I need a change of clothing, Abner, or I'll just die."

Their complaints spun like a spinning top gathering momentum with each turn, but however much they grumbled, the situation was controlled by the weather and no one was leaving the place anytime soon.

"I suggest you make the best of it everyone. There's nothing we can do about it, right now, but our hosts will try to make your stay here as pleasant as possible until we are able to travel once more." The sleigh-driver looked uncomfortable. "Breakfast is being served in the bar, please help yourselves."

After breakfast we sat as far away from the others as possible, wrapped in our coats we made for the enclosed terrace and found seats facing the forest. The snow still fell but not with quite the same intensity as last night.

"I think we'll be on our way later this afternoon."

"Do you, Ross? The drifts are still very deep."

"They know how to handle the weather, I'm sure they have contingency plans."

In silence we watched the flakes fall until I thought it might be the time to bring up the subject of his brother again. I'd had no contact from Red but was sure I'd be able to find him again, if Ross so wished."

"I've been thinking about your attempt to find out what happened to your brother," I said.

He turned to face me. "Good Lord, that's a bit out of the blue."

"Well, I've not liked to bring up the subject before. You've had so much on your mind lately."

"Don't you worry your little head about it. He's probably decided he doesn't want to be found anyway."

"I doubt it," I exclaimed, the words were out before I could stop them. I suppose it was because of his brief statement, said in such a detached manner, which had shocked me.

"What do you mean?"

I hesitated.

"Anna? Is there something you know about Harry that you haven't told me?"

"I'm not sure, otherwise, I'd have told you before. It's a long story and one which does me no favours."

"I'm listening after all we're not going anywhere, we have all the time in world." His blue eyes locked on mine and he smiled and patted my hand. I wondered if he'd still be smiling when I finished my story.

Chapter 67

He didn't interrupt me as the snowflakes stroked the windowpane and the sky began to lighten. Cakes and coffee were brought, we drank and ate without conversation and when we'd finished I resumed my narrative. His expression didn't change throughout, even when I told him about my week spent in Red's flat. I hid nothing, told him about the photograph in the silver frame and of Red's suspicions regarding Ross's involvement in the deaths of Diana and Ruby.

When I finished he was silent for a while. I was afraid to speak; afraid he would tell me he wanted nothing more to do with me. Then as a ray of sunshine broke through the clouds, he said, "And you have the strong feeling this person is my brother?"

I sighed, "I think he might be, Ross."

"I see, well when we return to London, I'll look into it. Fancy another coffee?"

And that was that. He didn't mention it again. It was not at all what I'd been expecting. No condemnatory speeches, no recriminations. I breathed a sigh of relief, there were no longer any dark clouds hanging over our marriage, we could move on.

Help arrived after lunch, in the form of a team who had opened up the road leading back to the hotel. This time there would be no picturesque ride through woodland; we were to be driven in a large vehicle complete with snow chains.

When we arrived back in our room at the hotel, we ran baths and dressed in clean clothes. Much as I'd enjoyed spending the night in the chalet I was used to a grander way of living now and missed the opulent lifestyle money could buy.

"I have some phone calls to make, darling. I don't want to disturb you so I'll take them downstairs," Ross said, from the doorway.

I'd been about to say he wouldn't disturb me, I was only reading but he was gone before I could reply. He was away for some time, the sky had darkened with the approach of evening and I was beginning to feel concerned when I heard the door open.

"Sorry, you must have wondered where I was. Actually I met an old friend. He was in the LSE with me, years ago and we got chatting."

"That's nice. Is he staying here? We could meet up after dinner if you like."

"Er, not possible. He's leaving, just packing up when I meet him, as a matter of fact. He took our number at Longacres though, said he'd be in touch, you know the sort of thing – never hear from him again, I shouldn't wonder."

"Right."

"Er, I…"

"What is it, Ross?"

"I phoned Miles to see how things were doing and he said he'd had a message from the publishers wishing to contact me about distribution rights or something similar. So I gave them a ring and there are some documents requiring my signature."

"And?"

"Sorry, I'll have to pop back to London for a bit, see to things that end, you know how it is. But you must stay on here; I'll be back in a couple of days, week at the most and then we can spend Christmas together."

I frowned. "I'm going to miss you."

"Me too, love, but it will fly by, you'll see."

The following day Ross departed for London, I continued with my skiing lessons, and on the day after he'd gone I met Maria.

Maria Kronberg was Swedish, blonde and beautiful. She was staying at the hotel alone, in order to recover from an unhappy love affair. Her parents were in business and from what I could gather Maria had no money worries whatsoever. In spite of being a child of wealthy parents, I found her to be unspoilt and the possessor of a wicked sense of humour. She joined me in the bar after dinner one evening.

"On your own, like me?" she asked, sitting in a chair opposite me.

"For a while, my husband has returned to London on business."

"Tough, fancy joining me for a tour of what's on offer as nightlife in Cortina? It's as dead as a doorknob in here."

"Doornail," I said, grinning.

"Ah yes, my English is lamentable, I think."

"Not at all, my Swedish in non-existent."

"All you need to know is Tak."

"Tak?"

"Yah, It means thanks. So when a handsome man offers to buy you a drink in Sweden you say Tak. It works of many levels you will find."

I spluttered and she joined in my laughter.

"Well tak for the offer but I don't think my husband would be too pleased, if the moment his back's turned, I hit the bars."

"When the dog's away!"

"Cat," I corrected but she just laughed.

"I knew that, I was just pulling you arm." She winked and I knew I'd found a friend, the first new one I'd made in ages.

"My name is Anna," I said, "and I think I would like to go into Cortina this evening, but nothing too exotic, perhaps a few drinks in a bar, somewhere in the centre of town?"

"Excellent. I'm Maria, pleased to meet you, I think."

Maria was good fun. The taxi dropped us in the centre of town near what looked to be the tower of a church. Shops, chalets, bars and restaurants appeared as if they'd been dropped from a great height towards the snow-covered town. The air was crisp and clear, the Dolomites rising majestically above us and I was glad Maria had warned me to wear stout walking boots, as the snow was thick underfoot.

"It's not Paris, London or Rome for that matter but it will do," Maria said. "Come on, there's music coming from down this street. Let's go explore."

We were young and it felt good to be with someone of my own generation, who liked the same kind of music, fashions and conversation. Ross was great and I loved him dearly but we did not share the same ideas, his being firmly entrenched in the nineteen fifties.

The bar was of the sort I'd seen the world over, smoky, lively, and with a small band playing pop songs. It reminded me of photographs I'd seen of the Cavern Club in Liverpool, where the Beatles had begun their careers and I loved every minute of it.

During the following days Maria and I spent long hours together discussing fashion trends, shopping and swopping make-up and hairstyling tips. She was like the sister, I'd never had.

The memory of our days in Italy together would have been perfect had it not been sullied by a newspaper report in the next day's newspaper. It was a day old by the time it reached us. The report was tucked away at the bottom of a page dealing with violent crime and it made my heart race with fear.

Chapter 68

"You are not yourself today, Anna? Is it something I can help?" Maria was painting her nails a vivid shade of red, whilst sitting on the end of her bed.

"It's this." I held up the newspaper and showed her the picture of the young man with his face battered and bruised. I had to tell someone and Ross hadn't phoned this morning.

"You know him, yes?"

"Yes. The report says he was attacked whilst leaving his flat and he could have died had it not been for a neighbour whose baby had been crying and she'd woken up and heard the disturbance outside her window."

Maria stopped painting her nails and looked up at me.

"This is very upsetting, no? He was a lover, I think."

"No, no, it's not that; he was, is, a friend."

"Do you know why this happen?"

I sat down with a sigh. "It says he was attacked by someone wanting to steal his wallet."

"But I see you don't believe it."

"I don't. They managed to catch the thief, thanks to a description given by the young woman who found him. He's well known to the police, a thug who has been in trouble many times before. He insists he was hired by someone to kill my friend but the police don't believe his story."

"But you do?"

I shivered; this was one question I didn't want to answer. "I don't know. Perhaps."

Maria stood up, shook her fingers in the air to dry the polish, and said, "I think, I help you to forget what has happened today. I will ring down to reception and see if we can join in an adventure."

I smiled in spite of my worries concerning Red, for it was his photo staring back at me from the newspaper. "An adventure?"

"A tour guide, I meet last night, told me there is a party going by bus to Venice today. He is very handsome and I think he will find room for the two of us for tomorrow. As for today, you and I are going skiing. The snow it is good. Your instructor is also nice looking I think?"

"You are incorrigible, Maria." I laughed.

"That is better, I see a smile. Go get ready and I meet you in the foyer in twenty minutes. My nails should be dry by then!"

She was just the person I needed to put things into perspective. I should accept the police's version of events and forget about Red, whom I hadn't seen for ages. Besides I was in no position to know what shady businesses he was involved in, and who might want him 'out of the way'. A trip to Venice, the following day was just what I needed.

I managed to stick to my resolve to forget about Red for most of that day but had no such control over my dreams. I woke in the early hours, bathed in sweat, his poor battered face still haunting me.

There were too many questions still unanswered where he was concerned. I couldn't make up my mind whether he had my best interests at heart, all along, or whether he was out to cause trouble for Ross at any price. And there was my strong suspicion that he was

A Tangled Web

Ross's long lost brother. That was another thing, why had my husband had stopped looking for him?

At four in the morning, I tossed and turned, aware that I had no answers and wasn't likely to get any more sleep that night. I ran a bath, dressed, and sat at my bedroom window looking out at the early dawn creeping over the snow-capped Dolomites. The sky was clear and I began to feel optimistic about our forthcoming journey. I'd never visited Venice before and was looking forward to it immensely.

Maria was waiting for me in the foyer, along with the others of our party. She was talking to Francesco, our tour guide, who was obviously infatuated with her. Dressed in a white fox fur jacket and marching hat together with tight black ski-pants she looked very glamorous. I felt dowdy by comparison.

"Ah, all ready? Francesco tells me he will show us the sights."

I bet he will, I thought, slipping my arm through hers and making for the bus.

"Miss Maria and Anna, you are to sit up front with me," Francesco shamelessly announced as we boarded the bus.

Maria gave me a sharp dig in the ribs and whispered, " This will be fun, no?"

I nodded, feeling my spirits lift from the moment we left the hotel, as the coach crunched over the impacted snow of the driveway and we reached the open road.

Blue sky, crisp alpine snow and good company what more could I want? The answer was Ross but he wasn't here so I was determined to make the most of the day.

A Tangled Web

"And now ladies and gentlemen I will give you a little flavour of what to expect from Venice in the run up to Christmas. But first let me say how honoured we are to have two famous film stars with us today. Miss Brigitte Bardot and Miss Audrey Hepburn have graced us with their presence." He turned to face us and we giggled like schoolgirls.

Francesco continued with his humorous report of the day's events, occasionally winking in our direction much to the delight of the rest of the coach party, who were ready to go along with the joke.

After a few hours the coach drew into a parking lot, where we were swiftly transferred to a waiting waterbus. There was a mist rising up from the water, the whole scene enchantingly ethereal, as we chugged down the waters of the Grand Canal to our drop off point near St Mark's Square.

There was a hauntingly beautiful quality to buildings, which rose up dramatically from the mist. St Mark's Basilica stood erect and proud as we assembled near the Doge's palace and looked around.

"As you may have noticed, people, this is, in my opinion, the best time to visit Venice, there are not so many tourists and the stink, it is not here." Francesco held his nose and we all dutifully responded with laughter.

We followed our guide, through the narrow streets lined with shops and festooned with Christmas trimmings, to the Rialto Bridge. It was decorated with sparkling Christmas lights that twinkled in the grey afternoon. It was magical, a memory I would never forget.

Francesco suggested we explore for ourselves, take a gondola ride, sightsee, do some shopping, and then we would meet up in two hours' time for tea, in a café near the bridge.

Maria said, "Shopping?"

I agreed and we hurried back through shop-lined streets, occasionally window-shopping but more often filling carriers with our purchases. By this time, we were back at St Mark's square and walking behind an older couple pushing a pram and cooing over a baby. It wasn't until a young woman with fair curly hair joined them that I recognised Nick and Jacky Ferris with their daughter and her baby.

"What is it?" Maria asked, as I stopped in my tracks. "You look as if you've seen a ghost."

I shook my head. "It's nothing. Hey, let's see what's down here." I pulled Maria down a side street far enough away from the Ferris's. Fortunately a shop selling jewellery diverted Maria's attention and I was able to hide my shock at seeing Avril with her baby. So they had relented, I thought, wondering if they had insisted on Avril marrying someone of their choosing. I thought this unlikely and hoped she was happy. Her involvement with my husband was in the past. But I wasn't sure what Ross's reaction would be when he heard the news that she'd kept the baby.

But however hard I tried, even I couldn't foresee the answer to that question.

Chapter 69

I was glad to be leaving Venice far behind as we stepped on to the coach to bring us back to Cortina. It wasn't because I found Venice not to my taste. I'd loved every minute of it up until I'd seen Avril Ferris and her baby. It disturbed too many emotions, which I'd hoped I buried and when we met the rest of the group on the Rialto Bridge for afternoon tea I found I was continually on edge in case I bumped into them.

If Maria noticed the difference in me she didn't comment, her good humour was unabated and as the coach left Venice far behind, I breathed a sigh of relief and started to enjoy her chatter, and that of our tour guide, once more.

We arrived at our hotel at half past midnight. Snow was falling as Francesco helped us from the coach and into the foyer. He was sandwiched between Maria and myself saying, "Thank you so much for your company my dear Brigitte and sweet little Audrey," as he kissed us both in turn.

We giggled, transformed once more into schoolchildren, waved him a fond farewell, and started to walk towards the lift. Ross was standing near the reception desk, his face thunder black.

"I was starting to get worried," he said, and there was no mistaking his icy tone.

"Darling, you're back," I said, unnecessarily.

"It would seem so," he replied.

"Ross, meet my good friend Maria. Maria this is my husband."

"I'm afraid, I abducted your wife today. She was missing your company and I suggested we take a trip to

A Tangled Web

Venice to raise her spirits." Maria was trying to ease an awkward situation and I felt thankful for her sensitivity.

"Well, looks like you succeeded, Maria. We'll say goodnight then." Ross took my arm, and we entered the lift, leaving Maria in the foyer alone.

Neither of us spoke until we reached our room. "You should have told me you'd be back today. Then I would have been here to meet you when you arrived."

He put both hands on my shoulders and kissed the top of my head. "I was worried that's all. I didn't know you'd made a friend. I was concerned you'd be all alone. It's OK now. Everything OK – we're together again – that's all that matters."

I felt his body relax against mine, and all thoughts of Red, the newspaper report, and Avril Ferris and her baby, slid from my mind like a slab of butter melting in the sun.

The following day, we made our way to the ski slopes as usual. Maria was standing at the ski lift when we arrived and made her way over to us.

"Hi you two, good snow today, I think." She smiled and linked her arm with mine. I don't think she noticed Ross's expression, or perhaps she chose to ignore it.

As the ski lift dropped us at the top, I made my way to the nursery slopes and Maria, calling a cheery 'goodbye see you later,' made her way towards the advanced run, followed by Ross.

Maria was right, apparently it *was* good snow and for the first time since my arrival in Cortina, I felt as though at last I was making some progress. "Excellent, Anna, there is a big improvement today," Antonio, my ski instructor said, "we will make a first class skier of you yet."

"Don't hold your breath," I replied but was secretly pleased at his praise and longing to tell Ross when we met for lunch at the hotel later.

I was dressed and drinking coffee in the lounge when Ross arrived. He was limping.

"What happened?" I asked.

He tried to wave it away as nothing but I could tell he was in pain. "Just an altercation with your friend, a minor accident, nothing more. Fancy something stronger, " he asked turning towards the bar.

I nodded, "A small brandy, please."

There was no sign of Maria and my concern for her welfare was growing. When Ross mentioned an accident all my past worries resurfaced, most of which I'd buried deeply in my subconscious in the hope of never having to re-visit them.

We'd eaten lunch and still there was no sign of my friend.

"What's the matter?" Ross asked. "You seem preoccupied."

"It's Maria. She usually eats lunch here after skiing. Was she injured at all in the collision with you?" I tried to sound as if it was a throw away question but was aware I having difficulty remaining calm.

"No, quite the reverse. She didn't even bother to see if I was OK."

"You don't like her?"

"Maria? I don't have to like her, she's not *my* friend." This remark didn't sound like him at all and he realised it by my reaction as he tried to make amends, "That didn't come out quite right, what I meant to say was I don't have strong feelings for her one way or another, like or dislike, it's all the same to me. Ready for an afternoon in bed, my darling?"

I'd missed him so much, missed our afternoons of lovemaking, "Of course," I said, but it sounded forced. If he was aware of it, he didn't comment as we made our way to our bedroom.

Later, in the bar drinking cocktails before dinner, I again searched for Maria but there was no sign of her. Ross was talking to an overweight man and his much younger wife about the stock market, when I put a hand on his arm. "Excuse me, I'm off to powder my nose, I won't be long."

In the foyer, I looked around but still there was no sign of my friend. Then the lift doors pinged open and a porter emerged carrying two large suitcases followed by Maria, dressed for travelling.

"What's up? You're not leaving, surely?" I asked with dismay.

She frowned. "I was hoping to see you before I left." She gave me a hug and whispered in my ear. "If you ever need a friend, please contact me." She slipped a note into my hand. "I have so enjoyed your company, my dear Anna. I do hope we meet again."

"Me too. You've been just great," I said, as she turned towards the door and the waiting taxi. I walked with her to the entrance and, as her feet crunched over the snow-covered path, she called out. "Tell your husband, he's good, but I'm much better!"

I waited until the lights of the taxi disappeared into the night and then went back to join my husband, her words dripping like melting ice as I tried to figure out whether there was a hidden meaning behind them but

A Tangled Web

decided not to complicate matters, I had something
more pressing to worry about.

Chapter 70

Christmas was biting at our heels when Ross suggested we go to Venice to do some pre-Christmas shopping. He knew I'd recently taken the journey with Maria so I was anxious not to show my reluctance. A nagging voice kept asking the question – did he know Avril was in Venice – but I hesitated to bring up the subject. I heard him ordering a car, there was no way he was going to travel by coach, and was soon swept along on a wave of his enthusiasm.

The journey was, I had to admit, less tiring or eventful than my previous excursion. I rested my head on Ross's shoulder and felt my eyes closing, being lulled to sleep by the purring of the limousine's engine.

We arrived in time for lunch at the Hotel Cipriani, which was a relatively new building, the inside of which was luxuriously furnished. Ross knew the maître'd and I realised there was so much I didn't know about my husband's past.

The lunch was delicious and soon we were in a water-taxi heading for the shops in St Mark's Square. I remember Maria telling me there were no prices showing in the windows of these shops, as in the jewellery boutiques in Monte Carlo, because it was assumed their customers need not worry their heads about such mundane issues.

Ross bought an emerald necklace for Velma, some diamond ear studs that I'd been admiring and a heavy gold chain with a sapphire and diamond dropper. He smiled at me as he asked the assistant to wrap the purchases in Christmas paper with the instructions that we would pick them up later. He was so enthusiastic it

A Tangled Web

rubbed off on to me and I joined in his excitement by finding gifts for the staff at Longacres and the couple who looked after the Belgrave Square house.

As the day wore on, I noticed Ross became more not less animated and as the evening approached, I said. "Well. I think we have completed our Christmas shopping satisfactorily, so what time are we leaving for Cortina? It's a long drive and it's getting late."

Ross swung me around in a pirouette. "I have a surprise for you, my darling. We are spending Christmas in Venice. I've arranged for our things to be transferred to our room at the Cipriani and we have only to take a short ride by water-taxi to the hotel then we can relax."

To say I was shocked would be an understatement. Dark thoughts as to his motive for moving us to Venice surfaced, along with a vision of Avril Ferris. He obviously had been keeping this a secret for reasons of his own, otherwise why wouldn't he have told me before? He wanted me to think this was a spur of the moment decision, as we had planned to spend Christmas in Cortina, but I wasn't too sure.

"You don't look very happy. I thought you'd be thrilled."

"Sorry, I'm just a bit surprised that's all."

"That's the idea. You'll love it, believe me."

"I do," I replied, knowing that it was the last place on earth I wanted to be as I was still not certain that the Ferris's weren't also planning to spend the festive season in Venice.

The hotel was splendid in every way; the views of the Grand Canal from the windows were magnificent and the décor luxurious. It was Christmas Eve and Venice was decked out like a princess at her first ball.

A Tangled Web

Christmas lights, reflected in the waters of the canals threading through the city, together with the veil of mist, which seemed to perpetually cloak the majestic buildings, produced a hauntingly beautiful scene and under normal circumstances I would have been captivated. However, the ghosts of Avril and her baby lingered.

"I'm going to leave you to your own devices, for a couple of hours today, my sweet." Ross was singing to himself as he emerged from our bathroom. "You aren't allowed to see what's in Santa's sack before the big day." His good humour was infectious as he swept me to my feet and danced around the room with me held tightly in his arms.

It was only afterwards, as I waved him goodbye from our bedroom window, that the green-eyed monster made an appearance. I hated feeling jealous and was determined not to let it spoil my day. I'd already bought my present for Ross on the day I'd visited the city with Maria, so decided to take a boat to the island of Murano a short distance away from the centre.

Murano glass is unique and I was looking forward to seeing the craftsmen at work. Stepping off the waterbus, I was soon transported to the glass factory and shop selling the beautifully crafted glassware and jewellery.

I spent a leisurely time watching the glass blowers as they transformed sticks of glass into ornaments, spellbound by their dexterity. Afterwards, I inspected the results of their labours, glassware, jewellery and ornaments, the colours of which were truly remarkable. Unable to make up my mind between a goblet fashioned in deep red glass interwoven with gold and an aquamarine glass wine stopper I finally decided to buy the both as an extra gift for my husband.

It was late afternoon when I sat in the waterbus heading for our hotel. The lights of Venice sparkled and I'd managed to forget my misgivings about Avril Ferris. Perhaps I'd been worrying unnecessarily, I decided. But I had no idea then that this was going to be the worst Christmas of my entire life and there was nothing I could do to stop it from happening.

Chapter 71

I was humming the chorus of Good King Wenceslas as I entered the hotel carrying my purchases. I was looking forward to giving them to Ross tomorrow along with the silk shirt and tie I'd bought with Maria.

I'd almost reached the lift when I saw them, sitting together in the lounge. Ross was bouncing the baby on his knee, his face wreathed in smiles, while Avril had her hand on his arm; they looked like a happy family and the bottom of my world dropped out as I watched them.

Something must have made Ross glance in my direction; perhaps he could feel me watching him. He raised his hand and beckoned me to join them.

"Anna, look, it's Avril and little Louie; they are spending Christmas here what d'you think of that?"

"What a coincidence," I said, trying to smile but failing miserably.

"Just what I said. Nick and Jacky are having a rest in their room and Avril was taking Louie for a walk before giving him his feed and putting him down for the night."

He was babbling, I'm sure he felt as uncomfortable as I but it was for a different reason. He'd shown no such discomfort before he saw he was being observed.

"Nice to see you, Anna, I hope to see you later, I must put Louie down for his sleep now." She took the child from Ross and cradling him in her arms walked away from us.

My husband was unable to take his eyes from them as they left the lounge, and I knew the prospect of spending the Christmas period in such close contact with Avril and her son would affect us both, one way or another.

"Well, I think it's time we got changed. Tell me, where did you disappear to after I left you?" Ross asked slipping my arm through his.

I told him he'd find out tomorrow and he accepted it without question. Later, we dressed and went down to the dining room and I saw Nick and Jacky Ferris seated at a table near the window. They smiled but I could see a wary expression on Nick's face. Thankfully there was no sign of Avril or her baby and we ate our meal alone and afterwards went into the bar. Nick and Jacky did not make an appearance neither did their daughter and I began to think that maybe things would work out OK after all.

Complacency is often the resort of fools for the morning had not yet come and although Ross and I spent Christmas Eve in each other's company, I felt that one of us was elsewhere, perhaps dreaming of another life.

We awoke to a slight dusting of snow covering the walkways, it was nothing like the snowfalls we'd experienced in Cortina but it produced a picture postcard aspect to the scenery enhancing the already magical surroundings.

I stood at the window and looked out at the Grand Canal, whilst Ross made a big display of having to 'find' my present. He returned from his dressing room with a beautifully wrapped gift, which he placed in my hands. "Happy Christmas, my darling," he said, kissing my cheek.

I unwrapped my present to find the diamond earrings I'd admired and which he'd bought in the jewellery shop in St Mark's Square, the other day.

They were enchanting and under normal circumstances I would have been delighted. But the question, as to where he'd been during Christmas Eve, hung in the air like a bad smell; he certainly hadn't been buying my Christmas present and the niggling feeling he'd been with Avril was too strong to ignore.

"Happy Christmas, Ross." I handed him my gifts and he unwrapped them with all the eagerness of a young child.

"Thank you, these are great. So now I know where you went yesterday – Murano?"

I nodded. "So where did you get to?" I asked, casually.

"What? Oh, just window shopping, you know, soaking up the atmosphere."

"Meet anyone?"

"Er, no, why do you ask?"

"Just wondered if you'd bumped into the Ferris's on your travels." I hoped I sounded as if it was the most natural question in the world to ask, especially as I'd seen them together when I arrived back from Murano.

"No. I didn't see them until I got back, just before you arrived, actually." He was walking towards the bathroom. "Oh, by the way, I suggested we spend the day with them today, if that's OK with you. Ma always liked company on Christmas day and I thought maybe you might be a little fed up of my company."

"Never," I replied indignantly. "Why would you think such a thing?"

He hung his head and look across at me. "Well you seemed as if you were having a really good time with that Swedish girl – what's her name – Marie? I thought you might be missing some female company."

"Maria. And no, I'm not missing female company and more than happy to spend our first Christmas just the two of us."

"Looks like I've put my foot in it then. Never mind, it'll be fun, you'll see."

There was nothing more I could say. I would be spending the day with the Ferris's and I was sure it would turn out to be my worst nightmare.

Chapter 72

Apparently Avril had asked to meet Ross at their suite at eleven to see little Louie opening his presents. Ross didn't seem to think it strange at all. I hesitated to point out that a baby, who was only a few months old, was unlikely to be able to open his presents unless he was a genius, in case it sounded catty to suggest such a thing. So I followed him disconsolately from the lift, down the corridor to the Ferris's suite.

I could tell by his expression that Nick Ferris was not happy. I had the strong feeling he disliked his daughter mixing with Ross and under the circumstances I could see his point of view.

Of course, I had nothing against the child, except that my husband for whatever reason had admitted to its parentage and the Ferris's obviously thought it to be the case. I felt the whole situation was awkward. Avril, however, had no such qualms, she was as happy as a sand boy and in some ways I couldn't blame her. It was I who felt the interloper.

Jacky, Avril and Ross fussed around the baby whilst I watched, unable to take my eyes off the gold necklace with the sapphire and diamond dropper Avril was wearing. It was the one Ross bought in St Mark's Square.

"Anna, what will you have to drink?" Nick asked, "Champagne?"

"Yes, thanks."

"How long are you staying in Venice?" He poured the champagne into two glasses, leaving the others cooing over Louie.

"I'm not sure. I didn't even know we were coming here until the day before yesterday. The plans were that we should spend Christmas and the New Year in Cortina because of the snow. Ross thought it would be romantic."

Whether it was something in my expression, I wasn't sure but Nick reached out and patted my hand. "It will work out, I'm sure of it."

I felt tears pricking behind my eyes and blinked rapidly.

"Well now everyone, I suggest we put Louie down for his morning nap or he'll be fractious for the rest of the day. Champagne anyone?"

My husband stood up. He was holding the baby, his expression making me sure that Nick's words were nothing more than feathers in the wind, insubstantial and unfounded; I knew at that moment that Ross had found the love of his life and it was wasn't me. This was a love with which I could never compete.

Nick stepped forward and took Louie from Ross. "Do the honours, please Ross, The champagne's in the Frigidaire. Avril, come with me, Louie will need his mother to put him down."

It was an order, Avril sighed and acquiesced but any fool could see she would rather be sitting alongside my husband discussing every minute detail of Louie's development to a captive audience of one.

Nick tried his best throughout the day. At lunchtime he ordered a buffet to be sent up to their suite. We drank copious amounts of champagne and as the afternoon wore on, he suggested we all retire for a nap in order to be fresh for the evening's festivities.

Ross and I made our way back to our room. He was uncommunicative and slightly drunk. In no time at all he was asleep on top of our bed and awoke two hours later with a raging headache.

"Perhaps we should ring the Ferris's and let them know we've decided to skip dinner," I suggested. But he wouldn't hear of it saying that, after taking some painkillers and having a shower, he'd be fine.

I wore my diamond earrings and a tight fitting black dress. Ross didn't comment, his eagerness to meet the Ferris's in the bar was obvious.

"Ready?" he asked impatiently, as I slipped my feet into a pair of high-heeled shoes.

To my surprise Nick and Jacky were alone, Avril and the baby nowhere to be seen.

"Louie's a bit overtired," Nick explained. "Avril's agreed to have dinner sent up. She didn't feel it right to allow the hotel staff to watch him, tonight."

I had the strong feeling that Nick had issued his instructions and Avril was in no position to disobey. His eyes met mine and I was certain I was right, as he gave a slight nod of his head and the ghost of a smile appeared on his lips.

Ross was agitated throughout dinner. He seemed distracted and unable to keep the threads of a conversation going for more than a second at a time. His gaze kept wandering towards the door leading into the dining room. The festivities, the music, the food, all passed him by without comment.

Eventually, he stood up. "If no one minds, I'll pop up and see how Avril's getting on."

Nick was about to say something but Jacky put a hand on his arm so he replied, "Fine but don't be too long, we don't want your wife feeling she's been abandoned on Christmas Day now do we?" He obviously meant it to be a light-hearted remark but he didn't quite pull it off. It sounded like a threat.

Chapter 73

Boxing day followed the same pattern, Ross took every opportunity to seek out Avril and the baby and I trotted behind like an afterthought. Nick Ferris suddenly announced at supper that evening that he was cutting short their holiday as there were pressing business matters at home, which required his attention. I didn't believe him for a minute but was grateful for his decision to effectively put some space between his daughter and my husband.

We saw them off the following day and from then on Ross appeared dejected. I tried to raise his spirits by suggesting we travel south in the hope of meeting warmer weather.

"In January?" he replied.

"We could visit the Canary Islands, if you wish?"

"I think I've had enough of travel for a while. Why don't we pack up here and go back home, to Longacres?"

I wondered why he would suddenly want to do such a thing, when the plan had been that we would stay away until spring. The answer was staring me in the face but I just nodded and replied, "OK, whatever you want. It's fine by me."

So we packed our things, left the hotel and headed back to England. Ross was uncommunicative during the journey and I began to wonder how long our marriage could survive and whether Christmas Day had ruined it beyond measure.

Joe and Esther were pleased and somewhat surprised to see us. Joe set about updating Ross on matters regarding the estate and Esther began cooking and making sure our bed was aired. In some ways it felt good to be home and not to have to spend every minute of every day in Ross's company. This would not have been a consideration before Christmas but now things had changed between us.

"There's a message for you Mrs Maitland. Your friend Lyn called just a week or two back. She said to ask you to give her a ring when you returned. I told her you weren't expected back for a while and did she want the number of your hotel but she said no – just pass on the message – whenever she comes home."

"I see, thanks Esther. I'll give her a ring tomorrow. I'm bushed. So I'll take myself off to bed. Perhaps you could tell Ross, once he's finished with Joe."

Before long I was fast asleep and dreaming. I suppose it was no surprise that I dreamt of them all, the Ferris's, and my husband. Waking sometime later, when moonlight was flooding into our bedroom, I saw that Ross's side of the bed was empty. I looked at the clock. It was three thirty four. Where was he? I felt so low I wanted to cry; with every moment that passed I was certain my marriage was on a track leading to disaster and I couldn't think of anything that would stop it from reaching its destination.

At breakfast, Ross explained that it had been longer than he'd anticipated getting up to speed with events on the estate whilst we'd been away, and not wishing to disturb me he'd slept in my old room. "I'm afraid I'm going to have to leave you for a few days, my sweet. There are some pressing matters to which I must attend, which means I'll be in London until the beginning of next week," he said, before drinking his coffee.

"I could come with you. I need to see Lyn, actually, I haven't talked to her for ages."

He put his cup down and frowned. "Not sure whether that would be a great idea. I'd be distracted from my work, for one thing and you'd be sure to be bored, for another."

"Right, no problem. I'll see you next week then." I'd suddenly lost my appetite so stood up, kissed his cheek and left him reading the morning paper.

In the study, I picked up the phone and rang Lyn.

"Fancy having a visitor for a day or two?" I asked, to which she replied, "Absolutely, I've got so much to tell you. It will be like old times."

Ross left for London by car later that morning and I followed by the afternoon train. I told Esther I was spending a couple of days with a friend. I didn't say where but said I'd ring her when I arrived.

Tom Trevellyn drove me to the station as Joe had sprained his ankle.

"Everything OK is it Mrs Maitland?" He asked, putting my case in the boot of the car.

"It is, Tom."

"Glad to hear it." I don't think I imagined the implication in his words or the way he said them.

"Is there anything you want to tell me, Tom?" I asked as we drove out of the estate and into the lane.

"Just take care, is all."

I could tell he wasn't going to say more but something made me reply. "I'm going to be staying with my friend in London, Tom. I'll give you her address and telephone number. Esther doesn't have it, only you. If you should need to contact me urgently, you know what to do."

"Right, I understand, you can trust me."

"I think I can, Tom, I think I can."

Later, during the journey, I wondered why I'd decided to take Tom into my confidence, and the only reason I could think of was that I needed a friend, now more than ever. I needed someone to watch my back, as I wasn't entirely sure my husband was fulfilling that role.

Lyn met me at the station and for the first time in ages I put my marriage and its constraints behind me. She hugged me with genuine affection and we chatted like old friends who hadn't been parted for nearly a year.

Her flat had been redecorated in vivid colours with sixties style furniture, her spare bedroom, thankfully, in more muted tones.

"It's so good to see you again, Lyn, I've missed you," I said, putting my case in her spare room. "We've so much news to catch up on."

"You are telling me. Did you know that Rosie married Dave from marketing?"

"No, you're kidding!"

This set the tone for the rest of the evening. We drank wine, talked of old friends and were still chatting as the clock struck one. Then Lyn said, "A couple of months ago, I met that friend of yours actually – Steve?"

"Steve?"

"You know, the one with red hair, the one who you were trying to get away from, remember?"

"Red? You met Red?"

"He was just out of hospital after having a severe beating. He was in a terrible mess. It was awful. He asked about you and we got chatting. In fact he's quite nice."

"You've been seeing him?"

"Yes, no, I mean, not like that. We've become friends. I'm with Jake now; he likes Steve too."

"I see."

"Anyway, Steve's worried about you. He wanted me to tell you, he'd found out something about your husband, which made him very concerned about your welfare. Sounded very cloak and dagger to me."

I picked up my wine glass and drank deeply before replying. "Take no notice. He's got a thing about Ross. It's old news. He thinks he means to harm me, ever since he 'saved' me from a fall in Saint Tropez. It doesn't mean anything. He was the one who kept me locked in that awful flat remember."

She leaned forward. "You've got him all wrong, Anna. I'm certain of it. Steve's one of the good guys, I'd stake my life on it."

I put my glass down on the table. "If that's so, then where does that leave Ross?"

"Well now, that's a question I can't answer. No one can, except you."

Chapter 74

Lyn had to go into work for a while but said she'd try and finish about two so we could spend some time shopping together in the West End. Both of us were nursing hangovers over a breakfast of toast and coffee and before she left she thrust a small telephone book in my direction. "Look under Steve. Give him a ring. He'd be stoked to hear from you."

"Not promising," I said, waving her goodbye from the doorway.

After I'd washed and dressed, I looked out through the window. Rain was falling in an unending stream down the windowpane and a cold wind swept through the stark branches of the trees in the road. Lyn's flat was in a area favoured by people who worked in the centre of London, it wasn't particularly fashionable but it was nowhere near as bad as the area where Red had his flat.

The atmosphere was warm and cosy and I was starting to get used to the patterned wallpaper in spite of the colours. The telephone book was where Lyn had left it on a side table. I picked it up and leafed through its pages until I saw the name Steve followed by a telephone number. I hesitated. Then I remembered the horrific photograph in the newspaper, when I'd been in Cortina and the effect it had on me. Ross was in London at the time and my imagination was working overtime. I suppose I'd owed it to Red to at least make contact. I picked up the book and dialled his number, not expecting him to answer.

"Hello," It was Red's unmistakable voice, the slight hint of an American accent, even stronger over the telephone.

"It's me."

"Anna?"

"Yes. I was sorry to hear of your injuries. I just wanted to see if you were OK." I didn't know what more to say to him.

"I'm getting there. Where are you?"

"At Lyn's flat."

"I'll come over."

There was no question as to whether I would see him, the urgency in voice brooking no argument. Twenty minutes later I heard the doorbell ring.

To say I was surprised at his appearance would be an understatement. His features still bore the marks of the assault. There was a fine scar running from under his hairline down to the corner of his eyes and another more pronounced gash across his throat. I gasped.

"If you think this is bad, you should have seen me after it happened." He smiled at me as I let him into the flat.

"I'm sorry."

"What have you got to be sorry about? It's nothing to do with you. These things happen in a big city. Hey.."

Tears were coursing down my cheeks. He put his arm around my shoulder and wiped them away with a handkerchief smelling of washing powder. "I'm OK now, promise."

I sighed. "Sit down and I'll put the kettle on."

"Sure thing, then you can tell me what you've been up to."

When we were seated alongside each other on Lyn's sofa, I told him about our trip to Italy, for some reason avoiding the fact that Ross had been in London when Red was attacked and finishing with our meeting up with the Ferris's.

"So, Avril kept the baby after all?"

I nodded.

"It must have been a bit awkward for you."

"You think Ross was the father?"

"There are many things I know about your husband, Anna, which is one of the reasons I was worried about you."

I bit my lip, fearing the tears would start again. "It isn't true," I said, wondering if this too was a lie.

"Well then, now it seems my fears were unfounded and you have a happy marriage. It is happy, isn't it?" Red asked.

"I was happy. I'm not sure about Ross, not since Christmas."

"I see."

"It's the baby, I can't compete, can I."

"You shouldn't have to. It's not impossible to love both a child and a wife, you know."

"Even if the wife's not the baby's mother?"

"Of course. Perhaps you are worrying unnecessarily."

His sympathy was one step too far, I found myself saying the words I vowed not to say. "He was in London when you were attacked."

"Pardon me?"

"Ross, he'd travelled back to London from Italy; he said there was business to attend to with his solicitor."

"Miles Cohen?"

"How…?"

"I can't tell you, not until it's all settled. You see your husband and I, well, we share a past."

So now I knew for certain.

"Your Ross's brother, aren't you?"

He looked surprised but just shrugged. "Yeah, you could say that, though I doubt your husband would admit to it. How did you find out?"

So I told him about how I linked the photograph, the American passport, the lie about being a Private Investigator working on behalf of Nick Ferris and the fact that he was so keen to follow Ross first to Beaulieu and then to Longacres.

"Perhaps you should be the one working for Weston's Investigations." He smiled.

"Why the lie?"

"About Paul? Well, I did work for the Agency for a while and I just happened to have one of their business cards on me at the time. It's not a complete lie; I still do some work for Paul occasionally, hence my supply of business cards, which you no doubt found in my flat."

"Why didn't you tell Ross you were his brother? At one time I knew he was desperate to try to find you, after Olivia's death."

"It's complicated. And I wasn't lying when I said I suspected him of being involved in Diana Huntley's death. Then there was you."

"Me?"

"I wasn't lying either, when I said I enjoyed your company, on the train. I like you, Anna, and if things were different, well...." He looked down at his hands before continuing, "Let's just say I was concerned for your welfare and wanted to keep an eye on you, just in case your fate mirrored that of Diana Huntley and Ruby Dent and leave it at that."

I stood up and walked over to the window. The rain had eased slightly and clouds were scurrying across the sky as if being chased by a demon.

"What will you do now? Will you tell Ross – about being his brother – or not?"

"As I said, it's complicated. Miles Cohen has given me some food for thought."

"Miles?"

"Yes, he wrote to me a while back."

"How on earth did he find you?" Realisation began to dawn. "Does Ross know where you are?"

"He does. And has known for some time."

"Since before your accident?" It was as if a spear of ice had penetrated my heart as I waited for his reply, whilst knowing it was I who had inadvertently led my husband to his door. "

Chapter 75

When Red finished talking, I rang Miles Cohen and confirmed his story. Part of me knew, without doubt, what his answer would be, whilst part of me was praying that I was wrong.

"What are you going to do now?" I asked, Red.

"I plan to leave things up to Miles to sort out. It's you I'm concerned about."

"You don't need to be. I'll sort this mess out with Ross and ask him what he wants. If the answer is Avril then our marriage is over."

He sighed and took my hand. "Believe me, Anna, I only have your best interests at heart. If you want your marriage to work, I won't contact you again. But if you ever need me, you have my number and you have a lifelong friend." He leaned forward and kissed my cheek.

"Thanks," I croaked.

Afterwards, when I was alone, I rang Lyn's office and told her I'd be leaving right away, as there was a family crisis, which needed my attention. I promised to ring her so that we could meet up again sometime. Then leaving money for the call near the phone, I rang Velma.

Without going into too much detail, I gave her a run down on events, beginning with our holiday, meeting the Ferris's, and my conversation with Red.

She listened, I could hear her slightly laboured breathing, then a sharp intake of breath as she replied, "I think it's time you learned the truth. I'd hoped to keep it from you but now there is no point. I'm near the

311

end of my life, it's a matter of months so the doctors say."

After the initial shock, I sympathised, feeling genuine sorrow, then made up my mind. "Don't say anymore. I'm in London. I'll get the next available flight over. You can tell me then."

It felt the right thing to do. I didn't want to see Ross at the moment, but more to the point I think he didn't want to see me. I was very fond of Velma and desperately wanted to see her before she passed away. She was an old lady, who had been Olivia's friend and confidante. I was sure whatever she had to tell me would be the truth. I was so sick of falsehoods, which had shaken my belief in everyone who was close to me. This time I needed to know the full story. She was the only person left who knew what happened when Olivia adopted two children and was left with one.

Next I phoned the Belgrave Square house and asked to speak to Ross. Apparently he wasn't there and the last they'd heard he was at Longacres. More lies piling up like autumn leaves gradually decaying, when would this ever end? Finally, I rang Longacres, told Joe I'd be staying with Velma for a while and didn't know when I'd be back. If Ross was looking for me, which I very much doubted, he would know where to find me.

The journey was unremarkable; I slept for most of the time trying to obliterate the past few months by putting the Atlantic Ocean between us both. Whatever Velma had to tell me it couldn't be worse than what I my imagination was leading me to believe. Red had told me he remembered Olivia and how she had tried to look after him but he didn't really know why she'd abandoned him in favour of his brother and now it was too late to find out. I saw the little boy through his eyes and wanted to weep for his loss, whilst hoping he could develop some sort of future relationship with Ross.

The cab dropped me off at Velma's flat and Carla opened the door to me.

"She's tired, she said to tell you she'll speak in the morning," Carla said, helping me inside and showing me where to put my case. It was the same room I'd slept in when I'd last stayed to read Olivia's hidden journal. "I'm off home now, Mrs M. You have my number on the pad by the phone and Lance's. Anything you need, just give me a ring and I'll get a cab and pop over. It's what we do, Velma likes to know she can call on me anytime so pays my fare – it suits us both – I don't mind, I've nothing else to do."

I thanked her and was grateful to be left alone until morning. But however hard I tried I couldn't stop thinking about Ross and how we were going to claw back the remnants of our marriage and make it work. Perhaps Velma could help. Perhaps what she had to tell me would make a difference.

Looking back, I had no idea how much difference Velma's revelation would make. It altered my life and the lives of both Ross and his brother. But I had to wait for morning to come to hear the words, which would be the catalyst for such changes to occur.

Chapter 76

I was shocked to see the change in Velma. She'd lost weight and her skin looked grey; a lifetime reliance on nicotine had finally taken its toll. Carla had washed her, made her breakfast, which looked as if she'd picked at it and left the rest uneaten, and was carrying the tray into the kitchen when I sat down at Velma's bedside.

"Good to see you, honey," she said taking my hand.

"And it's good to see you Velma. How are you feeling?"

"Better for seeing you, but all in all I'll be glad when it's over. I've had enough."

"I'm so sorry. Is there anything I can do?"

"Nothing anyone can. Anyway let's forget my problems. As I told you on the phone, there's something I need to say." The urgency in her voice made me shiver. This was something desperately important.

"I'm dying. You know that. It's the only reason I'm telling you this. I can't take this secret to the grave and beyond, whatever I promised Livia. Just pass me that glass of water, there's a dear."

She was sitting up in bed, her snow-white hair resting against two large plumped up pillows.

"When Liv knew her time had come she gave me the 'hidden' journal and asked me to make sure it was destroyed. But I knew it wasn't what she wanted and just before she died she admitted she wanted you to see it before her memoirs were published. She was adamant that the world should know it was she who was responsible for the deaths of Diana Huntley and Ruby Dent."

"I've often wondered why she did that. The police didn't suspect foul play; there was no need to make a clean breast of it – no one would know."

"It was an insurance policy."

"Insurance policy? I don't understand."

"She was making sure that, if at any time there was an inquiry into the deaths, there would be no need to look for a culprit – she'd owned up to being involved to save him you see?"

Icicles slid down my spine as I waited to hear the rest.

"She was covering for the real murderer. She was certain it was her son, but she would never let them take him. She was desperate to save his neck. She couldn't let that happen at any price." Velma coughed, a rasping sound that seemed to fill the room.

I wrapped my arms around my body to stop from shaking. There's no mistaking the truth when you hear it and I knew I was hearing it now.

"I had to tell you, before he decides he's had enough of you too. I couldn't keep my promise to Liv." Tears trickled down Velma's cheek.

I patted her hand and told her about Avril and the baby and how I feared Ross had already decided to supplant me in his affections.

"Then I've done the right thing at last. I do realise you can't tell the police; there's no evidence, other than the ramblings of a sick old women. And there's Olivia's confession, she knew exactly what she was doing when she made me promise it would be published."

"God, what a mess."

Velma bit her lip. "You could say so."

Now was the time for me to ask her the question I'd been mulling over in my mind during the flight.

"The other child; the one Olivia adopted with Ross. What happened to him?"

"Harry? He was a demon; at least that's what Olivia thought. If there was trouble then Harry was always at the bottom of it. It got so bad that Livia couldn't cope with the two of them so I took Harry back home. I knew someone who was looking to foster a kid, so I took him there."

I refilled her glass and handed it to her. I watched her laboured breathing as she drank the water and when she'd finished, she handed me the glass and continued, "But from the minute I took Harry away from her, he was a little darling. He was absolutely no trouble at all; and he was so cute, he had the reddest hair imaginable, it was like a fiery red halo sticking up around his head."

"Surely that was odd. I mean how could he have changed into an angel overnight?"

Velma sighed. "He could if the real demon had been making him a fall guy."

"You mean, you think Ross was the troublemaker and was blaming his brother?"

She nodded. "He was older, Ross I mean, and he looked so innocent."

"Poor Red." I'd thought he was older than Ross but then no one really knew their ages, it was all guesswork.

"What was that, dear?"

"I meant, poor child. To be taken away from another mother figure, to lose out on the lifestyle Ross enjoyed and to be thrown into another family so soon."

"Liv, when she decided to take the wrap for her child, also decided the time had come to make it up to little Harry. She felt so guilty at having abandoned him, even though she'd paid his foster family for his welfare until he disappeared. She instructed her solicitor to search for the boy. She decided to change her will. Once the boy was found he was to inherit half her estate and Ross's inheritance would be altered accordingly."

"Oh no!"

"What is it, honey?"

I stood up, unable to keep still and walked towards the window. The world was still turning; people going about their business, couples walking hand in hand. Turning around and facing the bed I said, "I know where Ross's brother can be found. Miles Cohen, the family's solicitor, knows who he is and that an attempt has already been made on his life a couple of months ago."

Velma sat forward, the effort it took more than obvious. "You've found little Harry?"

"His name's Steven Carter and he's living in London."

Velma smiled, "You've found little Harry, I can't believe it." The smile suddenly slid from her face as she understood what I'd been saying.

317

Chapter 77

Unable to get an answer at Red's flat, I rang Lyn.

"I think he said he was going to the south of France," she said vaguely. "He said he'd send a postcard. Why?"

"No particular reason, just thought I'd like to catch up with him when I'm next in town."

"Oh yeah? What's going on, Anna?"

"Nothing, I'll tell you later, got to go now."

Next, I rang Longacres and spoke to Joe.

"Is my husband there? I need to speak to him urgently."

There was a beat before Joe answered. "Er, no, Mrs Maitland. We haven't heard from him for a week or two, but I understand he is staying in the villa. I did try to ring him about a slight problem we were having with hiring someone to clean out the drains but Pierre said he hadn't seen him for a day or two and that's all I know. I expect he'll get in touch sooner or later though."

I could tell Joe thought this not unusual, although I knew he was beginning to wonder why I didn't know the whereabouts of my husband. I thanked him, assured him he was probably correct, and suggested that when Ross did contact him perhaps he'd tell him to ring Velma.

I thought he should know of Velma's condition, as I wanted him to make contact with the woman who had kept him away from a death sentence by her love for his mother.

I stayed with Velma until the weekend then left to fly to Nice. Knowing it would be the last I'd see of her,

I thanked her for trusting me with the truth, and kissed her goodbye with genuine sadness.

During the flight to the south of France, I considered how I would approach Ross, when he eventually showed up at the villa. I had no doubt now that he was with Avril and Louie and wondered how I was going to protect her, in the event he decided to move on. I knew there was no particular urgency and she was his son's mother and therefore held a secure position, at least for the time being. But was it a mistake to make such an assumption? Ross was a damaged individual at best, and a cool, calculating, murderer at worst.

My thoughts also focused on Red and what would happen when he confronted Ross with the truth. By now I was certain my husband knew of the inheritance issue from Miles Cohen in addition to which I had inadvertently told him about Red and the whereabouts of the flat, in which I'd been incarcerated. Putting two and two together it didn't require a gigantic leap of the imagination to realise that Ross was involved in the attack on Red, if not in person, then through a third party.

It took me a while to decide the first person I would make contact with, upon my arrival at the villa, would be Nick Ferris. Where our conversation would lead was anyone's guess, but at least a plan of action was forming in my mind. It was up to me to see that it was carried out successfully; I owed it to both Velma and Olivia.

It was spring now and the air in Beaulieu was pleasantly warm. Flowers were budding and threatening to break open and the sky was optimistically blue.

The taxi dropped me off at the villa and Pierre welcomed me and carried my cases up to our bedroom. I still thought of it as ours, although I shuddered at the prospect of ever again spending a single night in that bed with my husband.

Once, I'd bathed and changed and eaten a light meal, I took the short cut to the Ferris's property. There was the faint sound of someone singing and, as I drew nearer to the open French doors leading into the conservatory, I realised it was Olivia's voice coming from the gramophone.

Nick Ferris was alone, reading a paperback, as I stood in the doorway. He looked up, dropped the book in surprise, and stood up.

"Anna? It's so good to see you again. When did you arrive?"

I looked around. "Is Jacky here?" I asked.

"Jacky? No, she's in London, some get together with her girlfriends, a second marriage celebration, hen night, something of the kind. She'll be back at the weekend, so you'll see her then. Come in, don't stand there, sit down, can I get you a drink?"

"No thanks. It's you I've come to see and I'm glad Jacky isn't here." A look of alarm spread across his face as I sat opposite him. The scene was one of two friends chatting in comfort on a warm spring evening, but what I was about to tell Nick Ferris would soon dispel that impression.

I'd thought it out on the flight over to Nice. This wouldn't be the truth, the whole truth and nothing but the truth. I had to play my cards close to my chest but to also make sure he was aware of the danger his daughter was in by associating with Ross Maitland.

"Where is Avril?" I asked.

He shifted uncomfortably in his seat and I thought, he knows she's with Ross.

"Paris, I think."

"She's not alone, is she Nick?"

"Er, no, she's with Louie, of course," he coughed.

"And?"

"Sorry?"

"And Ross."

He sighed, "You knew?"

"Let's face it I'd have to be blind."

He frowned. "I'm not happy about it, Anna, not one bit, whatever Jacky says about them being a family. He's a married man and I don't trust him further than I could throw him."

Just as well I thought. So this might not be such a big shock to him after all.

"I'm not here to rant and rave about your daughter taking my husband away from me, believe me, I'm of the opinion you can't take anyone who doesn't want to go. I know our marriage is over and I've come to terms with it." Another lie but one which I would eventually make come true. "I'm here to warn you about Ross. I know he cares for Louie but I'm worried about his feelings for Avril. You might not believe it but I don't want her to be hurt. I know how it feels and he is quite capable of dropping her when he chooses."

Nick Ferris nodded. "I've always thought he was a spoilt, selfish boy; Olivia indulged him, spoilt him rotten."

"You're right, of course, so you see why I'm concerned. You must be vigilant, don't leave them alone together, if at all possible."

The urgency of my tone must have concerned him. "Anna! Is there something I don't know about?"

This was the part where the truth was necessary; otherwise he wouldn't take my warning seriously. "I won't go into details but I suspect that Ross has been involved in an attack on a young man in London. It's a long story and one which is not mine to tell but it's made me certain there is a violent streak in my husband which is extremely worrying."

He stood up, agitatedly pacing the floor. "Good God, and my Avril and little Louie are alone with him, this very minute."

"I'm sure there are no immediate concerns for their welfare, Nick. But I thought you should know. And before you dismiss this as the ravings of a 'woman scorned', perhaps you ought to read this." I handed him the newspaper report of Red's attack, which I kept in my handbag, as a reminder.

After reading it and inspecting the damage to Red's face, he said, "I see. Leave it to me, my dear. You need not worry about my daughter any more. I'll fix this."

Satisfied, I left Nick and took the short cut back to the villa wondering how I was going to find Red. He needed to know about Ross and how his brother had used him, when he was a child. He also needed to know that his suspicions about Ross being involved in Diana Huntley's death were correct all the time. He was the only one who would believe the full story.

The terrace was in darkness; the only light showing was from an upstairs window. As I approached the

A Tangled Web

French doors, a shadowy figure emerged from the darkness and placed a hand on my arm.

Chapter 78

"I'm so glad to see you," I said, relieved and amazed by his appearance. Red grinned and slipped his arm through mine.

"What's up?"

"Where do I begin? Come inside."

"I don't think so, walls have ears, my dear girl. Why don't we take a walk? It's a lovely evening, the moon is out, it's warm, what d'you say?"

Under the circumstances I thought his suggestion made sense. I didn't want to risk anyone other than Red hearing about Velma's disclosure. We walked, arm in arm down to the lower terrace, where the sea was as calm as a mirror coated with silver, reflecting the coastline and the moonlight.

"It's beautiful," I said.

"So are you, and surprisingly you are totally unaware of the fact."

I giggled. "I have missed you."

He pulled me closer and kissed my cheek. "That's the ticket," he said.

We sat for while, whilst I told him about Olivia's revelation to Velma, about Ross being the one who had caused trouble for him and her fear that it was Ross who had been involved in the deaths of both Diana and Ruby. I said I was worried about Avril and her child and my need to warn her about Ross. He listened, and without commenting, sighed, took my arm and led me towards the coastal path. A soft breeze blew through my hair and I felt his arm move around my waist.

When we touched the place where Diana had fallen, he whispered, "It was here."

A Tangled Web

"I know, I'm sorry, I know you were fond of Diana. But you haven't blamed him, even now, after I've told you the truth."

His sigh was blown away on the breeze as he turned to me and held my shoulders. "Ah, but what is the truth, my dear? It's just a variation on a lie. You think you know what happened to Diana but there are only two people who know the absolute truth, Diana and her murderer."

I could feel his fingers digging into my shoulders. "You mean Ross?"

"Do I?"

"What are you doing? Red?"

"Ha," His laugh was bitter. "You think you know me, you don't even know my name."

I felt my legs give way as the earth crumbled beneath my feet. An offshore breeze had strengthened and was sighing in the grasses. I knew now how Diana had met her death and it was not at the hands of my husband.

My body stiffened and I tried to struggle but he was too strong for me as I felt my feet reach the edge and step into nothing. Only dimly aware of voices I closed my eyes and prepared to meet my death.

In the darkness, I heard someone cry out and the rushing of displaced air close by, then I felt arms around my body, pulling me away from the cliff top and back to safety.

In the moonlight Tom Trevellyn helped me back along the path to the terrace, where he made me sit on the bench to recover from my ordeal.

"Are you OK?"

"I can't stop shaking. I don't understand. Did Red just try to kill me?"

He slid his arm around my shoulders and held me close. "We should go back to the villa. I'll ring Ross; he's the one to explain."

My first inclination was to say I didn't want to speak to my husband, so confused was I as to what had happened. But I let myself be led towards the house by Tom, wondering what part he had played in this scenario and coming to the conclusion he had just saved my life.

The French doors were open; Pierre stood in the doorway looking anxious.

"Brandy would be good, Pierre," Tom said.

"Yes sir, I've rung Monsieur Maitland. He's on his way."

"Good."

"Where is he - the other one?" Pierre asked.

"At the bottom of the cliff. He won't be causing trouble to anyone where he's going." Tom gave a harsh laugh and I wondered if I was the only person in the room who didn't know what had been going on.

The brandy hit the back of my throat and made me splutter but the alcohol finally contributed to me trying to make sense of it all.

"Why?" I asked, partly to myself, and not really expecting an answer.

"That's for Ross to explain. He'll be here tomorrow."

It suddenly dawned on me that Tom had been watching out for me all along and why was he here at the villa and not at Longacres?

"You're not a gardener, are you?" I said.

Tom gave a slow smile. "I know a bit about gardening, but old Ned Mason saw to most of the planting on the estate, I just weeded and kept the lawns in trim."

"Who are you then?"

"I work for Paul Weston Investigations. Ross hired me when he knew my boss was working for Nick Ferris. He wanted me to keep an eye on things; I failed to stop what happened to Diana but Ross was adamant that I should stick to you like glue whenever possible."

"So Ross suspected his brother was involved in Diana's death all the time?"

"Look, it's better if he tells you. You won't have long to wait. I'll only confuse matters." He called to Louise who was in the kitchen. "I suggest you make a milky drink for Mrs Maitland, Louise, it might help her to sleep."

"Sleep? I doubt if I'll be able to do anything of the kind," I said. "But Tom, I really do have to thank you. I daren't think about what would have happened if you hadn't been doing your job so effectively."

"My pleasure, Anna," he replied, and I noticed that at last he'd called me by the name I'd been trying to persuade him to call me so many times after my marriage.

Lying in the bed I'd shared with Ross, what seemed to be a lifetime ago and in spite of my insistence to the contrary, I drifted into sleep wondering what the morning would bring.

Chapter 79

In hindsight, I think Louise must have added a little something of her own to my bedtime drink because I slept soundly until ten thirty-five the next morning. There was a tray outside my bedroom door containing a coffee pot, which was still hot and a plate of warm croissants. Obviously she'd been waiting to hear me stir before leaving it there.

After devouring my breakfast with a hunger I found difficult to account for, I bathed, dressed, and left my room in time to hear a taxi drawing up outside. I was descending the main staircase when the front door opened and Ross rushed inside followed by Avril and the baby.

I stopped, not sure what my reactions to seeing him should be. He had no such qualms, he hurried towards me, taking the stairs two at a time.

"Thank God you are safe," he said, wrapping his arms around me so that I could his heart beating. "At last it's over." His lips found mine and it was as if the past few months were wiped away in a breath.

"Come, let's go into conservatory, you need an explanation. Avril, get Louise to fix up some breakfast for you and the baby and black coffee for me, there's a love, then come and join us.

Avril looked tired, there were dark rings under her eyes, but she didn't reply, just followed his instructions like an automaton. She aimed a weak smile in my direction then turned away.

This was the point in the story where I learned why Red had tried to murder me. Ross held my hand and began. It was a while before Avril joined us, she sat in a chair by the window looking exhausted and nursing a sleeping Louie, as my husband continued, "So, as you know, I had a brother whose name was Harry? When we were young, he was always trying to get me into trouble but it didn't work as Ma always saw through it that was until she could no longer cope with the two of us. You know what happened to him then and how he was fostered so I won't go over it all, except to say that the couple moved frequently and Ma and Velma lost touch with their whereabouts."

He stopped talking as if wondering how to continue, then as if he'd come to a decision, said, "I'd often wondered what had become of him. At one stage I know Ma tried to find him and I think coincidentally it was around the time Myrtle Strong died that I began to wonder if he'd found us."

"That was a bit of a long shot; why would you think such a thing?" I asked.

"It was the way Myrtle died, everything pointed to it being my fault. She fell down the stairs just after I'd replaced the runner. Ma wanted it fixed saying it was dangerous and, as Joe was in Kingsbridge visiting his sick uncle and Ned was no good at DIY, I said I'd see to it for her. But I was certain it was secure and knew it had been tampered with, even after the police came to the conclusion that she'd tripped and her death was accidental. Something kept niggling away at me and I remembered some of the tricks Harry used to play when we were little. Of course, I dismissed the thought as far-fetched and forgot about it until Diana met her death."

At this point Avril began to sob. Ross crossed the room to comfort her and I felt icicles slide down my spine as I watched him. When she'd recovered he sat at my side and I said, "He was so plausible. It's so difficult to think he could do such a thing."

Ross nodded and glanced again at Avril, "It wasn't only you he fooled," he said, bitterly. "Anyway, shortly before Ma's death Miles Cohen was visited by a Steven Carter who said he was Olivia's adopted son Harry."

"He was after Olivia's inheritance?" I asked, realisation having finally dawned.

"Exactly."

"I see." I glanced at Avril, who shifted uncomfortably in her seat.

"I think it's time I took Louie home, Ross," she said. "I need to explain it all to Dad. It will be easier if I tell him before Mum gets back from her trip."

"Of course, you must be shattered. I'll get Pierre to drive you over. Don't worry, it will all work out, once they know the truth."

Avril gave a wry smile, kissed his cheek and said, "Goodbye, Anna, don't blame him, he thought he was doing it for the best."

I watched them both walking to the front door, Ross's arm around Avril's shoulder, as he led them both to the car. When he returned he said, "Poor thing, she's got a lot of explaining to do."

"Do you love her?" I blurted out.

Ross did a double take. "What did you say?"

"Are you in love with Avril Ferris?"

"Is that what you think? I've told you before Avril and I are what we've always been to each other – we are good friends.

"Friends who have a baby together."

He sighed, took me in his arms and kissed me. "Louie's not my baby. He's Steven's. Louie is my nephew. The reason why I've been so protective of them both is because I knew what my brother was capable of doing to them, especially if he thought Avril would have a share in his inheritance."

"Nick thinks he's yours."

"I told you we'd planned it so that everyone would suspect I was the father. She didn't want to tell him the truth about Red and how foolish she'd been. Nick Ferris always believed I was the father, I could see it in his eyes every time he looked at me. But Avril wanted to keep the baby and, to her, it seemed the safest option at the time." He wrung his hands together. "I know what it must have looked like but I swear to you, there's never been anything like that between us. I love you, and have done from the moment I first saw you on your way to Longacres. This has all been such a dangerous mess."

"So Avril was meeting Red when she pretended to be Diana, when I first arrived at Longacres?"

"She panicked. It was stupid, it caused so much trouble; I wished I'd never agreed to let her stay. Harry was staying at a friend's cottage in Little Minnock."

I shivered, remembering the time I'd spent the night with him at the same cottage, when I was drunk.

"They used to meet there whilst she was staying at Longacres. Now you see why I had to help her. It was partly my fault she was in such a mess in the first place."

He bit his lip. "But at that time I had no idea he was my brother. It was only when we were in Cortina and you told me you thought you'd found him that put me on his trail. If you remember I made an excuse to travel back to London. But the attack on him had nothing to do with me, I promise you. He engineered it, after I confronted him. You see I went to the address you gave me. I recognised him as the man who pretended to 'save' you in Saint Tropez; everything else suddenly slid into place and I knew it was Harry."

"You said you didn't hurt him?" I asked incredulously.

"No, we argued but I didn't lay a hand on him. He got some thug to do that in the hope that I'd be blamed. He wanted to discredit me with my family, once they knew he'd been attacked. It was the way he worked, placing blame on my shoulders was something he always did."

I knew he was telling the truth. Red was a psychopath, charming, intelligent and lethal. He'd lied about working with the Weston agency, otherwise I knew Tom would have recognised him; to Red, the truth was a foreign country. He'd met Diana Huntley in London, heard she was working for Olivia Maitland and soon became her lover. I knew now that, on the day Red and I swam around the headland to the cove where my husband and Ruby Dent were sunbathing, her fate too was sealed.

"I tried to keep you safe, Tom was there, looking out for you whilst I was away. But it was when we bumped into the Ferris's in Venice that I was certain there was someone else in Red's sights. I knew that Avril and her baby were in danger. But I'll never forgive myself for not being here when he attacked you."

"You're not to blame. There's only one person who was responsible for this mess."

The rest of the story didn't seem to matter. I listened, the threads of the lies gradually unwinding to reveal the truth, Olivia, Velma, Diana, Ruby, Avril and myself were all victims of a man with red hair and a ready smile.

I knew we'd get over it. With Ross in my life anything was possible. The truth would remain a secret, and only I would know the real reason why Olivia had written her hidden journal. Ross thinks it's because she suspected Harry was responsible for Diana and Ruby's deaths and was protecting him because she felt guilty about abandoning him as a child.

But this was one secret I was happy to keep.

Chapter 80

My son shows me to my seat. He's in his early thirties and looks the image of his father when I first met him. There are occasions when he takes my breath away, as I remember those days when I was young and was thrown into a web of intrigue. His father indirectly saved my life and I owe him for that and so many other things.

"Dad's furious he's missing your BIG moment." The light from the overhead spotlight turns his dark hair red and for a moment, I catch my breath.

"He'll watch it on TV with Amy and the kids," I say, making myself comfortable in the seats reserved for the celebrities. I watch the actors taking their places and can't believe I'm in such elevated company. I feel like pinching myself to make sure I'm not dreaming. "It's his own fault," I add, "He still thinks he's twenty-one. If he hadn't insisted on attempting the advanced ski run with you and kept to the nursery slopes with Selina and Lucas, he'd have been fine. A broken arm is no joke at his age."

"I'm not complaining; pity they could only give you two seats, though."

"But I'm only the ghost-writer," I reply, as the buzz of conversation dies. The film begins, the credits roll, and Olivia appears holding the hand of a young boy.

THE END

A Tangled Web

If you have enjoyed reading this book please pass on the word and if you can spare some time to leave a review on your amazon site, it would make all the difference.
If you are looking to read more from me, visit www.kjrabane.com.

Many thanks, K.J.Rabane

K.J.Rabane has written for local newspapers, had short stories published in magazines and an anthology of crime fiction, in addition to which she's written television scripts for an on-going drama series, which is ready for submission. She is also a commissioned contributor to the Food & Drink Guide and works as a freelance supporting artist for film and television productions.

Her main interest is in writing crime fiction and psychological thrillers but her novel According to Olwen falls into neither category. All her books are full of idiosyncratic characters and her crime fiction novels are plot driven.

Her poem Luminous socks was a finalist in the 2012 All Wales Poetry Competition and her novel, Who is Sarah Lawson?, reached the quarter finals of The Amazon Breakthrough Novel Award 2013 Competition. To check out a comprehensive list of reviews on all of K.J.Rabane's books visit www.amazon.com.

Follow K.J.Rabane's page on Facebook and K.J.Rabane on Twitter and Pintrest

CPSIA information can be obtained at www.ICGtesting.com
Printed in the USA
LVOW07s1956040315

429274LV00033B/1232/P